PERFORATED HEART

A NOVEL

ERIC BOGOSIAN

SIMON & SCHUSTER   New York • London • Toronto • Sydney

SIMON & SCHUSTER
1230 Avenue of the Americas
New York, NY 10020

First Simon & Schuster hardcover edition May 2009

SIMON & SCHUSTER and colophon are registered trademarks
of Simon & Schuster, Inc.

For information about special discounts for bulk purchases,
please contact Simon & Schuster Special Sales at
1-800-456-6798 or business@simonandschuster.com.

The Simon & Schuster Speakers Bureau can bring authors to your
live event. For more information or to book an event contact the
Simon & Schuster Speakers Bureau at 866-248-3049 or visit our website
at www.simonspeakers.com.

Designed by Dana Sloan

Manufactured in the United States of America

1   3   5   7   9   10   8   6   4   2

Library of Congress Cataloging-in-Publication Data
Bogosian, Eric.
Perforated heart / Eric Bogosian
p. cm.
1. Authors—Fiction. 2. New York (N.Y.)—Social life and customs— 3.
Publishers and publishing—Fiction. I. Title.
PS3552.O46P47 2009
813'.54—dc22
2009008414

ISBN: 978-1-4767-3895-6

For Henry

Yesterday is not a milestone that has been passed, but a daystone on the beaten path of the years, and irremediably part of us, within us, heavy and dangerous.

—SAMUEL BECKETT, PROUST

PERFORATED
HEART

PERFORATED
HEART

December 12, 2005

Last night Leon dangled the carrot of a fancy literary award before my greedy snout and I, like the pig I am, lurched for it.

Arrived on time for the Humphrey, freshly shaved, in suit and tie, and joined the throng of hipster literati milling outside the ballroom. I was shown to a table near the back of the room. Not a good sign. An aging socialite stinking of chardonnay and Chanel No. 5 leaned in, "Are you a writer? I hope someone at this table is a writer!" I beamed as if we were sharing a witty joke. A salad adorned with flower petals was put in front of me. Wine was poured.

I spied Leon seated three tables closer to the front of the room. He waved. I nodded. He turned away. My own editor could not be bothered to come over to my table and say hello. Of course, Leon wanted me there because he can't waste precious bucks promoting my new novel. No budget means there will be no display ads. No audio book. No parties given in my honor at Balthazar or the Four Seasons. All I will get is an abbreviated book tour (flying coach and residing at budget hotels). No NPR appearances. No magazine covers. If I'm lucky, I'll get two or three guest lecture gigs at second-rate colleges. It's all nickels and dimes to him.

At my table for eight, the chocolate mousse lay unforked and the decaf cooled as the jovial movie stars onstage speculated on the names of the winners present in the crowd (forgetting to mention *me*, of course). An honorary award was given out to a publisher of progressive children's books. A eulogy was intoned for the CEO of a major media corporation who had died rock climbing a week earlier. And so the circus dragged on and on. Finally, a winner was announced.

Upon hearing a name, *not* my name, my neighbors dropped their eyes to inspect their silverware. At adjacent tables, heads turned to gauge my humiliation. An obese publicist to my right patted my hand in consolation. "I'm sure your book was *much* better, Richard." His pupils dilated with the thrill of witnessing my pain.

The winner, a tweedy, aging Ivy Leaguer, florid-faced and wet-eyed (due to the quarts of vintage wine he has consumed daily since his first literary bestseller) jogged up to the podium. The lickspittles leapt to their feet and applauded. With his usual tennis club jocularity he snatched the prize from Catherine Zeta-Jones, took her in his arms and kissed her on the mouth. I shivered with disgust.

The victor leaned into the microphone, thanked his wife, his agent, his housemaid and, of course, *Leon*, who digested this morsel with beatific slit-eyed joy. I could only think, don't thank *me*, motherfucker. Your writing is vapid and ironic to no purpose. It is a wretched blend of overwrought creative writing school frosting. It is "cute" and it is pointless. All designed to sucker in the peanut gallery. I could never write what you write my friend. I don't "do" sentimentality and I don't do glib. I don't do cliché.

BUT WAIT, what the fuck had I been smoking? I forgot our hero's spot on the *bestseller lists*! I overlooked the most important aspect of this enterprise, that we're all in it to get RICH! Of course! The true measure of the artist. Does your stuff SELL? Why would anyone be doing this, making all this effort, if not to sell millions of "units" so that the author-hero can become a *wealthy* author-hero! Then the author-hero can attend *more* dinners and receive *more* awards and sell *more* movie options to the corporate leviathans, and spend more time at more Hamptons get-togethers to cluck and kiss the other author-heros' bronzed cheeks, dazzled by the reflection of the collective genius present. The artist is the antenna of the race and the race is venal and shallow.

When the speeches finally sputtered out, young people in black T-shirts and slacks, Secret Service earbuds wired to their skulls, herded the crowd toward the exit. The literati scrabbled like fiddler crabs, snatching their swag bags packed with glossy consumer magazines, CDs and bad perfume, pinching and clawing, then scuttling off to flag a cab. I was aiming for an exit when one old fool sneezed on me! For a moment, I wanted to beat his face in, but then . . .

Success has its price. But it also has its rewards. And here she was, my compensation for enduring this trial. Brown-eyed, smooth-skinned, scented like the spring flower she was. She smiled shyly at me and said, "Richard Morris! I can't believe it! I . . . I . . ." She actually stuttered as she pretended to be awed. This goddess wore designer glasses, signifying erudition. Her hair was smooth and perfectly cut, her face unblemished. Her fragrance was like wine before the first sip. Before I said a word she blurted, "I read your book. It was so wonderful! The judges have their heads up their asses!"

Out of the corner of my eye I spied Leon laughing it up with the winner. I turned my back on them and ingested the lovely praise. When my new friend was a student at Amherst or Princeton or wherever, she wrote her thesis on my first novel, blah-blah-blah. But wait, there was more! With cocksure vigor she launched into a debate of magical realism (she had read my pointed essay in *The New York Review of Books* last year) and announced "You're full of shit"! She argued her case with a verbatim quote! Nothing in the world is more erotic than a beautiful stranger uttering one's exact words. I fell into her eyes, the pact was sealed.

I had a car and driver for the evening so I offered her a ride home on my way to my own uptown pied-a-terre where I would be staying the night. As we maneuvered the traffic, she chattered on about aesthetics and style, theme and structure. I focused on the aquarium world drifting beyond the tinted windows where people strolled, lapped ice cream cones, hailed cabs, entered and exited buildings. Each individual represented a single priority, living from moment to moment, fleeing or pursuing, praying or narcotizing.

In a deep reverie by the time we stopped outside my building, I discovered that my acolyte had decided she didn't want to go home just yet. I understood. She was curious, eager to see my unique two thousand square feet of living space. She had an urge to visit my library, my art collection, my media center, my kitchen. My shower cabinet.

Earlier in the evening, I had dimmed the lights and thrown open the drapes, anticipating a guest. I never do this for Sarah but upon re-entering the apartment, I thought of her. It was her fault she was being replaced this evening. She couldn't join me tonight and I was forced to go stag. Her loss. Thus orchestrated, the apartment lay before my visitor like a movie set: vistas, twinkly lights out there in the black, the rising moon. I flipped on the stereo and poured brandies. Everything proceeded per usual.

She was a writer, of course. And marginally interesting because twenty years ago when she was eight years old, her father accidentally shot her mother in the leg, severing the femoral artery. This brilliant young woman, then a brilliant little girl, witnessed her mother's death as she bled out on the living room floor. I brought up my own mother's premature death and we discussed that for a while until I sensed that tears were imminent and I changed the subject. After endless all-night sessions with various ex-girlfriends and lovers, I am no longer available as therapist to fucked-up beauties. I want my perquisites with no strings attached.

The awards dinner was a fading memory as we flirted. It was fait ac-compli, wasn't it? We were striking a deal. She would permit me to caress those mysterious thighs, nuzzle those breasts and enter her. In return I would grant her access to the inner sanctum of a great man's life. She would be allowed to entertain the illusion that she had melded with a great mind. (A mind not unlike hers, of course.) This entitlement would nourish her grandiosity, which she mistook for authentic talent.

My venerable cum was still cooling (or warming?) in her somewhere when I began to get restless. (No, no condom. I'm fixed. Furthermore I always make a pretense of being a person who rarely gets laid, ergo, the logic is, I carry no STDs. Girls like my new friend are usually clean and so am I. I hope.)

At two A.M, I let her know I had an early morning appointment and invited her to depart. She seemed surprised by this. As she redressed, I killed time scanning the latest issue of *The New York Review of Books*, then escorted her down to my driver, who had been waiting patiently under the awning of the building. Something simultaneously chivalrous and vulgar about that.

I handed her an autographed copy of *A Gentle Death*, slammed the door of the car, blew a kiss, turned on my heels and marched smartly back into the mild glow of the lobby, where my stoic doorman kept vigil. His face betrayed nothing.

In the elevator I discovered myself in a mirror. I am in my mid-fifties, almost handsome, gray-haired, bespectacled. I have the bearing of what? A successful man of the city. Or just one more putz? I am a Jew, an "Eastern intellectual"—the kind of man the conservatives hate. Unlike my numerous uncles, I am neither overweight nor short. Like them, I wear the mask of one who is both focused and bemused, benign and angry. A wry smile and a furrowed brow lend an enigmatic quality. Here I am, as the world sees me, as I see me. No matter what I do, I can't get past myself.

There's nothing like the relief of reentering a vacant apartment after a date. It was as if I'd been holding my breath for hours and could finally exhale. All the disturbances had been cleared away, life was calm once more. The storm had passed, the rain had fallen and the sun was peeking out. I washed down a tab of Ambien with a mouthful of Fiji water and hit the sack.

I must have been asleep for twenty minutes when the phone rang. For a moment I had no idea where I was, or even who I was. Total disorientation. My companion's scent garnished the sheets. The early morning gloom of my bedroom was deep and soporific. I swam back to wakefulness and reached for the phone thinking that the call must be from the young lady. She'd probably left something behind. Wanted to come by in the morning to pick it up. That old trick.

Ready for a fight, I picked up the phone. But the voice on the other end was unexpectedly male. As the shadows congealed into solid reality, I caught on that my father was speaking. I tripped through a list of potential emergencies including a car accident, a brain aneurysm, even death. That he could call me after dying of a heart attack did not at that moment seem illogical. I groped for a light switch and the room exploded, yoking a band of pain around my skull. Only at that point did I realize I'd spent most of the previous evening drunk.

My father was neither dead nor ill, not in any trouble at all. He was calling because his aged aunt Sadie (my great-aunt) had died. She had resisted to the end. He described a gruesome final few hours, in which she had to struggle for every breath. Things had resolved as they do. Ninety-six years old and Sadie was at peace at last.

I assured him I would drive up in the morning. I had planned to use the day to lay out the bones of an essay for the *Times* op-ed page, another tactic on the part of Leon to billboard the book sans expense. But I didn't want to write it in the first place ("Literacy and the Internet") and now I had an excuse to postpone it. In the world of contemporary publishing, there are two emergencies that are never questioned: a death in the family and a request to fly out to Hollywood to "take a meeting." The *Times* would wait.

December 13, 2005

I'm up here at Dad's place, immersed in the old homestead aromas—the lingering redolence of fried fat and stale coffee grounds, rug dust, a hint of something pickled. First thing today, I snatched him up and drove the two very familiar miles over to Sadie's. In my late teens, I traveled this route countless times while hanging out with my high school buddies, smoking joints, chugging beers, wallowing in emotion and laughter. A long time ago, when I was a know-nothing kid.

My sister called. She would not be attending the funeral, wouldn't even sit shiva. "Okay," I said. "I got it covered." My sister's not crazy, she's just sensitive and has no outlet. With me in town, she's happy to leave me in charge of Dad. We wouldn't see each other this time around. I'm not that sure she likes her big brother anyway. Now that we're all grown up, we don't have to pretend anymore.

When Dad and I arrived at Sadie's weathered double-decker, we found a gaggle of unidentifiable friends smoking and gossiping by the front steps. One hailed my dad as we approached. "Morrie! I see you have the writer with you!"

"Yes. He drove up."

I shook hands with some guy dressed in a camel's hair coat. I repeated. "I drove up."

A big-nosed character puffing a cigar chanted: "Morrie Junior! How's the Big Apple? Still mishuga?"

Another dropped his cigarette onto Sadie's immaculate concrete steps. "This your son, Morrie?"

"My son. Richard. He's a writer. One of his stories was made into a movie."

"Really?"

Etc.

We entered the gloom of the house. Most of the mourners were from distant suburbs, even Rochester and Philly. Few young people (i.e., anyone under fifty). The "kids" didn't know Sadie because she neither married nor had any children of her own. Nonetheless her death cast a long shadow upon the holiday season, and already my aunts were whining about how it "won't be the same this year." I gave a private prayer of thanks to Sadie since attending this funeral would allow me to wriggle out of my annual holiday pilgrimage. It's unprofessional visiting the extended family. Does Russell Banks visit *his* family? Richard Ford? Richard Price? I doubt it. The difference is, those big wheels have their own brood. I don't.

In the cramped living room, soft, sad faces rose up from the hushed velour murk like bloated cadavers from a muddy lake bottom. Someone had lit a fire, making the room too warm. Borrowed folding chairs lined the walls of the back bedroom and the hallway. In the kitchen, dishes covered with aluminum foil formed a traffic jam along the narrow Depression-era counters: Stroganoff, cabbage rolls, casseroles, roast chicken, wild rice, even kasha.

As I greeted the wizened faces of the *alte kaker*, I saw the future. What was happening here would repeat itself over and over again in the next decade or so, like a remake of a bad movie, with different protagonists cast in the starring role of corpse. They'll all go, one by one, including Dad. Including me.

I came face-to-face with the rabbi, who stood much too close to me as he spoke. His breath reeked of Manischewitz and I noticed hair sprouting from his ears. How soon will I have to shave *my* ears? He intoned homilies about Sadie and life and irony and all that and then abruptly turned the conversation to the subject of his nephew Randy, who is an aspiring screenwriter living in Brooklyn. "That's near you, right? Perhaps you could spare a few minutes to give Randy a call and give him some pointers?" I squeezed the rabbi's shoulder and insisted he have his nephew call me. Then I absentmindedly forgot to write down my number.

My aunt Norma wandered into the living room clutching a bundle of tinted photographs. A guessing game ensued, everyone trying to figure out the who's who of eighty years ago, when Sadie was a teen and when the gang of long-lost uncles and aunts sported oily black hair and tightly layered buttoned-down clothing. Here was a picture of Dad as a baby, bare-bottomed on a bearskin rug! Here was my ancient grandmother when she was a shy girl, her whole life ahead of her. Here was Sadie wearing gloves and a pillbox hat. Others too, the elders of that bygone era, stiff and anonymous and grim. No one present could recall their names.

My family immigrated from the village of Polinka, west of Kiev, long before the two wars, so were spared the wrenching legacy of Nazi horror. We were and are simply Jews in America, what the others back in the old country dreamed of becoming when they raced for the barb-wired borders. In fact, I've always detected a certain arrogance attached to this fact, as if "our people" were smarter than those others because "our people" got the fuck out of Dodge before the shooting started. But of course, that's a lie, there was plenty of shooting in good ol' mother Ukraine.

Picked from the pile, a sepia print. A real old-school bris, the baby laid out across the laps of the proud parents, the mohel standing behind them. Everyone stares vacantly at the camera with the nonreflexive eyes of traumatized Upton Sinclair–era immigrants freshly arrived from the shtetl. Every single person in this photograph, including the baby, is not only long dead and buried, but completely forgotten. On the day of that photograph, perhaps ninety years ago, each individual was immersed in the thick soup of his or her anxieties, blood and breath—and are all now dust. They are gone, the photographer is gone, the rabbi is gone, their children are gone and their children's children are gone.

They say it takes three generations to forget. Is anyone remembered? Only the artists and killers and kings.

I was in Sadie's living room, eating pound cake. Someone was shuffling through a sheaf of her personal correspondence. I snatched the letters to my lap. I am the literary representative of the family, I am the keeper of words. Something like a cantor, they all defer to me. ("Richard, what did you think of the President's speech last night?" "Richard, what do you think of *The Da Vinci Code*?") They know I've made money with my writing, been written about in *Newsweek*, won prizes, although not one of them could tell you why, nor has any of them ever made it all the way through one of my novels, but they do know I'm a somebody "out there"—they know I am of the world.

Sadie's life had been so obvious for so long—her cleaning, her crumb cake, her soap operas—that whatever we thought we knew about her couldn't possibly be the whole story. And my family didn't want Sadie's secrets. They'd rather sentimentalize the old woman who never said much, poached a mean gefilte fish, and worked as a secretary in a now defunct office building on a now defunct street in a now defunct downtown, fifty years ago. My gut told me to hang on to the letters.

Later, alone on my king-size bed at the Marriott, I read them.

They fell into four categories: first the oldest, when Sadie was a schoolgirl and had a pen pal, in Argentina. In a flowery cursive, the pal wrote about horses and sheepdogs and sunsets and school.

The next pile was a collection of letters of commendation. Sadie was a WAC during World War II, stationed at the Army air base in Reykjavík, Iceland. When we were kids she would regale us with stories of the midnight sun. She obviously made a big impression on her superior officers.

The third pile was correspondence between Sadie and a kibbutz near Galilee. Perhaps this had been her great dream, to join the Zionists and pick apricots. These letters petered out in the mid-fifties.

The last twenty-one letters were from a woman in Stroudsburg, Pennsylvania, named Angie Demarco. These dated from 1961 to 1967.

They followed or anticipated visits between Sadie and Angie. I thought of the Proulx short story "Brokeback Mountain" (now a major motion picture). The letters didn't give anything away. It's possible the two women were friends and nothing more. I never met this Angie, and I don't think anyone in my family ever did.

I was happy I didn't let them have the letters. Sadie's life, including its mysteries, was safe with me.

December 14, 2005

Day of the funeral. Dad was strangely dispassionate about the whole thing. I noticed he had missed a patch of cheek while shaving. There was a grease stain on his overcoat. He wasn't even dressed in black. When was the last time he got a haircut? At his age he must be thinking: I'll be taking my own dirt nap soon. Which must be tough.

At the dinner, Dad got antsy and wanted to go home. Everyone understood. Dad's an old guy, he can do what he wants. On the way back to his place, he announced that he was hungry. Interesting. So we stopped at a diner where they serve oversized portions of greasy pasta and meat. His rich son was picking up the tab, which put him in a great mood. Hey, whatever turns you on, Dad. Family tradition, counting our pennies to the death.

Dad's eighty-something, and he was flirting with the waitress. Obviously women feel safe around the old, dying lion. He's adorable because he's toothless. Nothing endears a man more to a woman's heart than impotence. But could that winsome waitress ever imagine the lion's dreams? The violence, the trespass he would love to wreak? Really, what more could an old guy want than to get it hard one more time? To be in there, pitching fast balls, curled into that existential jackrabbit thrust? This is all the male animal needs. To get lost in the fucking. To fuck. To fuck hard. Men kill so they can fuck. They run for high office so they can fuck. I fuck therefore I am. Middle-aged men fall for young women because youth revives the walking dead.

Leon found me on my cell. He didn't mention my not winning. No, he wanted to hear the dope on the girl I had met at the awards ceremony. Turns out she's the daughter of a Wall Street tycoon. I told Leon that my aunt had passed away three days ago and I didn't want to discuss the girl. There was a pause on the other end of the line. Leon was trying to gauge what Aunt Sadie meant to me, so he could respond accordingly. Curtly I said, "Have to get off Leon." And with that I punished him. I hung up and ushered Dad safely into his house.

Taking a break, I went for a walk along an old path behind Dad's yard through what was once a familiar ten acres of scrub and saplings landlocked between the subdivisions. For some reason the developer missed this chunk.

I was alone in the thicket when I realized I didn't know the town anymore. Someone could waylay me on this desolate path and cut my throat. But I was not apprehensive. Instead, surrounded by the serene winter environment, I felt a kind of peace, almost elation. The black branches of the winter oaks fissured the high orange sky, wisps of altrostratus clouds reflected the dimming sun. I took in a lungful of frosty air and felt high.

I pulled out my cell phone to call Sarah. I wanted to secure the experience by sharing it with someone, preferably a woman. Then I stopped. To pretend that Sarah was my "soul mate" was an insult to the moment. (A tiny, tiny voice mumbled something about how I was wrong to have sex behind Sarah's back, but then I remembered that it was Sarah's fault for not coming to the ceremony with me. She "had to teach." Maybe. Maybe not. So—it was no one's fault.)

I cautiously resumed my walk. Dead leaves crunched under my feet. Probably foxes or skunks around somewhere. No snakes this time of

year, I was pretty sure of that. Stillness. Beauty. I said to myself, "Here
you are." Here I was, placing myself in the thicket, in the beauty, in the
moment. I continued, "This is it, a perfect moment in the center of a
perfect life. You have it all: money, fame, security, health, sexual satiation,
work to do. A new book coming out. An award nomination. Just take it
in. Breathe it in. The sun setting, health, wealth, life. WHAT MORE DO
YOU FUCKING WANT?"

I heard my own voice, followed by silence. Then a huffing under the
stillness. Breath, not human, behind me, approaching quickly. I turned,
not fearful, more curious to see whatever was coming. A deer? A bear?
Death?

No, it was a chocolate Labrador retriever outfitted in a tight-fitting
Day-Glo vest. He flashed a wet smile of appreciation, sniffed at my shoes,
circled me once, then loped away down the path, indifferent. Keeping
pace, two oldsters (probably about my age) appeared, gripping collaps-
ible L.L. Bean walking sticks. They smiled as if this was the moment
we'd been waiting for all day. Had they heard me talking to myself? I
meekly said, "Nice sunset!"

They blew past, grins frozen with exertion. They'd tricked me. I felt
I should say hello and I did, but now they did not return the courtesy.
Deaf-mutes, perhaps. They were only intent on tracking the dog with
their rapid, health-promoting step, pumped full of high-omega fish oil.
Fuck 'em.

I scanned the horizon and the sunset, found my path and noted how
dark the woods had become. By the time I was in Dad's backyard once
more, the streetlights had clicked on. I found Dad asleep in his armchair,
left him there and drove back to the Marriott. Locked in for the night, I
sipped minibar whiskey from a bathroom glass and watched the may-
hem on the evening news.

December 15, 2005

In an attempt to achieve some kind of intimacy with Dad before leaving town, I drove over to his place and spent the morning with him. Not that there was anything to do or say. We'd said it all. In his living room, we drank instant coffee cut with nondairy creamer. Suddenly Dad stood and pronounced "Time to go." He had a doctor's appointment. I thought, what the hell, and tagged along.

Dad insisted on introducing me, even though I'd met his doctor thrice before. Dad loves the rush of saying "Have you met my son, the writer? He's been nominated for the Pulitzer. Twice." My bile rises whenever he utters those words. Back in the day, my father fought my ambitions with undiluted venom. "Get a real job! You're wasting your time!" I will never forget the patronizing sneer. He even walked out of one of my readings claiming he had indigestion.

That was when Dad was young and strong and bristling with plans for me and everyone else. We battled hard then. I cursed him. He slapped me. I threw a teakettle at a wall. The dent is still there. He never missed an opportunity to cut me with his dismissive attitude. I returned the favor by riffing on his own neurotic existence in my second collection of short stories. Which he never read.

Fame heals all wounds. Old Dad has been crushed into nonexistence by the sediments of time. New feeble Dad is invigorated with the power of my notoriety and that's all there is to that. "You know my son, the bestselling author?"

"Yes. Hello Richard."

"Did you see the movie they made from one of his short stories? *The Philosophy of Paradise*? Not my sort of thing, but it won a special prize at the Cannes Film Festival. Did you ever see it?" I extended my hand to the doctor. He was ignoring my father, which was okay with me. Why bother with something as boring as a proud parent, when you can mix it up with an actual somebody?

As I clasped my dad's doctor's smooth, dry hand, his brow furrowed. He searched my face with mock compassion and said, "And how are *you* doing, Richard?"

"Very well, thanks." I girded myself to repeat for the umpteenth time a synopsis of *A Gentle Death*. He might have found my new book of interest. But no, that's not what he was after. He had much bigger fish to fry.

"Richard, when was the last time you had your cholesterol checked?"

"What?" I was sorting my mental Cliff Notes, preparing my opening statement. ("This time I wanted to write something about personal history . . .") But he wasn't talking about that.

"You are your father's son after all."

Cholesterol—the key word. Oh, I got it. He wanted to play in *his* court. As his deceptively mild eyes searched mine, I had an urge to slap the professional smile off his face. Or maybe just give him a quick cuff behind the ear, and say "Cut it out, asshole. You're not talking to one of your groupies now. I don't buy your scare tactics." Just one more high priest, this guy. Reminding every person he meets that only he can save them.

But I didn't say any of that. Instead, I meekly hopped up onto the examining bench and perched like a schoolboy while he pumped the blood pressure collar and pressed a stethoscope against my chest. I humored him. As if this was something I *wanted* to do.

Why would I have wanted this? Because I had an urge to bond with my dad before we had lunch and this is how I was going to do it. See? Me and Dad, we're just two old guys visiting the doctor! Used to pee into the toilet bowl at the same time, now we're giving urine samples together! And however we bond, we bond. A visit to the doctor is no more different than strolling through a car dealership to check out the cool new Mustangs.

And dear reader (whoever the fuck you are, I'm probably dead if you're reading this) you know what's coming, you're ahead of me on this one, right?

The doctor frowned. Something wasn't right. He wanted more testing. Right then before I left town. I told him that was impossible. Almost dragging my father after me, we escaped the clutches of the condescending quack. But not before I had sincerely promised Dad that I would visit my own doctor and endure a stress test when I got back to the city. Of course I was concerned too, but no way would I give this self-satisfied physician the gratification of being right about anything.

For the remainder of the afternoon, Dad wouldn't drop the subject of my heart. He gobbled up his pasta quickly, so as not to delay my return to New York. I wanted to explain to him, there was nothing wrong with my health. It was fatigue. It was the wine and the stress of awards ceremonies. I promised to call after I saw my guy.

December 20, 2005

Well, this is going to be a fun holiday season. I had the stress test, failed miserably, and, surprise, surprise, I'm scheduled for surgery in eight days. (Maybe I died on the table, which is how you came to be reading this?) Something called "minimally invasive direct artery bypass" (MID-CAB). They will cut me open and stick a scalpel into my beating heart. Graft a vein. All that. What makes it minimal is that I will never legally be dead during the surgery. My heart will keep beating. No machine will be required to keep the blood coursing. It's a no-brainer. They perform hundreds of these every week. Yeah, right.

The surgeon was reassuring. Very little chance of a problem. I did some research, learned that Philip Roth had heart surgery and came out of it okay. He wrote like a speed freak for the next ten years. I have no choice in the matter so it makes no difference what Philip Roth did or didn't do.

I will have to take time off to recuperate. Supposedly I will be able to return to "normal activities" two weeks after the surgery. The bad news is that my book tour is coming up and anything that involves getting on airplanes, let alone passing through airport checkpoints, is considered stressful.

I informed Leon of this new development. He clucked and made a big show of disappointment. He assured me that as soon as my heart is healed, I'll have my tour. He insisted that strategically this will work out for the better in the long run. Fuck him. More money saved. But I can't think about Leon now. My life is on the line. A major medical event. I have insurance, so what more can I do but lie down and let them stick a knife between my ribs?

Now and then I sense a slight ache in my chest, something I've never felt before. The more I try to ignore it, the more it makes itself known, a sensation that beats like a distant lighthouse in deep fog. I've also developed a form of insomnia that tenaciously fights the Valium the doctor has prescribed. I lie on my back for hours, rolling a single thought back and forth: "Maybe I will die." Of course, I *will* die, sooner or later, but will I die this week? This month? Before spring? Before summer?

And when I do die, will I be able to think as I disappear? Will I lie there, clinically dead, still capable of cognition? Paralyzed but powerless to halt the slide into darkness? That moment will be the longest moment of my life. Hopefully I will be unaware of my own death. Go to bed, fall asleep and somewhere in the wee hours of the A.M. simply cease to exist. Cease being. That would be better, right? Or not. Wouldn't I want to know beforehand? But there is no way to know, unless you're on death row.

It is certain beyond any certainty that I will one day cease. And all the information in my brain will cease. Memory will cease. Knowledge will cease. Skill will cease. Personality will cease. This is what I think about as I lie in bed. Terrible jaws of fear grip me for hours. Then, the pills gain traction and I slip away and I'm asleep.

December 25, 2005

There's a chance I will die during surgery. This would be such a gift for Sarah. She likes drama because she thinks it makes her a better writer. She's still young, she doesn't understand that what doesn't kill you *doesn't* make you stronger, it wears you out and weakens what little integrity you have. She seeks authenticity and gravitas. Why else would a woman in her late twenties bother with an old fucker like me? Of course if I passed away she'd mourn. But in the end, it would be a big gift, my death. She'd write a piece for *The New Yorker* and there's a very good chance it would get published.

I had planned to spend Christmas alone but Sarah showed up and insisted on giving me a present. (I'd been too busy to get her anything. Which only deepens her affection for me. She feels closer to me when I exhibit my faults, especially when I don't acknowledge them as such.) She brought me a scarf and a book about Rembrandt by Simon Schama. I didn't spoil the gift by telling Sarah that I'd read it. We ate a light meal, I drank one glass of Napa cabernet sauvignon. We made a fire and hunkered down on the couch.

I was trepidatious about the sex act. Would it kill me? I forgot to ask the doctor, couldn't call him on Christmas Day. Sarah was of the opinion that we could "snuggle." She was anxious about my health, but she was also anxious for my attention, as usual. She beamed me with her big brown eyes. Despite my own (more pertinent) anxiety, a wonderful erection came easily. Alive again!

Sarah administered ridiculously slow fellatio which raised my blood pressure so high that when I did cum, I exploded into ecstasy, my limbs rigid, my chest convulsing for lack of air. As I was drowning in a sea of pent-up endorphins and spasming nerve endings, my pulse blipped erratically and I whirled into a chasm of fear. My enormously swollen heart muscle was holding the reins of my very life. I was cumming and dying synchronically! My mouth and tongue went dry, my breath shallowed, charging the finale with even more weirdly terrific energy. Sarah swallowed and I thought, "That may be the last one you get, kid."

For the remainder of the afternoon, she was incredibly contented. I watched my young girlfriend as she bustled about—young, fertile, confident, warm, supple, lithe, brimming and optimistic.

January 2, 2006

So it happened. I survived. A big chunk of still respiring, still pulsing organism. Surgeon said it went very well. The graft will last ten years, blah-blah-blah. Oh really? And what happens then? Hey doc, what happens after ten years, huh? Twenty? thirty? Oh right, I die anyway. Too bad.

The pain is not overwhelming. The stitches itch and there's some swelling, but I'm not in agony. Generally I'm mired in a diffuse torpor, something like a hangover, but lacking the bite of alcohol poisoning. I'm on anticoagulents and tranquilizers but under it all, I know my heart has been punctured like a bald tire and my soul doesn't like it one bit. No matter, it's done.

Leon sent flowers. The publicity person called to let me know my airline tickets for the book tour had been canceled. I will have a lot of time on my hands. I think of old Aunt Sadie and her letters. I have no letters. I have nothing. I spent the afternoon lying around listening to the Renaissance choral music of a guy named Guido, a singer at the papal court in Avignon. Wonder what his last hours were like.

January 5, 2006

Still in the city. I wander the apartment with nothing to do. Can't even masturbate or enjoy a low-tar cigarette. Against doctor's orders, I unwrap the wound. It is garish, black and red, fierce like a revolutionary poster. It speaks to me and tells me that "it" is much stronger than I am. That "it" can kill me at any time. This scar has the authority of being the visible manifestation of a much greater scar, one I honestly can't comprehend.

I picked up *If This Is a Man* by Primo Levi. I'd read his Auschwitz journal before but for some reason, I relished every terrible detail anew, couldn't put it down. And yet it was probably the worst thing I could be reading right now. I am completely engaged with my core self and what was this book saying but that there is no core self? When he arrived at the camp, Levi asked a guard why he couldn't slake his thirst with a small piece of ice. The guard brutally answered, "Warum? Hier ist kein warum." ("Here there is no 'why'!")

Levi's reasoning was simple: Take away a man's every possession and you take his memories. Steal his clothing and shoes, shave off his hair and you take his dignity. Take away his hope and you take away his desire. When all that is gone, there is no man left. What is a man but memories and desire and hope? I wonder what Emily Dickinson would say to Levi if they were to meet?

When I first read this book thirty years ago, Levi's story was about something distant and foreign and as such, awesomely fictional. Like Borges or Kafka. I didn't understand that he was telling the truth. Because thirty years ago, any failure of mind, body or humanity was what happened to and by others. It could never happen to me. I couldn't comprehend death, real death. But life does end. And when it does, complete anonymity arrives and smothers each one of us.

January 6, 2006

Kirkus and some of the national press have weighed in on my new book, *A Gentle Death*. Not particulary enthusiastic. One review was absolutely hateful, as if I have devoted years to writing a novel for the sole purpose of irritating the reviewer's delicate sensibilities. Doesn't matter. Fuck him. Fuck all of them. All that matters is that the book be read. By someone, anyone.

I'm no good in the city. Can't write, can't think, can't sleep. Every day I grow more disconsolate. Sarah suggested a drive up to the country house. I made her promise not to touch me.

January 7, 2006

Sarah and I are in the country. Recuperating from heart surgery makes more sense here. Sarah mothers me to the best of her capacity. It's not her thing. She can't cook, she can't give a good massage, she can't even change the dressing on the wound. Her most comforting aspect is her ample bosom. Large breasts generate calm. This morning, as she leaned over me to adjust my bedcovers, a breast brushed against my cheek and I was an infant all over again. Maybe I have a mother fixation because Mom died so young. Was she young? She died when she was my age.

Later, I stood before the mirror, contemplating my naked, saggy self. The wound improves my appearance. Such a beautiful scar. Diligently stitched up, red slice/black thread. Obviously, something important happened there. This wound signifies survival. If a mugger's knife had made it, I'd be dead. It's like a badass tattoo, but better because it is authentic. Sarah wanted to kiss it, but I warned her off. Last thing I needed was an infection.

We ventured out to the Old Mill for lunch. Brilliant sunshine, bitter cold. We ordered brook trout, wild rice and zucchini. The waitress was peppy and bright-eyed. I now divide the world into those with problem-free hearts and those living on borrowed time, like myself. The waitress trotted back to the kitchen and the werewolf in me rose up. I wanted to grab her from behind, tear her chest open and taste her pulsing blood. I had to content myself with the trout and zucchini. I enjoyed the food, but waves of depression continued to ripple through me and wear me down. I was crushed with fatigue. Couldn't lift my fork. The meal, like every meal now, was accompanied by a cocktail of pills which only served to remind me how fragile I was. Sarah and I exited the restaurant, me creeping like a retiree. The waitress waved to Sarah as we left, mouthing "Bye now!" I realized she thought Sarah was a dutiful daughter taking her old dad out for an airing.

January 10, 2006

The New York Times review yesterday used words like "compelling" and "insightful," which is critic code for "Don't even bother reading the dust jacket." The killer line was: "A less heavy-handed writer would have given this material a much brighter treatment." Of course it was compared to the short story collections from twenty-five years ago. The Philosophy of Paradise was also mentioned. I have written five novels but I will forever be a "renowned writer of short stories one of which was adapted as a film, directed by Paul Schrader." Read: "not a major talent; negligible; a clown." Tell that to Kafka, to Nabokov!

The critic missed the gist of the book, of course. Completely ignored the themes of biography and anonymity and personal reinvention. Didn't mention the assassination sequence, probably the most exciting chapter. Skirted the shopping mall subplot.

That's how they get you, by synopsizing the plot incorrectly and then criticizing you for *their* mistaken sense of what the book is about. Or focus on the weakest chapters, in this case, the dreary relationship between Carin and her son, something I added at the last minute only as a background to Frank's story. Roth and Ford can digress all day long and every syllable is fawned upon. Me? I'm a dartboard.

I complained to Leon but he insisted it's a positive review and said the marketing department was delighted. They're calling it a "thinking man's thriller" (whatever the fuck that means). Leon claimed my agent, Blake, has already sent copies to Brad Pitt, Johnny Depp and George Clooney. He quoted the "compelling" line. I said, "Leon, no one ever bought a book because it was 'compelling.'" He changed the subject and started blathering on about how Bush choked on a hot dog yesterday.

In a sinister mood, I insisted that Sarah go back to the city. Against her protestations, I drove her to the train station and kept the car. She doesn't want me to drive, afraid I'm going to seize up while sailing the two-lanes, but I feel fine, physically. Emotionally is another story. As the Amtrak diesel chugged in I thought, "One step is all it takes." (Then the book would sell like hotcakes! Nothing like suicide to get stacked at the front of the store.)

On the platform, Sarah and I kissed tenderly. All clichés, all the time! Even my self-destructive thoughts are clichés! As she trotted off toward the conductor I contemplated her backside and almost forgot why I wanted her in my life. Then I remembered: She's a beauty, she's mine. And my next thought was, so what?

January 11, 2006

If I got myself a dog I could adopt the dog's priorities as my priorities. I could name him Zuckerman and he would stand patiently by the door, waiting and watching. He'd know when I needed to go out. He would become my boss. Then I would never have to think.

In the late afternoon, I allowed myself one glass of wine and became instantly drunk. Found myself in the middle of the living room singing my lungs out before a roaring fireplace. I was deliriously happy about nothing at all and it seemed so obvious that I should always feel this way, that nothing was so important that I should ever *not* feel this way. Then, in a span of ten minutes, I fell from total elation to thrumming despondency.

The juncos and black-capped chickadees raise a ruckus around the feeder as the squirrel industriously steals their lunch. My heart feels like gray meat.

January 12, 2006

I woke this morning refreshed and ready for the day (I slept like a log), I was even slightly motivated. I couldn't write but at least I could move around, do something. Maybe it was the glass of wine. Wine's good for the heart, right?

For no particular reason, I unfolded the little ladder that drops down from the bedroom ceiling and clambered up into the crawlspace which serves as an attic to the house. When Elizabeth and I were putting this place together almost twenty years ago, we had hauled all sorts of stuff up there. Under the bare lightbulb I recalled that Elizabeth had carefully stowed away boxes of my research, manuscripts and books under the eves. Perfect place for them in case of a fire.

Good old Elizabeth. The cardboard boxes lay just as she had arranged them, in rows, labeled and sealed. She was in her supportive mode then. She worshipped my work. And so they waited for me. Carton after carton. I attempted to wrestle one box down the ladder but it was too much for me in my condition. How had she gotten them up here in the first place? I descended, gingerly. I'd had enough exercise for one day.

I should have it carted away. The accumulation of my life. What am I saving all this for? The museum wing that will house my papers? Fuck me. I was exhausted. I'd lost my appetite altogether. Couldn't even piss. I took a nap.

January 13, 2006

I've phoned Leon five times in the past week and today he finally returned my calls. Pretended to be very positive about *A Gentle Death*, then immediately changed the subject. Insisted I should take it easy. I wanted to query him about sales, but if they were any good, he would have been the first to tell me. I didn't ask him about Brad Pitt or Johnny Depp. Lots of long pauses.

After a particularly long pause Leon dropped me onto hold, then returned to say his daughter, who recently graduated Brown, was on the other line and he had to take the call. Yeah, right. Whatever.

I've been here before. I built a career on bad reviews. On rejection. Me and Bukowski. Or somebody. They can't kill me. I hope. But they have set me adrift one more time. What's the alternative? Figure out what "they want" and write the same shit over and over, move those units, make those bucks for the Man? If I was smart I'd do that, right? Stick to the tried and true, the formula. That's what all the successful artists do. And in my case, that would be what? What is *my* formula for success? I knocked 'em dead with a collection of short stories twenty-five years ago. What was I writing about that was so appealing then? Anger? Ambition? Drugs? Sex with my movie star girlfriend Elizabeth? Maybe I was dumber then, more outspoken and thus easier to read. Doesn't matter, that voice is no longer my voice. I'm not that guy anymore. Can't do it.

I write my novels because I have to. That's all. And Leon publishes them. And now the new one is out there languishing. That's the way the artistic cookie crumbles. Not that anyone gives a shit. Just my own thing. Absurd, isn't it? Writing for my own benefit. What's that? If no one's interested in what I have to say, then my writing is nothing more than the inner monologue of a lunatic, right? Might as well be pacing the streets of Manhattan in an old overcoat, flinging my arms about, ranting. What's the diff? Yes, I'm a petty, self-involved egotist. But I've dedicated myself to this thing. What does Ian McEwan call it? This "writing project." It *is* important. It has to be important or I could never stick with it. What difference does it make what they think? My conviction is what makes the art. (Spoken like a true mediocre artist.)

I want to get drunk. I want Sarah to come up here and kill me with her mouth.

January 15, 2006

Back in the crawlspace, I broke into the boxes, my life, entombed in crumbling cardboard. What could I have been thinking? No one gives a shit about this stuff. Storing the detritus of my personal history, as if I'm a Hemingway and everything I've ever touched will someday be prized by scholars. Old report cards, essays, newspaper clippings. Photos of classmates: Mike, Rich, Larry. Susan. Where are they, right now? A flat, dried prom carnation, a rusty lapel pin piercing its faded stem. An arrangement of DNA and memory. But forgotten.

Volumes upon volumes of journals, one to a year. I know I wrote them, but I don't recall so many. They begin in high school, continue sporadically through college and continue to when I first moved to New York in the seventies. For the most part spiral-bound notebooks, the sort you'd need for a "101" college course. All carefully inscribed in black ink. I remember now, I had that fountain pen I would lovingly refill. I thought the flowing ink gave my words greater weight. Where is that pen now?

Crouched in the crawlspace, I tried to read but the light from the one bare bulb was too faint, so I grabbed up five and carefully made my way down the ladder. I brewed fresh coffee, settled onto the couch and began.

The writing was hilarious in its way. Portrait of the Artist . . . etc. Embarrassing. Awkward. The most terrible aspect was that the young me had no idea what a total idiot he was. He thought he had some kind of insight when he had none at all. Of course I wrote all this for posterity. The ultimate absurdity. But here and there I found nuggets of personal history embedded in the writing and so these things have some worth.

They are half-diary, half-journal, contain all kinds of information about what I was *doing* then. I had forgotten how I spent my days. I remember I had some fun, but these entries were specific. Names, places, acts.

I will read them and burn them in the fireplace. My more recent journals are worthy. These are an embarrassment. *My* funeral is coming soon and I don't want anyone going through this stuff.

September 11, 1976

I saw a man wearing an old-fashioned signboard on the street, handing out leaflets to the passing parade. He looked like someone out of Puritan times. I wonder if he was being punished? He was advertising custom-made suits.

I like to peek at people in parked cars. All kinds of private stuff going on in there, all kinds of stories. People kissing, talking, arguing. I even saw a guy shooting up drugs. A few days ago I saw a bald man crying while a young woman held his head to her chest. Maybe they had had an affair and were breaking up. Maybe he was telling her he couldn't leave his wife. Or she was leaving him for another guy. Who knows? Stories. It's all stories.

Finally got settled into the new apartment. Complete and total feeling of a new beginning. Like the start of a new school year. Except it's not school, it's the rest of my life. My future. I'm taking one step into my future.

Living in Times Square was very stimulating, but in the long run, dangerous. After eleven P.M., there is no law. The police disappear and I could get my throat cut and everyone would just stand by and watch me bleed. Besides, I knew it wasn't permanent, they weren't going to let me stay in that attic forever. This is much better. No transvestite prostitutes outside my new Upper East Side apartment!

And I start the new job on Monday, which gives me all day tomorrow to finish unpacking and go grocery shopping. Have to remember to pick up vitamins and ginseng powder and tea. And a toothbrush which I seem to have lost along the way from there to here.

The new roommates seem like okay people. Haim and Dagmara. He's an Israeli and she's from some Eastern bloc soviet satellite, either Hungary or Poland, I'm not sure. I don't think they're a couple, but they haven't been very clear about that. (I think Haim wants to have sex with Dagmara, but she's not into him.) They live in the bedroom together, which has a door, and I'm going to live out in the dinette area where I will be exposed to the comings and goings of anyone who visits the apartment. I'm going to build some kind of bookcase/wall to block off the living room. Altogether the three of us live in about seven hundred square feet. But it's a modern high-rise so we have big windows and a view.

Dagmara is some kind of Slavic femme fatale. Nice round breasts, very white skin, big blue eyes. I think she bleaches every hair on her body. She's sexy in an Eastern European way, which takes a little getting used to but she actually *is* sexy.

Haim is a doppelgänger for the guy from *Fiddler on the Roof*. Big bald shtarker with a bushy beard. He sells fine art posters (e.g., Modigliani's nude, Van Gogh's *Starry Night*, da Vinci's *Mona Lisa*) on the sidewalk in front of the Metropolitan Museum of Art. They both speak perfect English but have accents, so hanging around them is like being in a foreign country or something.

This journal will track what I see and hear in New York. Who knows how long I'm going to stick it out, but I figure I should keep a careful notation while I'm here. *Portrait of the Artist as a Young Man* etc. etc. The things I see on the "mean streets" (M. Scorsese) will provide a foundation for my future writing. Can I remember everything? Kerouac is the pole star. Remember everything, write everything.

So back to the journal: Once I got all my stuff moved over from the first apartment, I ate a quick lunch with my new roommates (Haim is loud and boisterous, Dagmara smiles shyly at me) and then I went out for a stroll in Central Park, and roamed under the leafy oaks and maples. It's a beautiful place, this park. But I've been warned to stay away at night. While I was walking I saw a few people who looked like they might be dangerous. Not only is our apartment close to the park, it's close to Harlem. 96th Street. After Times Square, I'm both less worried and more on alert.

When I got back to the apartment, Haim was gone, so Dagmara and I hung out, drank some Darjeeling tea and had a nice talk. She's a poet, but while she's waiting for her poetry to be published she works at a real estate agency here in the city.

While we sat talking, she smoked cigarette after cigarette. And she kept gazing deep into my eyes and then looking down at her lap and taking these long pauses. A terrific gravitational pull was happening between us but it would probably be a bad idea to have sex with her. Especially if she and Haim had something going. I asked her if she wanted to smoke a joint but she said she didn't do drugs.

Eventually we ran out of things to talk about, so I went up to the roof of our building (we are on the twenty-third floor of a forty-three story building) and smoked the joint by myself. I realized that coming to the city is part of some kind of destiny fulfillment. That this day would be the first day of an adventure, no matter where that adventure led. One way or the other, many things are going to happen to me, this is obvious. And I want to embrace every single one of them. When I said goodbye to everyone up in Stoneham, it was like saying goodbye to a life. Like saying goodbye to myself. Whether I ever get any attention for my writing isn't important. The important thing is that I am here. And I will keep a journal in which to collect my thoughts and my writing.

September 12, 1976

Haim split the apartment very early today to sell posters in front of the museum. Sunday is his big day. He's famous in his own way because everyone who visits New York City visits the Met and everyone who visits the Met sees Haim selling his posters out front. He owns a beat-up old Cadillac and stores the posters in the trunk. He sells them for five dollars apiece. He told me that on some days he makes as much as three hundred dollars.

Dagmara and I went out and got bagels and lox at a deli. Food here tastes fantastic compared to back home. I felt like a real New Yorker, surrounded by other New Yorkers all talking a mile a minute and drinking coffee and eating smoked fish on a Sunday morning. Back home almost everyone I know is Catholic and they all either go to church on a Sunday morning or are nursing hangovers. So it's nice to be "Jewish" on a Sunday.

The day was sunny, but not too hot, and we ended up strolling through the park. We bought ice cream. Brilliant sunshine and crazy breezes foretold something wild was about to happen.

So guess what, something wild *did* happen. After the walk we ended up back in the apartment. Outside the windows the sky grew black and the rain started spitting down, then pouring, then drilling. Lightning flashed on the horizon. So we decided to watch some TV together. Then we smoked some cigarettes. Then we started making out. *Butch Cassidy and the Sundance Kid* was on the TV. Dagmara unbuttoned my Levi's and nature took its course. I was watching the movie and thinking, *Welcome to New York*. We didn't fuck because Dagmara was afraid that Haim would catch us.

For the rest of the afternoon, Dag was very quiet. I told her I had to write, which is why I am sitting here at my desk in the dinette area of the apartment while she rambles around the place fiddling with her cosmetics. There's really no way to escape each other.

I made some coffee and smoked half a joint and got some writing done. My mom called (Dad on the extension). She said, "Are you all right?" I wanted to say, "I'm stoned, I'm in New York and I just got a blow job from a beautiful woman."

At the same time, I'm not all right because I'm never all right. Underneath it all, there is a sense of wrongness. Like I did something wrong. What did I do wrong?

LATER, SAME DAY:

I'm back. I realized that Haim would be coming home soon. Dag likes to make dinner for him like they're a married couple. The weird thing is, we didn't even fuck and she was being all weird. I did get her shirt off though and she has a pair of very excellent breasts. She's very proud of them, as she should be.

I refuse to worry about whether this is going to be a great love affair or not. I've only been in New York City for a month! Let's put it this way, I read some of her poetry and she's going to have a great job at Hallmark Cards someday.

So I split. The city had been scrubbed clean by the hard rain. Not many people out. But the amazing thing about New York is that it never really stops—it's always going, one way or the other.

First I visited my old neighborhood, Times Square. Hit the porn shops. Some amazing stuff in there. There's a "straight" section and a "gay" section in each shop. Piles of glossy magazines with titles like *Shaved Splits and Open Clits* (whatever that could mean)! And then there's these things called "live peep shows." You enter a little dark booth that stinks of Clorox and drop a quarter into a slot and there's a whirring sound and then a little metal shutter rises and you're looking through a small square window into this circular space about twelve feet wide. And right there, on a platform are two live people, naked and fucking. They look really tired, probably junkies. It's like a mini-arena so across the way are all the other little peep windows and the feverish eyes of the other men observing in the darkness. Perverts watching hookers fucking. Nice.

I was hungry so I stopped in a place where they serve soda and pita bread sandwiches stuffed with greasy slices of meat that some angry guy with a thick black mustache carves off this gigantic hot dripping meatball turning on a massive spit. It's called a gyro or a souvlaki or something like that. The guy with the mustache was Greek I guess. But the stuff had amazing flavor. Probably not kosher. I sat at the counter and devoured my pita sandwich and while I was sitting there, these three young black guys wearing tight-fitting caps wandered in, leaned over the counter and started stealing éclairs from out of the display case. Right in front of the Greek guy, like they were daring him to try and stop them. I assumed they must be gang members. The Greek guy acted like he didn't even see them. They walked out like kings.

A bum showed up who stunk like a chunk of blue cheese. He asked for a glass of water. The Greek picked up this huge chef's knife and told him to get lost. The old bum told the Greek to fuck himself, then the Greek made a move like he was going to jump over the counter and the bum slipped out the door. Then the bum stood outside the plate glass window staring at us and cursing, the glow of the neon painting him an eerie blue and red. Finally, scratching like he had rabid mice under his rags, he wandered off, cursing.

I bought a coffee in a paper cup emblazoned with an image of the Parthenon and the words "We Are Happy to Serve You" and walked about fifty blocks southward to this strange part of town where the streets are all cobblestoned, empty and dark. Even saw a couple of rats. I ended up down by the World Trade Center, these enormous towers that shoot straight up into the sky. The whole area was completely deserted. Probably not safe but I liked the feeling of danger. Eventually I came to a park and to my astonishment realized that I was surrounded by water, looked up and what did I see? The glowing green Statue of Liberty standing out in the bay. (I guess it's a bay. New York City Bay?) She was so familiar-looking, it was hard to believe she was real. I was shocked by the symbolism of everything.

I ended up in an alcoholic hangout called the Blarney Stone. The place was all dark wood and mirrors and stank of stale beer and boiled meat. The grinning cardboard leprechauns and four leaf clovers from Saint Patrick's Day were still Scotch-taped to the walls.

I drank six glasses of forty-cent beer and got a little fucked up. I tried to keep up the conversation with the old guys at the bar, but they were too haggard to bother with me. Still, it seemed like a good place to collect my thoughts. I should go back there again.

On the subway, I fell asleep and overshot my apartment by thirty blocks. Had to walk back through Spanish Harlem to get home. Lots of burned-out buildings, cars in the streets up on cinder blocks, hoods popped, tires and wheels long gone. Saw some black people and mostly Puerto Ricans but I didn't get mugged or killed! It was like I had some kind of drunken aura that protected me.

In the apartment I could see light under the door to the room that

Dagmara and Haim share. I could hear them talking in their thick accents. (They talk in English because they don't understand each other's language.) I could have listened by the door, but didn't.

I lay on top of my bed, the world swirling like a carousel. Later I heard Haim in the kitchen, rummaging around. Then I heard him in the living room, devouring a bag of plums, watching TV with the sound down. I'm in this half-drunken, half-caffeinated state, sort of excited and very tired. I just lay there listening to him. Fell asleep, woke, fell asleep. Thought about the future. The new job. My work. All the obstacles.

Haim finally lumbered off to bed and I got myself up, drank a ton of water and wrote all this down. Tomorrow's the first day at work. I'm going to be completely burnt-out.

September 14, 1976

I got up pretty early. Ran into Dagmara in the bathroom, working on her cosmetic alchemy. When she saw me, she didn't smile. Like I raped her or something. Damn. I guess there will be no more Sunday afternoon blow jobs.

I wolfed down some granola, then sprinted to the subway. I had to leave about eight-thirty, because my new boss wanted me there at nine. There were a million people crushed together waiting for the train. It was hot. The graffitti-covered subway car raced into the station just missing the people on the packed platform. The train was crammed even before we tried to wedge ourselves in. As we squeezed into the cars, ancient crud-encrusted loudspeakers over our heads blared incoherent announcements.

In the jammed car I was immersed in the syrupy stink of coffee breath and deodorant and farts. Men read creased newspapers (a special fold that takes up the smallest space possible because there's no room to spread out). The women were slathered with makeup like they were headed for the disco. Most of the people stared ahead in the screeching din, some nodded in fake sleep. Twice I caught a girl checking me out. Not sure what I was supposed to do with that. Talk to her? Ask her out? Being so close to so many strangers creates anxiety, I think.

So I got to Jonathan's loft at nine A.M. Turned out this is the same neighborhood I was in last night! SoHo. Looks different during the day. It's an abandoned neighborhood, just cobblestoned streets, a few cars, one diner and a bunch of art galleries. There were plans a few years ago to knock the whole thing down to make room for a highway. But the city doesn't have the money and now artists live down here.

I waited in the stairwell for almost an hour before Jonathan, my new boss, showed up. He didn't smile, didn't apologize. Just turned a key in the center of the door because the fox lock is actually a gear mechanism that releases massive metal prongs from holes in the door frame. Everything in this neighborhood is nineteenth-century like that. The stairwells have banisters covered in hundreds of coats of paint, every door is heavy and reinforced with riveted metal, the lofts are enormous, floored with dark planks of ancient wood. The cavernous ceilings are sheathed in patterned tin. The building facades are cast iron.

Jonathan's place is called Erehwon Video. (Erehwon is "nowhere" spelled backwards. Get it?) We specialize in video art, which is the new cool thing. We assist artists who use Sony Portapaks to make their art. My job is to sit at a desk and answer the phone and inventory our video equipment and the videotape library. People come and go all day. Plus Jonathan has a viewing room where people can watch these videotapes on a monitor (TV set). He also wants me to write publicity releases about stuff we're doing. I don't really understand what the big deal is about, but Jonathan's going to pay me a hundred and thirty-five bucks a week, so it's worth it.

Most of the "video artists" who come by are hippie types: long hair, bushy beards. I guess they see themselves as revolutionaries who are using video to change the world. (Don't hold your breath.) These artists video-tape everything they can. Some are documentary filmmakers. Sometimes they show their tapes in art galleries, even museums! This Korean guy came by who didn't say much but laughed a lot. Jonathan says his stuff is in the Museum of Modern Art. Nam June Paik is his name.

We leave a monitor running in the front room all day with video art playing on it. Most of the stuff is pretty boring. Once in a while there's some nudity which I appreciate. There was even one in which a guy was discussing philosophy while this girl with tattoos sucked his dick. I guess the point was that after a while the philosophy lost out to the orgasm. Some point, huh?

So anyway, I made it through the day. It's easier than loading boxes on a truck dock. After work I didn't really have anywhere to go, so I headed for Times Square again and had another gyro at the gyro place. I shouldn't eat so much of this stuff, it's going to wreck my skin. The Greek guy with the mustache didn't recognize me. He must see a thousand people a day. No gang members hanging out this time. A lady with bleached gray hair was hunched over the counter, sucking on a droopy cigarette and slurping a cup of coffee. After my sandwich, I gobbled down a New York City éclair—swollen and perfect, almost obscene, packed with yellow ooze.

The streets around Times Square were filled with three-card monte guys and dealers selling nickel bags and loose joints and pills. There were women who seemed to be prostitutes and there were transvestites who I *knew* were prostitutes. Jamaicans clanging on steel drums, jumpy hustlers hocking watches out of briefcases, sleepy-looking guys snapping flyers, or just weirdos asking for the time of day. There's always someone walking around talking to himself or yelling at the air. I think the crazies intentionally put on a show so people will identify them as crazy. It's big business in New York City.

At home Haim was sprawled on the couch watching *Little House on the Prairie*—I'm sure he thinks this makes him more of an American. The apartment was rank with perfume and hairspray. Dagmara was in the bathroom powdering her body parts in preparation for a date. She posed before the mirror perfecting her eyebrows (she plucks her eyebrows off and replaces them with a thin black line). While Dag works on her face she leaves a lit cigarette on the edge of the sink. Her concentration is total. I wonder what she's thinking about? Getting a husband? Blowing me? I said hi and she said hi and that was it. Now she acts like she never touched me. I told her she looked nice and she smiled a tight smile. Basically, she lives in the bathroom.

I rode the elevator up to the roof and smoked a cigarette. When I came back down (to write this), Dagmara was gone. Haim and I had a conversation about life. I said it bothered me to see the winos and junkies lying around on the sidewalks. What I meant was it *doesn't* bother me to see them and the fact that it *doesn't* is what bothers me. Haim got all Talmudic and stroked his beard and said that all humans form themselves into tribes and it's natural that I shouldn't concern myself with anyone who isn't from my tribe. When he said this I realized that Haim considers the two of us to be from the same tribe. Deep down, I don't think of myself as a Jew, the way Haim thinks of himself as a Jew. I think of myself as a suburban American kid (trapped in a Jew's body). Fucked up.

I asked Haim if he wanted to smoke some grass and he said the Arabs smoke hashish back in Tel Aviv, it's not something he does very often. After about three tokes Haim started giggling like a little kid. Then he went on and on about how beautiful Dagmara is, what unbelievable tits she has, how he wants to suck on them, how he wants to fuck her cleavage, have her sit on his dick, how he's going to cum on her tits, etc. Obviously he's clueless about what happened between her and me. And clearly she's not fucking him. Which is just as well.

Work tomorrow.

January 20, 2006

The book is moribund. Sales are in the hundreds, not thousands. Leon is off at the Cairo International Bookfair (God only knows why. He's not selling *my* book there.) so we're not in communication. Whenever Leon is overseas he acts like it's 1850 and there's no way to reach me. Wants me to believe he's staying in a hotel without telephones. Thinking about Leon wears me out.

My ex-longtime girlfriend Elizabeth has gotten hold of *A Gentle Death* and discovered that some of the chapters feature a character reminiscent of her (Carin). So she e-mails me daily, insinuating a lawsuit. After the last e-mail, I answered her, filling her in on my recent cardiac surgery. I concluded by saying I would be in touch as soon as I felt better. I owe her that much. I loved this woman. And with the knowledge that I did indeed love her, she held me hostage for fifteen years.

We woke every morning in the same bed. We read the paper together, shopped for antiques together. We drank wine from bottles carried up from our own cellar. We drove long distances in the Lexus, sat face-to-face across starched tablecloths, and at the movies, picked popcorn from the same box. We held hands. I always loved her. Just because I gave in to temptation, should I be condemned? Because I didn't conform to her idea of the way things should be, I had to be punished?

Of course, living with a former acclaimed actress means you never know where you stand. Elizabeth would argue the term "former," but once we moved to Connecticut, she retired from the Hollywood shuffle. Nonetheless, every time we entered a supermarket or a shopping mall, we were always reminded of "who" she was. I would stand idly by while she signed autographs. Toward the end, I simply walked away and let her do what she had to. She resented me for this too.

Her favorite weapon was accusing me of selfishness. There wasn't a move I could make without thinking about her resistance to it. If

I couldn't add to her happiness, she wanted me guilty. She claimed I was "stunted" emotionally and spiritually. (Elizabeth was a New-Ager long before it came into vogue. Always seeking "answers" and "personal growth." "Personal growth" in our society means greater and greater congruence to the expectations and needs of others.

My love for her wasn't enough. She wanted slavery. As soon as I stopped worshipping her ass, she began a self-improvement course which demanded total obedience and very little sex. We could never reach stasis. Not possible for either of us. What did I ever do to her? "Cheat" on her? Yes, I did cheat on her, what else could I do? She had lost interest in me. God help the man who *marries* a beautiful actress. At least I avoided that! "For sweetest things turn sourest by their deeds: Lilies that fester smell far worse than weeds."

January 21, 2006

I can't put the confrontation off any longer. Elizabeth called the house. After she stopped screaming at me, I reminded her that I haven't been well and that she was only making me more ill. She said she doesn't give a shit about my heart. The truth is my weaknesses only encourage her. Perhaps she hopes if she can get me agitated enough, I'll croak right now.

Leon said there's nothing to lose, everything to gain by having coffee with her. Pointed out that Elizabeth can cause more trouble than she realizes. He shared all this with me in the smooth tones of his tobacco-sanded voice. On speakerphone, probably drunk. What he doesn't say is that publishers are skittish these days and according to my contract (unbeknownst to Elizabeth), if I in any way cause the book to be withdrawn from circulation, then not only will book sales cease, I will be compelled to return the fucking advance! *And* pay for the legal proceedings employed to get that money from me! They'll take my country house! My 401-k! Fuck me.

September 25, 1976

A guy named Jack has been in and out of Erehwon picking up and returning tripods and lenses for the past couple of days. He's not a video artist, but he works for a guy who makes videos. Jack is a "camera assistant" and he's twenty-six, like me.

Anyway, he told me there's this club, Max's Kansas City, where you can hear live bands. It's mostly punk rock, which I have absolutely no interest in. People who push safety pins through their lips are losers. I told him I haven't been into rock since Hendrix died but he insisted that this place was different.

So the point is, it's nine A.M. I just got back to the apartment. Haim and Dagmara are asleep. Me and Jack went to this Max's Kansas City place and it was actually very interesting and crowded (Jim Morrison used to hang out there with Andy Warhol!!!). The band was punk but really they sounded like any old band from back home. Very loud. They were called the Dead Boys and they put on a good show. I guess the lead singer hangs out with the Sex Pistols and is a heroin addict.

This guy Jack likes to drink, so after a set we split to a Polish bar where the booze was cheaper. From there we headed to another bar (Old Town), and finally ended up in this basement speakeasy over in the East Village (I think). Then around two A.M. Jack asked me if I wanted to go dancing, and I suddenly thought, oh, *that's* what this is all about, another gay guy! I said, "I'm not gay."

Jack said, "That's okay, they'll let you in anyway. They let me in."

We walked ten blocks east and ended up in what appeared to be a completely abandoned block. No sign of life on the street anywhere.

Jack lit a fat joint and passed it to me. Then he coughed out the words, "Follow me," and we entered this gloomy warehouse building. Inside we were in a long empty hallway, strung with bare bulbs in the ceiling. At the end of the corridor, bathed in murky blue light, an old guy sat at a little table. We handed him ten bucks each. Then he pushed a button and a door in front of us opened a crack and a roar flowed over us like the crashing sea. A throbbing beat, flashing lights, sweat.

The place was an enormous cave called Infinity. Probably the biggest indoor space I've ever been in. Like the old gym at my high school, but with really high ceilings and everything wrapped in pulsing neon. The way it was laid out it gave the impression of extending in every direction, limitless. On the main floor were about five hundred people dancing to the loudest music I've ever heard. The sound was like a vast molten sea and everyone was drowning in it. The beat was so strong it shook my guts.

Jack wedged himself into the crowd, dancing with nobody in particular. The throng swallowed him up and I lost him. Lots of gays were there, dancing with each other. But lots of women too. (Lesbians?) Everyone happy and wild. People wearing cowboy hats, some in shimmery sequins, other folks naked from the waist up. Dancing was all there was. I timidly imitated Jack, and danced by myself, as if anyone could give a shit. After I built up some confidence, I danced with women, sometimes with men. But if I tried to talk to any of the women, they smiled deafly and danced away.

It was like everyone in the place was on a mission to dance themselves to death. I caught the fever and didn't want to stop either. Any sense of time disappeared as one tempo flowed into the next. Then someone handed me a tiny brown bottle of liquid and indicated that I should sniff it. Before I could react to the strong chemical smell of the vapor, the room exploded like massive mirrors shattering. The splinters spun into cyclones of color. The walls fell away.

I thought I was going to have a heart attack. I was surfing on a kaleidoscopic euphoria swirling into oblivion. My knees went weak. My heart pounded. My brain roared. I tried to hang on to my senses, then realized that even if I did collapse the gut-thumping music was so powerful it would prop up my physical body. I was safe! Pretty soon I was reaching out for the little brown bottle whenever it passed by.

I got very fucked up. But by dancing as hard as I could, I burnt the intoxication out of my veins. I was high but in a totally physical way. And even though I didn't know one single soul in the whole magnificent place (besides Jack) I was an essential part of this gigantic endeavor, like a bee in a swarm. The place was a hive and we were bees on speed going faster and faster and faster.

I got thirsty and went looking for Jack and found him upstairs in the middle of a vast mezzanine overlooking the dance floor. He was lying on a kind of bed-couch with someone, a woman. I approached him, all smiley and shit and then realized that Jack wasn't just *with* this woman, he was actually having sex with this woman. Right there in the middle of everything with people coming and going all around them. No one gave a shit. Jack glanced at me sideways but keep pumping away. He didn't smile.

Later on, Jack came dancing up beside me. The woman was gone. He didn't say anything about me seeing him flagrante delicto. It was as if I had caught him eating a slice of pizza. Not worth mentioning. He disappeared a couple more times and then hours later shouted into my ear, "Time to go home."

We stepped out of the warehouse onto the street, where pigeons pecked at the night's crumbs and spills. The sun was edging up over the rooftops. We made our way down Broadway as the tense workers flowed up from the subway entrances ready for another day of boredom. Jack and I were like the invisible dead, seeing but unseen.

We shambled east along Houston Street, thick-headed and semi-blind in the morning glare. Insomniatic winos burned scrap wood in iron barrels. Buses and cabs roared and honked and hissed. Everyone was on a mission to contribute to the new day. Jack tugged me into the doorway of a diner. We sat down at the counter and ordered fresh coffee and fresh doughnuts. What could be better than this? I was deliriously happy, like a jet-lagged tourist.

Jack nodded toward a gaggle of girls dressed up in sequined blouses and tiny cutoff jeans. Lots of eye makeup. I knew these were hookers, having a quick bite before heading home to shoot up drugs and hit the sack. One girl smiled at me. Flattered, I smiled back until Jack whispered in my ear, "She thinks you're a hustler."

In one corner, a muscular black guy stood alone, having a conversation with nobody in particular. Every so often, one of the girls would drift up to him and bring him coffee, or a sugar doughnut, and he would touch her face gently with the back of his hand and then she would drift away again. Of course he was wearing an enormous diamond on his pinkie. Clichés are built on some kind of truth, right?

I tried to hear what Superfly was saying, but all I could pick up were non sequiturs. His words flowed like bubbling champagne: "See, that's what I'm saying, that's what I'm talking about. I'm not into the specifics. I don't want to know the specifics. I just want to see the stack. Because there might be, might be some kind of, you see what I'm saying here, situation, in which, on occasion, I just might not be around. Could be anywhere. Connecticut, New Orleans. I don't know. I don't want to commit myself like that. But under that specific occasion, see what I'm saying, the business has to be able to run itself. You get too close, see what I'm saying, you get too hands-on, well, then that's what gets a man killed. If everything is organized right, you never gonna have that problem, you hear what I'm talking about?" He must have said "You know what I'm talking about" or "That's what I'm saying" at least fifty times. And I'm not sure that anybody did. I don't even know who he was talking to.

Suddenly I was back home crawling into the cool sheets of my bed. I closed my eyes and then what seemed like two minutes later blasted out of bed and raced off to work. I had a surprisingly huge amount of energy all day. Jonathan was sucking up to someone he thought was an important artist so he left me alone. Jack called around five and asked if I wanted to "hit the beaches," his expression for barhopping, but I told him I had already made plans. Which was a lie.

About an hour later this woman came by Erehwon. She was using one of the duplication video machines we own and as she squatted down to loop some tape onto a reel, she had an almost perfect bum, so I started up a conversation with her. Turns out she's really into Thomas Pynchon and I've been reading *Gravity's Rainbow* so we're seeing each other tomorrow on my day off.

January 27, 2006

Elizabeth did not rise as I leaned down to kiss her on the cheek. Like kissing marble. She wouldn't meet my eyes. Her looks and celebrity, as usual, attracted attention from those seated around us. The waitress drifted over and we ordered skim cappuccinos.

Once upon a time, her beauty was unleashed upon me in all its raw, unadulterated, fully naked power. It was a gift. But it was also the weapon she used to bring me down. Beauty is a double-edged sword. What did Dostoyevsky say? "The dull edge is the worst"? Back then, I exalted and suffered simultaneously. Now, all I get is the unforgiving hammer of the dull edge. She knows that even now as I despise her, I ache for her. So she hides herself behind a dozen frigid veils, refusing to meet my eye the way I want her to.

Elizabeth asked, "How's your girlfriend?"

"Sarah?"

"Is there a new one?"

There's no upside in being honest with Elizabeth. So I told her that Sarah and I weren't seeing much of each other. I steered the conversation to my heart surgery, making sure to impress her with the bloody details. Building on her revulsion (empathy?), I painted in broad strokes the portrait of a man, alone, ill, softened by his encounter with death. I wanted her to understand that I'd "changed."

I could see she was confused.

Because she's never, ever thought of me as vulnerable. Such a thought would bring the whole house of cards down. Bitterly and over time, Elizabeth has constructed a mental Richard voodoo doll into which she can stick pins of resentment and accusation. This voodoo doll, fully dressed in my sins, is essential to her worldview. Elizabeth needs to be certain about me. The Richard in her mind behaves in a certain way. He is an evil force. Without me to hate, Elizabeth might have to look at herself. What use am I to Elizabeth with my weak heart, my mild demeanor? I saw an opening, so softly I asked, "Are you okay?"

Perhaps she was visualizing my funeral, wondering if she would attend. I would have liked to know the answer to that question too. "Elizabeth?" She lifted her chin and I saw that her eyes were clear and hard. I'd misunderstood her silence. She wasn't buying this new Richard.

She launched her attack. "I hate this book Richard. I like it less than anything you've ever written."

How is it that some beautiful people remain beautiful for their entire lives? She was a beautiful little girl and she'll be a beautiful old lady. It is the eternal passport that gets her through all borders. Her all-day ticket. Her license to kill. But like the proverbial fish that doesn't know it's wet, she takes for granted this feature of her reality. It is the common denominator in every equation she shares with every person.

Fact: It is the undying hope of every physically beautiful and highly intelligent heterosexual woman that she will someday find a man with whom she can commune as deeply in mind as in body. But the ancillary truth is, beauty, the very passport that opens all doors, contaminates any real intellectual communion. It is a distraction when it is in full flower and a headache when it begins to wilt.

I said, "You'll have to get in line, Elizabeth. Many people hate my book."

"Really?"

"I must be doing something right."

She stirred her coffee and tightened her mouth, as if saddened by my failure as a writer. "Doing something right? Is that the way you look at it, Richard? You are pathological!"

"You mean, fucked up."

"Yes. Fucked up. Disconnected. Weird. Whatever."

When we were first together, she had a real appetite for my work. She'd snatch up pages of manuscript, find a quiet corner and dig in. Total concentration. Wouldn't let me interrupt her. A better reader than any editor, any fan. And then she would share her thoughts, which were always to the point and always perceptive. I don't know what excited me more, knowing her criticism would make my work that much better, or knowing that I possessed this amazing woman. Entering her mind was almost as thrilling as entering her body.

She tended my garden and my work thrived because of her. (Maybe. No. It did.) But her influence extended beyond that. Not only did my writing grow sharper because of Elizabeth, but so did my personal style. I matured because of her. I spoke more carefully in public. I was funnier when I sensed she was listening. I dressed better. My sideburns were trimmed properly. And my friends envied me because Elizabeth was mine.

Elizabeth knows all of this. But if I ever read her the paragraph above, she'd claim she had no idea what I was talking about. She doesn't see things the way I do and that's what gave her so much insight to me and my work. The irony is that even though I'm delighted she's been reading my work again, I can't allow her to see that. It would concede too much. Concede that when I was writing the book, I was always thinking of her.

She continued her attack. "There are people called 'empaths.' These are people who feel emotions of others deeply. You're the opposite, you don't feel them at all."

I gazed into her lovely eyes and said, "There's no such word as 'empath.'"

"Richard! The book is not that interesting. Can't you see that? It's one-dimensional. There is no insight. There's no interplay between the characters, no subtext. I don't know who these people *are*. They are disconnected from any specific circumstance or consequence. They have no context."

"'Context'! 'Empathy'! You sound like a therapist on Oprah! I have a reputation for being objective. That's my value to the world. I am unsentimental. I am honest."

A million years ago, when Elizabeth and I were first seeing each other, sleeping together, touching each other, glorying in the unaffected experience of being near one another, she had her opinions and I hung on her every word. But in the beginning, her braininess, which is indeed considerable, only made me love her more. We would dissect my writing as part of a larger, ongoing dialogue on politics, art, philosophy, science, love, humanity, even spirituality. This was before every gesture and remark we shared had become infected with our mutual animosity. By the end, I stopped giving her my opinion on any subject whatsoever. I wouldn't even bring up a new movie, because any remark of mine, anything at all, would trigger a nasty argument.

Did I just call her "brainy"? Well, she was. But intellect was never a priority for her. She had nothing to prove. She was a fine actress, lauded for her work onstage and in film. She was too good for Hollywood and she knew it. When she tired of me, the intellectual discourse only served to piss her off more. After a while, I think she played dumb to hurt me. And so it ended.

"Elizabeth, I hope we're not having coffee so that you can critique my book. I thought you wanted to see *me*. I thought this was personal."

"It is personal. Personal and public, obviously. And know this, this is not a vendetta on my part. The book is bad. Bad for you."

"And bad for *you*?"

"Yes. Bad for me. Obviously."

As if reading my thoughts, she tried to dam the stream: "This character, this pathetic, neurotic nymphomaniac, is me. Right? I mean off-the-record, she is, right?"

"Elizabeth, we lived together for fifteen years."

"Which gives you a right to invade my privacy? As if my life is something you own? A franchise?" It interested me that Elizabeth was absolutely sure of her position. How can anyone be so confident? Intellect creates this assurance. But beauty seals the deal.

I was forced to attack. "We lived together. We have discussed my work many, many times. We have discussed other people's reactions to my work. You've attended readings of my work. You've heard the idiotic questions. I'm sure that on several occasions, in response to one nitwit or another—and this is not a verbatim quote—I have, in your presence, responded with something like: 'These are not actual people, these are *constructs*.' Constructs, Elizabeth, constructs. I am an artist, I contrive, I build a thing out of words. To make a statement like 'This character is me . . .' what could you mean by that? You're a woman, yes. The character in my book is a woman. Beyond that, how can a fictional fabrication be a 'real' person? No such thing. Scribbling on a page. A person is not two-dimensional. Every portrait is an abstraction."

"Stop."

I waited for the tears. She may be smart and cool but she cries "just like a woman." "Elizabeth, do you want an answer to your question or not?" It was imperative to herd the dialogue back to the fundamentals. My power versus her power. Once upon a time, this turned her on, my hold on her. Now it only angered her. But it was the cornerstone of our relationship. If I lost this argument, I might as well let her stick a knife in my heart as I sat there at the café table. Get it over with.

She lowered her chin, so that she was looking up at me. One of her most intense expressions and she knew it. "You are a bully. You possess zero empathy. That is why I was so happy to have you out of my life."

"Is 'empathy' the word of the day?" I was reminded of how much attention she once required. Like babysitting a four-year-old.

"I wake in the night and try to understand how I could ever have loved you."

"But you did. You did love me once Elizabeth. And I think whatever feelings we had for each other, they can never be completely eradicated."

"Richard, you do *not* want to go there. Not today. I will walk out of this café and you will never see me again." An empty threat. Because she did love me and no matter what she said, she couldn't change the past. The historical record was clear. I cheated on her. I broke her heart. She left me because I hurt her. Because she loved me. If she loved me deeply enough, we'd be together still.

I said, "If it makes you feel any better I ponder the same question." I was lying. I never ponder the question as to why we loved one another. I know why I loved her. Why I still love her.

There was a pause and the waitress pounced. "Get you folks anything else?" I glanced at the girl. Said nothing. She got the message and moved off, but not before I noticed the blond peach fuzz of her freckled upper arms. In the gaps between thoughts, I wondered what this waitress would look like naked and goose-pimpled on my bed. I wondered what her little avenue tasted like. How old was she, twenty-five?

Elizabeth was watching me. Could she read my thoughts? I said,

"What we felt for each other can't be altered. Whether you wish it never happened or not. Whether we understand it or not." I dared her to look away. I should have leaned over and kissed that mouth. Picked her up, laid her out on the table, let it all flood—the love, the desire, the overwhelming truth of what we were to each other. Fucked her right there. My intensity melted her momentarily, incrementally.

She said, "You repeated the story about me and my father."

"That story's been told a thousand times in a thousand different ways."

"Not *my* story. How much I loved him. How he would tuck me in at night. How gentle he was. How my world imploded when things changed between us. How cold everything became. You even used the word 'imploded'! That's *my* word. *My* personal history and *my* word."

"So if you use a word, I'm not allowed to use it?"

"Richard, anyone who knows me, even people who *don't* know me are going to understand that you are describing me. You detail our sex life, you describe our sexual intercourse! Things we said to one another, the way you would touch my back. You even describe the shape of my bum, the pucker of my *asshole* for God's sake!"

"You have a divine asshole, the Platonic asshole. No pun intended."

"What's that supposed to mean?"

"Plato said that there is a perfect thing after which all things are modeled. Your sphincter—"

"Plato had zero interest in my body! Shut up about my body! Don't be a jackass!" I was impressed by her restraint. There was a time when I could tease her into throwing things. "So look, Richard, Russell says I can sue you."

"Don't tell me what Russell says or Russell wants. What do *you* want me to do here, Elizabeth? Spell it out."

"I don't know. If I sue, it will probably just bring more attention to your pathetic exercise."

"Have to agree with you there." Beat. "Look, Elizabeth, I'm sorry if you are uncomfortable with my writing." I placed my hand on hers. It seemed like the right thing to do. She didn't take it back.

Her eyes reddened. Was she going to weep into her skim decaf cappuccino? "Richard, is that all I was to you? A pair of breasts? A cunt? A sphincter? Those words of yours, those passages came at me like an ambush. Fortunately I was home alone because I literally had to race to the bathroom and throw up."

"You threw up? Really?" No one else will ever react to my writing the way she does.

"I felt like throwing up. No, I didn't! Okay? But I felt like it." Beat. Her brow tightened. She disengaged her hand. "Maybe I should write a book about your cock."

She was losing the argument. "Elizabeth, I don't expect you to see things the way I see them. But no matter how you parse it, I did love you. I still love you. But I can't and could never love you the way *you* loved *me*. I'm me, not you. And my love is carnal. It's just the way life is. And I write about life."

"Whatever we were or did, you didn't have to tell the whole fucking world!"

"I thought those passages were very flattering."

She wilted. "So now the book is out there. And I guess you have me checkmated, Richard, because you know I can't sue you without bringing even more attention to the fucking book. But you must be punished."

It was time for me to let her run with the line. Easy, easy, let her think she was having her way, and finish this. I attempted to look contrite. "I'll write another book and put your side of it in there."

She unlocked her gaze from mine, fiddled with her spoon. "You want to make things right, pay me."

This is what she had come to say. "It's that simple?"

"I don't want or need your money. I only wish you hadn't done this in the first place. But it's done. You hurt me. I have no idea *why* you wanted to hurt me, but you did. So pay me. I can't think of any other way to hurt you. Or I will sue."

"How much money do you want?"

"I don't know. A percentage of the royalties."

"I've already spent my advance."

"Russell will figure it out. He's good at that stuff. As you well know." Russell was once my lawyer, before Elizabeth pirated him away. She gazed into his eyes. That's all he needed to follow her to the ends of the earth. I doubt she pays him a retainer.

"Elizabeth, you and Russell draw up some kind of proposal. Don't even send it to me. Send it to my new guy. He's good at that stuff too. We'll all do what we can to work this out."

"I don't trust you." She was pouting. My God.

"I can ask Leon to recall the book. I will if you want me to." I had to make it clear she has no fallback position. It was a nonoffer offer.

"That would be the same thing as suing you. The minute Leon recalls the book, everyone goes out and buys a copy. Quotes will be posted on the Internet."

"So have Russell call my guy."

"I'm exhausted. Just seeing you exhausts me." She looked tired. It hurt me that I could do this to her. But it was her own fault. She should have forgiven me when she had the chance.

Now that we had the negotiation part behind us, I felt like we were on the same team again. That somehow she'd won, even though she hadn't, so now we could talk to each other like grown-ups. The woman has always had absolutely perfect lips. Lips I kissed thousands of times. Those lips belonged to me, and because they belonged to me once, they belong to me forever. So I said, "You're tired? You can come by my place and lie down for a while."

At this, her eyes narrowed and sparked. "Right!" She stood, leaving the bill for me. She didn't say goodbye. She was gone.

I exited the café, ignoring the curious glances from the crowded tables.

Were they recognizing me, or recognizing Elizabeth and so wondering who I might be? No matter. I took a long walk by the river. I delighted in the symmetry of the landscaping and greenery that didn't exist when I first arrived in the city. It occurred to me that I cannot conceptualize a relationship without thinking of it as a transaction. "I'll give you this, if you give me that." Perhaps it's because I excel at transactions. Problem is, once the transacting's over, I don't know what to do with the damn relationship. I want to keep bartering. Something, anything. If my prick no longer interests you, how about pain? We can give each other pain.

I could have pretended that I didn't give a shit about Elizabeth, but we both knew something was still there. Or at least I knew that she touched me in a way that no one else ever has. When it was good, we were like children together, at least for a while. But I couldn't be a child. Not in this world. And so I couldn't stay in that dreamworld she wanted to inhabit. There were wars to be fought. Kudos to receive. Interesting women to know. Elizabeth fell in love with the anarchic side of me, but couldn't stand living with it. And that's that.

September 26, 1976

Got up this morning and did fifty push-ups and a hundred sit-ups. Also did some yoga and meditated.

Jennifer and I went on a "date." After we saw a movie in the Village, I picked up a bottle of wine and we ended up at her place, which is in a part of town I don't know very well. We made out on her couch. She was really into sex, right away. Her hair had a faint chlorine scent, she must be a swimmer. Her body was small and tight. Her admirable butt was muscular. We fucked, but I was kind of drunk and still tired from my night out with Jack so I was slow getting it up.

Finally after all kinds of soothing sounds from her I managed a soft erection and we kind of stuffed it in. By then my whole effort was focused on staying hard and this made me even more nervous, so I pounded away and came too soon. She didn't seem to care. I left her place feeling pretty unsatisfied.

When I got back to the apartment Dagmara was out. I found Haim slouched on the living room couch watching *Mannix* reruns and eating ripe tomatoes as if they were apples. I told Haim the story of my lousy sexual peformance with Jennifer. It felt like a confession.

Haim thrust out both tomato-slick hands and grabbed an imaginary girl. "So what do you care if your prick is soft! You have a beautiful girl in your arms, you eat her, you squeeze her, you suck her toes, you lick her legs." He illustrated all this with a fat tomato. "Don't worry about the prick. The prick is boring, it's a schlong, a schmuck, a piece of meat, worth nothing without your passion. It gets hard, it doesn't get hard, so what? It just goes in and out, in and out. Every man has a prick, but how many men know how to *love*! Kiss her! Fress her! Give her all you've got. That's what a woman wants." He finished the tomato in two huge bites.

I smoked a joint, took a bath and then wrote this down. While I was writing this, Dagmara returned with her date for the evening, a Slavic guy wearing a shirt three sizes too small for his hairy barrel chest. He was in heat over Dagmara, perspiring and tongue-tied. Obviously she's not fucking this guy either. She's got everyone on a string, my Polish blond bombshell. Am I the only one to get lucky with her? Note to myself: Get another blow job from Dagmara if possible.

September 27, 1976

Day off for no particular reason. That's the way it is down in SoHo. Downtowners are hippies. Jonathan has decided he wants to go to New Orleans and he let me have a day off.

Been writing most of the day. Trying to capture some of my impressions of the city on paper. The goal is to build a montage of layers, of images, one on top of another. Voices, sounds, pictures. Swirling around, jumping from one to the next. Pynchon is a great inspiration. Also Kerouac, of course. They write cinematically. That's the way to do it, in cuts like a movie. James Joyce was way ahead of the pack with this. That's what writing has to be in the future. Undeniable. Blazing. Majestic.

The videos at Erehwon are an inspiration too, ironically. They jam things together in a cool way. There's a word they use around here, "interface." The energy of the work is in the "interface and the frame." (Just finished reading Susan Sontag's book of essays, *Against Interpretation*.)

I have to energize my writing, like the music over at Max's Kansas City. Like a machine gun. Blam-blam-blam. My writing must be lethal. My words have to threaten. Most writing is about what people are thinking. Like something from another century. It's dead. *Real* people don't think, they *talk* and they *act*. Without knowing *why* they talk and act. Thoughts have nothing to do with anything. Thoughts come *after*. No one in a movie has a thought. You can't *see* thoughts, why *read* about them? Psychology is as dead as a Freudian cigar butt.

I have to experience life so I can know what I'm talking about when I write. I have to dance and fuck and get high and see everything! My life should be rock concert and my writing an Altman documentary of that rock concert. Make it dense and well made, but entertaining at the same time. Like Shakespeare—entertain the royalty *and* the groundlings. Is it possible?

There's so much shit out there. Why do I bother? Kerouac ran into so much resistance. All writers do.

Anyway, I am trying to write this short story about a guy and his pet cat. He's incapable of love with a human being but he's in love with his cat.

Almost a sexual thing, but I don't want to be clear about that. Maybe he kills his next-door neighbor over the cat. I don't know, it's not really working.

LATER:

I was writing down the above when Haim came rolling in with his friends. He's best buddies with the other street vendors who work in front of the museum: the hot dog guy, named Joe, of course, and the ice cream man, Tony.

They had a woman with them. The woman was not particularly young or pretty, in fact she looked worn-out and depressed. Like they kidnapped a housewife off the street. She could have had rollers in her hair or wearing an old bathrobe, that's how suburban she looked.

When she entered the apartment, she didn't say a word and didn't seem curious about me at all. But Haim and his buddies were in a boisterous mood. They were lugging huge grocery bags of beer and chips and cigarettes. I tried to ignore them. But it was impossible to write while they bustled around.

Next thing I knew, Haim was setting up a little movie projector on the coffee table. Then he drew the blinds, flipped on the projector and started screening a movie on the wall of the living room. It was a porn movie, poorly shot and filled with really sudden cuts. It began with a woman alone in her apartment. She was dusting her furniture. Then I guess the doorbell rang (the film was silent) so she trotted over to her front door and there was a delivery man standing in the doorway carrying a box. She let the guy in. And then the film cut to an extreme close-up of this greasy purple hard-on sliding in and out of a dark hairy vagina. It was so close-up that for a few seconds I couldn't grasp what I was looking at. Really gross.

Obviously, by this time, I'd given up on my writing and emerged from my "room" to hang out with the boys. Haim had thrown a thick arm across the shoulders of the depressed-looking woman. He was all friendly with her, like they were at a movie theater on a date. He waved me into the room. "Richard, come in, come in! Watch the movie, it's good!" I tried to avoid staring at the woman, I couldn't understand why she was watching this porn surrounded by leering men.

Haim got up off the couch and threw his arm around *my* shoulders. In a hoarse whisper he said, "You want to get your cock sucked? She'll fuck you too!" Like I was a co-conspirator with these guys. Over Haim's shoulder I spied the woman on the couch, who looked like she was in mourning. Tony and Joe sat on either side of her, stupid grins pasted on their faces. Maybe they always looked like that. I didn't know, I had just met them.

This woman should have been home serving her kids a tuna casserole. She should be answering phones at a bank! It was obvious she should have been anywhere on earth but here in our high-rise apartment with Haim, his roommate and the vendors. I thought, she hates us. I say "us" because I was now a member of this group of assholes.

I whispered to Haim "I'm kind of working right now."

Haim shrugged and slapped Tony on the knee. "You first, Tony, you go."

Tony grabbed his beer, and took the woman by her hand. Haim pointed the way to the bedroom door with a nod of his bald head. Tony took a last pull on his beer and led the lady into the room and out of sight. The slamming door made a sad hollow sound in our tiny apartment. I returned to my desk and began to write this but it was impossible to concentrate.

After about ten minutes, Tony emerged and Joe took his place. Another ten minutes passed and Joe emerged wearing a sheepish smirk. The woman darted into the bathroom. Haim leapt up and bellowed at the bathroom door, "Hey, let's go!" The woman emerged from the bathroom looking lost and frightened. Maybe she wasn't a professional hooker and did this on the side when she wasn't housewiving. Haim murmured something and, like a sleepwalker, the woman slipped past him into the bedroom. The door slammed for a third time. The situation had the erotic aura of a barbershop. "Next!"

After a pause of about a minute, a tremendous rhythmic booming began to shake the wall. I expected cracks to appear in the plaster. Neighbors could have heard all this, but it was the middle of the day, only the aged were in the building. Finally, thankfully, the booming ended. A muffled moan. A pause. Then Haim threw open the door of his bedroom (the bedroom he shares with Dagmara), grinning, mopping the sheen of perspiration off his bald head.

"Now your turn. We warmed her up for you."

"Nah, it's okay, Haim." I was standing in the kitchenette area, pretending to drink a glass of juice, spying on Tony and Joe.

"We have her for an hour. You don't have to pay."

"Yeah. I . . ."

"She's a nymphomaniac. You don't want to hurt her feelings, do you?"

Was it possible she's a sex-starved female who has a thing for street vendors? Didn't matter. I whispered to Haim, "Tell her I'm gay. Please?"

From the corner of my eye I again saw the woman skittering from the bedroom to the bathroom. A snap and click as the door locked. It creeped me out to think she might be using my soap. My towel. Maybe my toothbrush! When she finally emerged, the men were arguing about a soccer match.

The woman stood waiting for their attention. I said, "Haim?"

As if he were paying a cabdriver, Haim dug into his trouser pocket and found a wad of bills. He carefully peeled off several twenties and thrust them into her hand. Without meeting his eye, she said "Thank you" and slipped out our front door like a melancholy ghost. Haim and his buddies guzzled the rest of the beer, rewound the film and watched it one more time. Finally they all left.

I was happy to see them go, but I guess their presence satisfied my curiosity about hot dog vendors and ice cream men. They hadn't said much. All I really got was that they are regular guys. Regular heartless guys. Like me. Because I realized after they were gone, that if they weren't here, if I had been alone with her, I would have had sex with her. Just to get to know her better.

February 1, 2006

I continue perusing my journals from the seventies. It's beyond me how I was able to survive in New York City, let alone set down roots as an author. In passage after passage I spout the most conventional wisdom, conceptualize in the most irksome way and go on and on about how I'm going to "conquer the world." What an ass! The young man I was did nothing exceptional other than drink and get laid. I'm embarrassed by my former self.

Lately I've been enjoying William Kapell recordings from the fifties. Exquisite pianist. Brahms, Chopin. You can feel the fire under the form. He died at thirty-one in a plane crash and now he is barely remembered. Gould made it to fifty. Because one man lived longer, he is better known? Each work of art is the protector of the earlier effort. Kapell did not record enough to shelter his own output.

Also been making my way through a Randall Jarrell translation of Goethe's *Faust (Part One)*. Jarrell was about my age when he died in a car accident. Suicide? Who knows? Spent years translating Goethe's poetry for the simple reason he felt it had to be done. Probably didn't make a penny. Beautiful job. Listen to this:

> *Care nests here at the heart's core, uneasily Hatching out secret*
> *miseries, spoiling all happiness, all peace, Putting on, always,*
> *her new masks: She comes as house and home, as wife and child,*
> *As fire and water, dagger and poison; You tremble at all that*
> *doesn't happen, You weep for everything you've never lost.*

Nice huh? Goethe, on the other hand, lived to be about nine hundred years old. Him and Tolstoy and Shaw. These guys, unlike most of those old-school European cats, did not contract syphilis and did not die raving lunatics, kept writing right to the end.

Goethe wrote about the essence, the thing that can barely be touched. TRUTH! But couched the problem in a story about a guy who wants to get laid. This is a play written almost two hundred years ago. In Goethe's world, the sexual urge lives inside of all other urges. Like nested Russian dolls. Freud said this too, didn't he? Underneath it all, *sex*. Under that, infancy. Or for some, "God." Freud claimed the spirit was only an illusion. Said our innate sense of spirituality is nothing more than memories of the amniotic womb-sea. The music of the spheres is only a vague memory of mom's belly juice sloshing around.

I've spent my entire life surrounded by the artistic giants of literature. Like mountains along the horizon, viewed from a distance, I've taken them for granted and imagined climbing them one day. But they were so far away, when I finally got close enough to climb them, only then could I appreciate how truly immense they were. Why bother writing at all?

Sarah keeps calling. I think she figured out I was in the city with Elizabeth. Maybe someone saw us together. How did I end up married to Sarah? Oh, that's right, I *didn't*. So she should fuck off. My great-aunt Sadie has bequeathed to my sister and me five thousand dollars each. I cried when the lawyer called to tell me.

October 1, 1976

Jack, who I think is an alcoholic, wants to go barhopping every night. But I need time to stay home and write! This is complicated by the fact that Dagmara's always wandering around the apartment smoking or bleaching her upper lip or cooking. Also, she has gotten into the habit of bringing a female friend home with her, Anita, also from Poland. They hang out in the living room and drink cups of Turkish coffee and smoke and nosh chocolate cake and whisper. Every so often they laugh like they're drunk. Anita always gives me the eye as she's leaving the apartment. If Dag isn't hanging around, then Haim is watching TV in the living room. This place is too small.

Jack and I barhop either Greenwich Village or the Bowery. I like the Bowery. Lots of dark little places that have been there since Eugene O'Neill was a young alcoholic. Crumpled white-haired men cluster around the bare wooden tables. The bartenders grimly pour and move on, feeding the old drunks like pets. This crowd is not chatty or easygoing like in TV shows and movies. The old men are like zombies. Jack told me they sign their Social Security checks over to the bar and live in the tiny rooms upstairs until the next check comes. They never see the money. Drink it all. Pretty horrific. I should interview one of these guys and write a story based on that. Am I a bad person for wanting to do that?

Oh, and by the way, I got mugged. I wasn't frightened until afterward. Just walking down the street and a skinny black guy brushed past me. I forgot about him in an instant. Then I half-noticed him up ahead of me, talking to two other guys who were leaning against a car. They all turned and one nodded at me, like he was saying hello. The first guy said something to the two at the car and then they all started walking toward me and then another guy I hadn't seen before jogged over from across the street and before I knew what was happening I was surrounded by four men and could feel the blade against the back of my neck. I was trying hard to think. Trying hard to come up with a plan in case they started hitting me. The main guy said, "Look down! Look down at your feet!" So I did.

I gave them the twenty bucks I had. Plus my watch. When I got back to the apartment, I told Dagmara and she suddenly got all mothering and loving. It broke the ice that has formed between us. I think she realizes I'm not a terrible person. Did she fall in love with me? Is that what this is about?

I didn't call Dad. He would only yell at me and tell me to move back home.

October 4, 1976

After work today, I cruised up to 42nd Street to write in the library without the chaos of Haim and Dagmara. So I was sitting at this giant oak table and this scruffy guy sat down across from me. I thought he was talking to himself. But then I figured out that he was talking to me. His face was all dark like he'd been in the sun for weeks. He was wearing four layers of clothing. Said he hasn't eaten in two days. His hands had sores on them. His bloodshot eyes were boring holes into me. He wanted money.

I said, "If you're hungry, I'll buy you something to eat."

In an angry tone of voice, like I was lying, he growled, "Where?" So I said, "I know a place." And I got up and left the library with this guy tagging along. He didn't say anything while we walked and I didn't either. I was making my way along 42nd Street with an impoverished street denizen. I didn't even know his name. We headed into Times Square to the Nedick's. This place is like an emporium, it could be a betting parlor, but instead people swarm around chomping on hot dogs and huge soft salt pretzels. I bought the guy two hot dogs and a root beer.

I watched him while he picked at his food, chewing slowly. He had a furious knot in his brow. When we left he didn't say "Thank you," he just walked away and blended back into the crowd. One more anonymous New Yorker.

I'm glad he didn't shake my hand. He probably had fleas. But why was he angry at me? It was as if I had done him wrong by not under-standing that what he was really asking for was money. Like *I* was the asshole.

Doesn't matter if he knows it or not. I will write about him someday. He will live on in my pages.

Been reading a novel by this guy J. G. Ballard. *Crash*—absolutely per-fect book about a guy who wears black jeans and intentionally crashes cars into other cars and has an orgasm each time he does it. I wish I could write like that.

October 7, 1976

So I was at work and this woman was returning a tripod while I was wrapping these packages with twine and I needed to wrap the twine somewhere, so I spooled it around this little teddy bear that Jonathan keeps on a shelf. I made a joke to the woman about the little "bondage bear" and this woman, Sally, turned to me and said, "Are you into that?" And perversely (again trying to be funny) I said, "Sure." She invited me out to Ken's Broome Street Bar for a drink.

She was blond, pretty in a tough way, nice body. So we had a drink and while we were sitting there she pulled out this paperback book and dropped it onto the table. It was *The Story of O*. She looked deep into my eyes and asked me if I've ever read it. I said, "Of course." She said, "What O is into in this book? That's what *I'm* into."

We left the pub and shared a cab and when I dropped her off at her place, she kissed me on the mouth. I was like wow, I have a girlfriend!

Anyway, long story short, we got together the next day and surprise, surprise, she really *was* a masochist! Which was interesting.

We met up to go to a movie but we never got to the movie. She asked me up to her place. It was a cramped, glum railroad apartment. Macrame on the walls. Tiny kitchen with a spice rack on the wall and dirty dishes in the sink. Everything had a greasy film of dust on it.

Sally pulled me into the bedroom and a cat scooted out. I was standing there, not sure what I was supposed to do, and she started rummaging around in the closet and pulled out a coil of clothesline. Then she stripped naked and had me tie her hands and ankles together. I barely knew her. I didn't even know her last name. We were supposed to be going to see this new Lina Wertmuller movie, *Seven Beauties*, and instead here I was tying her up. I was trying to figure out the right attitude to take toward all this, but she was being very serious. Moving things right along. Not smiling or even looking at me. On the other hand, she was acting so submissive it was getting me hot. And she was naked and I wasn't.

I tied her wrists together and then I tied her ankles together, which was a very intimate act to perform with someone I'd just met who was naked when I wasn't. Once she was all tied up, I wasn't sure what the next step should be. But she rolled onto her side and I just opened my fly and entered her from behind which, because she couldn't move her hands very well, was extremely awkward. Plus she wasn't particularly wet. But she seemed to like it. She said she did anyway.

After I came, she wanted me to hit her, but instead I untied her. I needed a break, the whole enterprise was exhausting. We smoked a j. Then she demanded that I spank her. It was surprising to see her white ass-skin turn pink. But I wasn't really into this spanking thing, especially since I had just had sex and wouldn't have minded lying down for a while. She didn't want to stop, but since I was the boss she had to do what I told her to do. That's part of the domination thing. So I dominated her into taking a break.

The situation was ironic because sometimes when I masturbate I fantasize about tying up beautiful women and having sex that way but while I was actually doing this stuff with Sally it didn't feel like anything special or exciting. It just felt clumsy and nonerotic. Too much thought had to go into it. Kind of ruined the mood. As far as I was concerned we were just goofing around. Except we were not "we." It was just *me* who was goofing around. Sally was very serious. She *really* wanted me to hurt her. Badly. She had this determined look in her eyes.

The good news is, I got laid. Also she likes to drink, which compensates for the nonsatisfying sex. Plus she wanted to be my slave so she cooked a meal for me after we fucked. The downside was that she's not a very good cook. Plus she's smart as a whip (sorry, couldn't resist) but she didn't seem that interested in talking about anything other than sex and bondage and other ways I could torture her. I wanted to discuss Pynchon and Ballard, but it went nowhere.

October 9, 1976

After work, Jonathan dragged me off to a concert by some friends of his, the Philip Glass Ensemble. A clarinetist and keyboards and a sax. Very loud. And very repetitive. Like a massive wall of sound, like a tidal wave of sound. About halfway through, I floated into a trance state. Which according to Jonathan, is the whole point. It's called "minimal" music. I liked it, I think. Not the kind of stuff you'd dance to, but interesting. I guess this guy Glass is some kind of genius. I met him and he seemed more like a very tired nice guy than a genius. Actually I don't know what a genius should look like.

Everyone in the audience was wearing black.

Jack was there, videotaping the event, looking very professional. After he packed up his stuff, we all walked down to Spring Street to this underground hangout called the Byrd Hoffman School of the Birds. It was surreal because the streets in SoHo are cobblestoned and the door to this place was very small, maybe half the size of a normal door. I had to crouch down to enter. Made me think of *Alice in Wonderland.*

Inside the space people were dancing to normal music, but not the normal type of dancing. They were spinning with their arms out straight, while staying in one spot. And in the middle of all this spinning was this mildly retarded guy named Christopher Knowles. He's what's called an idiot savant. He is the leader of the place. This petite woman with jet black hair was always by his side, and seemed very suspicious of anyone who approached him. I tried the spinning for a while. Finally Jack and I escaped to Fanelli's and had some beers.

Tried to read a book about "structuralism" by this guy Roland Barthes. About ten pages in, I realized I had no idea what he was talking about so I stopped.

February 6, 2006

Today I can't get Sarah out of my mind. A little voice says, "Watch out, keep her, she may be the last one. Eventually the sexy grad students will lose interest in you. And Richard Morris will not find a female like Sarah again. Because he's old now." Because sooner or later there *will* be the last one. And I don't want my last "love" to be some wheelchair-bound, thick-nosed crone camped beside me in the sunroom of a stinking nursing home. You only get so many trysts in this life, and if I still have a chance to touch a living, breathing, vital feminine female, I should take it.

Sarah's good in every way. Thank God for her patience. Thank God for her enthusiasm, because I don't have any. Thank God for her moist womb, her rich flowing tresses, her pink skin. I can almost get sentimental about this girl. All she wants is to *be* with me. She doesn't infringe on my freedom. She doesn't even want exciting sex from me. She's happy to nurse me and blow me and feed me. The problem is that I find any desire on her part annoying. At times, her very existence irritates me.

Why can't she just take a break? What's the old country song? "How can I miss you if you won't go away?"

There is a kind of defeat in totally surrendering oneself to what women desire. In that surrender, you lose your mystery. The truth is, in the larger context, in order to survive, mystery *must* be preserved. As I give in to her, she starts forcing her domestic agenda on me and I become a mediocre artist. She becomes bored and leaves me. So I can't give in to her. She claims that "underneath it all," I'm a nice Jewish boy. How does she figure that? "I know you," she says, "deep down." But she's wrong. She doesn't know me.

The affable artist is the bad artist. Only the ornery artist is the good artist.

October 10, 1976

Out with Jack until four last night. Tremendous hangover. My teeth hurt. Drinking gin with some tall blond Dutch guy who had the most intense green hashish. We got completely wasted in the Dutch guy's room at the Chelsea Hotel. He insisted he is going to bring me to Amsterdam as a "visiting artist," whatever that means. Not even sure how I got back to my apartment.

In the morning, I woke up to the sound of yelling and screaming. But it wasn't actually screaming, it was just Haim and Dagmara making breakfast, clattering around in the kitchen, only a few feet from where my head lay on my pillow. I have to get out of here.

I spent the afternoon taking it easy, sipping herbal tea and smoking. Dagmara perpetually buzzing around. Haim was at work. I think Dag and I have made some kind of peace. But no way is she going to let me have sex with her, that's pretty clear. It's like she lost the battle but won the war.

Dagmara's friend, Anita, came by. She's more savvy than Dag. She's been in the States longer. She's married to a truck driver. Huge breasts. While she waited for Dag to come home, Anita hung out with me and we discussed literature. She actually knows who Franz Kafka is! She's read everything by Dostoyevsky. She also smokes nonstop. I'm curious to see what her nipples look like.

Dad called. Wanted to know why I don't call him more often. Said he's "worried about me." I lost my temper and hung up on him.

Dagmara came home, then she and Anita finally left the apartment and I drank four espressos and wrote a bunch of shit which I got really excited about, then threw it all away. I investigated Dagmara's underwear drawer and found her panties and jerked off. It's like I'm falling in love with her because she won't sleep with me.

Sally called, wants to go see this movie everyone's talking about: *Taxi Driver*. It's playing at the discount movie theater down on St. Mark's Place—why not?

I've been reading Stephen King, *Salem's Lot*—kind of cool. Listening to Queen and Bad Company a lot. I ended up smoking a giant spliff while reading and fell asleep on my bed. Woke up, wrote this, ran out the door to see the movie. Work tomorrow.

October 12, 1976

Broke up with Sally, but before I get to that, I have to notate here that *Taxi Driver* is, in my estimation, the greatest movie ever made. This guy Robert De Niro is completely fearless. Can't imagine what he is like in person. I had seen him before in this Harvey Keitel movie, *Mean Streets*, and he was pretty great but in this movie he is like Christ reborn. Plus Cybill Shepherd is so intensely blond and perfect I get hard watching her onscreen.

After the movie, we went over to Sally's place. Sally wanted me to fuck her in the ass. So we worked that out but then her butt started bleeding and it was gross and I lost my erection. She saw the blood and got all turned on. She wanted to suck my dick with the blood and microscopic shit on it. I had a mini-breakdown and told her I cared about her and that I could never hurt her. She got angry at me. She said she didn't need a psychoanalyst for a boyfriend, that she just wanted to get beat up. She said I had really let her down. It made me feel impotent. Not hitting her is like not getting it up.

The confusing thing is I have feelings for Sally. It was nice hanging out with her. Having some kind of companionship with an intelligent woman. But it was doomed from the start. And deep down I know the value of every experience is that I can write about it someday. My life is only a by-product of my writing.

Got home and for some unknown reason Dagmara gave me a shoulder massage and made me tea. She's so sweet to me. We ended up falling asleep in front of the TV and didn't wake up until Haim got home. He found us on the couch. After that he didn't say much, then I heard him banging around in the kitchen roasting chicken legs in the broiler.

So now Dagmara's all happy because we had togetherness without sex but Haim isn't speaking to me. I'm getting no work done in this apartment. I'm lonely even when I'm around people.

A list of people I need to observe:

Heroin addicts
Pakistani cabdrivers
Old Irish guys
Sexual braggers
Old Jews
Club punks
Doormen

Wall Street fatsos
Subway tellers
Post office clerks
Pizza countermen
Catholic schoolgirls
Black kids on the subway
Businesswomen with padded shoulders and bow ties
Dancers
Chain-smokers
Mafia guys who sit in front of clubs
Chinese butchers
Bartenders
Barflies
Winos on the street
Bodega owners
Dogwalkers (poodles, large dogs, nasty dogs)
Porn store clerks
Three-card monte dealers
Leafleteers
Strippers
Steerers
Pot dealer philosophers
Techies
Skateboarders
Joggers
Ladies who lunch at the Plaza
Businessmen in suits and sunglasses
Transvestites
Retarded messenger boys
Nickel bag sellers in the park
Cops

November 15, 1976

Haven't written for a while. Been working long hours for Jonathan. I got him to give me a raise. Yay!

Dagmara's buddy, Anita, showed up one afternoon when no one was home and we started kissing and then we had sex on my bed and then she left. Her breasts are more interesting when they are hidden under her clothing. They're so massive they slip into the space between her arms and her chest when she's lying down. Plus she must be at least twenty-nine or thirty. I don't think I'm into older women.

On that subject, Jack says that he always uses condoms because there's this thing, "herpes," going around. Plus of course the usual syphilis and gonorrhea. But who gets those diseases?

Jack gave a party at his loft. Jack's crowd is sarcastic and competitive. More people wearing black. Mainly visual artists and filmmakers. The filmmakers make work on Super 8 and video, not regular film (35mm?). This white-haired guy named Jim showed a short film on the ceiling. Everyone is into New Wave music and punk. And everyone drinks as much as they possibly can. Especially this writer, Zim, who explained to me that he is an alcoholic and will probably die by the time he's twenty-eight. He drank four large tumblers of whiskey. I could never do that.

Zim isn't like the others. He's more serious, more dedicated to getting fucked up. But also very intelligent and insightful when discussing work. He knew all about J. G. Ballard. He's also read *Finnegans Wake*— or says he has.

Zim also had cocaine.

Cocaine is an excellent drug. Especially combined with pot and vodka. There are all these misconceptions about it. The truth is that it's not physically addicting and, in fact, you can work while doing it. It's typical of our culture to try to prevent us from using anything that feels good. God help us if we feel good! The dominant culture is invested in shackling our imaginations. The artist must be free.

I spent the night trying to talk to this artist, Katie. Small breasts, big eyes and amazing hair. I'd catch her staring at me from across the crowded room, but when I'd approach her, she wouldn't say much. In a blink she'd be gone. Later Jack told me that she's a lesbian. I don't think she's a lesbian, I think she just doesn't like me.

I stuck around until all the booze was drunk and helped Jack clean up. Then Jack and I strolled around the Village till dawn. That's when I like New York best. It's like we're adventurers exploring another country. I said I was hungry and Jack knocked on an unmarked door at the back of a building. Inside was a cavernous room filled with stacks of aluminum trays being tended to by bakers all dressed in white, wearing hats made of folded newspapers. White flour dust covered everything. They were baking bialys. Jack bought a dozen in a paper bag for fifty cents, then he and I rambled down the dark streets munching on the fresh bread and belting out "We are the Champions!" as the steam leaked from under the manhole covers and echo-y sirens wailed through the canyons. Doesn't get any better than this. To be young and drunk and full of bread. Got home and played Pink Floyd really loud. On my headphones, of course.

Reading about the CIA. And trying to read Yeats. Read Allen Ginsberg's *Howl*. Not sure if he's a fake or the real thing. He walked by me one time in the East Village. Also saw Andy Warhol with his friends. Just walking around.

February 18, 2006

Sarah has stopped calling. Leon e-mailed, wants me to drive into the city to do press interviews. Why bother? The book is dead. No one wants it.

I told Leon I'll give interviews over the phone. Leon and I are playing a game here. If I don't do the interviews, someday he'll remind me that I did nothing to "support" the book. That it was *my* fault the book did no business. So I have to go through the motions now to protect my ass in the future. So I will do the interviews.

Why do I have to support my own book? Wasn't writing it enough?

I spent the day sitting by the window tracking the winter birds as they pecked at the crusted snow beneath the feeder. Rachmaninoff and Beethoven string quartets on the stereo. Every day I push myself and go for strenuous walks in the clear freezing air, my breath hanging in wisps behind me. Hopefully my heart doesn't burst and they find my frozen body on the path.

This morning I opened my eyes and couldn't move. No motivation to get out of bed and make coffee and write. There's nothing to write, because there's nothing to write from. The surgeons cut into my heart and now I've only got half a heart. The bad half. The petty half. The vivacious half is dead. Can't even jerk off. The best part of the day is late morning after coffee when I peruse my old journals. "Portrait of the artist as a young idiot." The most ridiculous aspect of my younger self is the supreme confidence. Particularly the sexual confidence.

Truth is, I was never a great lover. Possibly not even a *good* lover. Average in every way. Then and now. This is the meaning of anonymity. To be nothing special. The pain of this acknowledgment stirs me. I thought I was special, but I wasn't. I was only one among many. To acknowledge the anonymity of one's own effort? Isn't that a kind of death? The nonspecialness. Total merging with the billions. One more molecule circling the sucking drain. Exactly that anticipation of nothingness, exactly that pain of awareness that goads me forward. To keep writing. To assure myself that I am indeed something special. (Rousseau: "I am not made like any of those I have seen; I venture to believe that I am not made like any of those who are in existence.")

Now. I am, now. Now I am unique. I wasn't then. Then I was a naive idiot. A wannabe. But because I was so certain of my existence, I existed. A mirage.

Every life is an arc. Begin as infant. Die a corroded old soul. Everyone reaches an apogee at some point. I'm past that apogee now. I will never again be as smart as I was, as strong as I was, as attractive, as fast as I once was. Never. I'm losing, day by day. And I have a lot to lose because I've had it all. The fame, the money, the women. No children. Could have had the children, I guess. But even if I did, dying alone would have been in the cards, because as an artist I would have compelled them to hate me. This is what all great men do. So it's better they never existed and never knew me. Leon's going to get what he wants. I'll go back to the city and endure the charade. What choice do I have?

December 15, 1976

Bought along a little tape recorder today. Just left it on and taped people talking. Great way to capture the rhythms of speech. Taped Haim and his buddies. They will go on and on and it isn't until I transcribe them that I find the totally Beckettesque aspects of their speech. For example (the following is verbatim):

Tony: "All the time."
Joe: "Bullshit."
Tony: "I'm telling you."
Joe: "When?"
Tony: "Yesterday."
Haim: "I believe him."
Joe: "I don't."
Haim: "What's not to believe?"

Joe: "Fuck?"

Tony: "That's what I'm saying."

Joe: "Not even talk to you?"

Tony: "Talk and fuck."

Haim: "It's happened to me."

Joe: "Bullshit."

Haim: "It did."

Joe: "Both of you."

Haim: "It's true. You don't believe?"

Joe: "I don't believe."

Tony: "It's statistical."

Joe: "What?"

Tony: "You ask ten. Five walk away. Two slap you. Two just stare and one says 'Okay.'"

Joe: "'One says Okay'? Okay, what? What 'Okay'?"

Tony: "Okay, let's go."

Joe: "Go where?"

Tony: "Her place. Or a hotel room."

Haim: "You pay for a hotel room?"

Joe: "So you say, 'You wanna go to a hotel room?'"

Tony: "Something like that, not that exactly."

Joe: "What exactly?"

Etc. Etc. Kind of like Joyce. Right? (They were discussing Tony's system for propositioning women.)

Ran into that artist Katie on 13th Street. In contrast to the night at Jack's, she was amazingly friendly. She took me by the arm and we had coffee. Then we walked all the way down to SoHo where she shares a loft with a girl named Lila. We smoked a joint and had sex. She has the nicest peach-colored skin. Smooth. I was so stoned when we screwed I barely remember it. I kind of fell asleep and when I woke up, she was dressed and talking to someone on the phone. I went into the kitchen and her roommate was there. Maybe beautiful Lila is Katie's lesbian lover? While I was in the kitchen, Katie shut the door of her bedroom and after a while I left. I've wanted to call her, but I forgot to ask for her phone number.

February 23, 2006

Raccoons have taken up residence in the barn. If I had a dog, they wouldn't dare hang around the place. Without a canine presence, I think they're setting up house out there. I run out to the barn a dozen times a day, hoping to catch one of them. At night I shine my flashlight into the pitch-black and toss bits of driveway gravel at their glittering eyes. I told Sarah I was buying a shotgun. Everyone has a shotgun up here. She was horrified, of course.

The sad thing is that it's a beautiful old barn. Filled with a miraculous dry aroma of ancient hay and wood. Tiny, barely visible bats hang high in the rafters. Mice skitter under the floorboards. Spiders weave in the corners. And the raccoons? What do the raccoons do? Fuck? Dig holes? Write books?

Why do the raccoons bother me so much? Because they are sneaky and they are occupying something that is mine. I've run out of people to get pissed at, the raccoons are substitutes.

Still, I like spending time in that barn. I once thought I'd turn it into a studio, a serene place in which to write, but the sheer pretentiousness of the move turned me against it. It's an old-fashioned affectation. Something that "serious" writers did back in the day of the federal work programs. Arthur Miller. Clifford Odets. The "artist" migrates from the smoke-filled city, finds a run-down farm, then writes in "the country." Bellow was different, he remained in his beloved Chicago. So Jewish to find resonance in the "country." Why is that? Because Jews are afraid of the wilderness, in it they see danger. Raccoons.

It's all gesture. Turn a barn into a writing studio. Turn a country house into an office. Everything represents something else. Even my money is symbolic. What is money? Sure, for the poor it's a solution to a problem. But for me? A symbol only. I lose sleep over this new book. Why? Because it's not selling? What should I care? I don't need the royalties *or* the kudos. I need the symbolism of the sales. It would be better if I didn't care anymore. Like a dog who has been fixed and lies on the couch all day. Forgets what he once was.

I write at the kitchen table. It's enough.

January 20, 1977

Jack and I have been out toasting Gary Gilmore's death (by firing squad). I like this freedom. When I was at school or living with my folks, all nights ended safely in bed. Not something I ever questioned. But now, hanging with Jack, I realize that I never have to go home. Ever. It's up to me when I come or go.

We migrate from club to club, apartment to apartment, bar to bar. We end up in the most interesting places. We are explorers, nightcrawlers. The city is our home. Every fluorescent pizza parlor, every empty park bench, every private nightclub, all-night diner, hurtling subway car, every spit-stained sidewalk and bloodied pavement. It's all a home away from home. Because the city is our home.

Jack and I split up around two A.M. the first night out this week and I ended up at this girl's place down on Elizabeth Street in Little Italy. Nice girl, pretty. She's a modern dancer. Tall, strong. We got high. Talked. But man, her place was like something you see in those Jacob Riis photos of immigrant slums. Tin ceilings and walls. Roaches scurried across the floor while we made love. The roaches were probably sucking up my cum the minute it hit the sheets. If I wasn't so stoned and drunk, I don't think I could have handled it. Couldn't sleep all night, kept waiting for a roach to crawl up a nostril.

In the morning, we had a quickie, then she made espresso in a soot-blackened aluminum demitasse pot. No food. No nothing. Just one small bitter cup of coffee and a cigarette. I gulped it down, then took a lukewarm shower in her mildew-smeared bathroom, shook the roaches out of my underwear, got dressed and split. Now I'm hoping I didn't catch one of those venereal diseases Jack's been talking about. He says it's the sweet-looking ones who are carriers.

So I was blasting back to the watering hole on Spring Street and who did I run into but Katie with the peach-colored skin. Having just been fucked by aforementioned modern dancer, I had this weird idea that Katie could sense that I had been cheating on her. (When in fact, since we are not boyfriend/girlfriend, wasn't really cheating.) The point was, I wanted to keep moving, so I finally got her number and told her I'd call her. She seemed intrigued as I ran off. Probably a good thing. And now I have her number.

I found Jack at the bar hunched over a whiskey glass, unsurprised to see me, as if I'd been gone for two minutes to take a piss. I ordered a short beer for my breakfast. In the pissoir, we snorted a couple of lines of coke, knocked back a nasty shot of tequila for luck and charged out the front door into the cold morning air looking for real food down in Chinatown. Jack never asked me about the dancer, wasn't curious at all about where I'd been for the last twelve hours, and in a few minutes I too had forgotten all about her.

Yesterday, I finally made it back to the apartment in the late afternoon, jumping into the insane subway rush, making sure I got back home before Dagmara did, showered off the sex residue, changed my underwear and then shot back downtown and hooked up with Jack again around six. Espresso, cocaine, cigarettes, pep pills, Four Roses whiskey. Better living through chemistry. It works until it doesn't. And then I crash.

Sometimes it's so easy to believe I'm the center of the universe.

January 22, 1977

Met this interesting guy, "Big John."

Last night, after I cashed my paycheck Jack informed me that we had to restock our inventory of marijuana. "Replenish the arsenal," is the way Jack puts it.

We caught a subway that crosses the East River to Brooklyn which spit us out in a neighborhood called Williamsburg. Jack dragged me through the mean streets of Brooklyn (I was freezing my nuts off because all I had on was my peacoat and a sweater). We trudged up hills and down dales finally ending up in this dark, dark neighborhood. It was a typical loft situation, old warehouse mid-nineteenth century, standing on what seemed to be a desolate overgrown alley. Not a soul could be seen.

We entered through the typical anonymous door and ascended a massive staircase leading up to a metal door which in turn led into a humongous loft. At first, I thought we were in an abandoned factory. Camped out in the midst of this anarchic interior landscape of half-painted canvases and bookcases and mattresses and scrap lumber and a disassembled Indian motorcycle were four men draped over armchairs and old broken couches. The tang of righteous weed seasoned the air.

It was obvious that Big John was the big guy in the Barcalounger, talking. I wasn't introduced to the others. All the focus was on John.

When we entered, John halted in mid-sentence, turned to face me full-on, squinted as if I were hard to make out, then popped his eyes wide and said, "You a *narc?*"

I glanced at Jack, who shrugged. I said, "What? No!"

John thrust a gnarled hash pipe at me and said, "Here! Smoke the peace pipe and we'll ignore your shortcomings." I grabbed the pipe and as I took a hit, he nodded, as if to say, "That's right. I know what's good for you." I instantly trusted this "Big John." He looked exactly like a stoned Santa Claus. Bearded, long-haired, cherry-cheeked and jolly.

I dropped onto the couch and passed the pipe over to Jack. The three anonymous men had their feet up on the coffee table, so I put my feet up too. A TV stood off to one side, but no one was really watching it since the sound was turned off. A stereo somewhere was playing Dylan.

I had assumed we were stopping by John's to pick up the grass, then continue on our merry way. But I guess you don't hit and run with John. You *must* get wasted to the point of cerebral paralysis. And then, once you're in that state, you *must* listen.

John was in the middle of a mini-lecture on "the heretical fucking proto-Protestants of southern France" and the bold knights and the invention of chivalry and romantic love and the mindless, bloodthirsty Crusades and fierce Saladin and the pathetic Children's Crusade and the heretic Meister Eckhart (who, according to John, said, "Man must live without 'why'") and the hermit Walter Hilton, who wrote *The Cloud of Unknowing* (later I found this same book under my feet on the coffee table).

Wait, before I go any further, I have to add that John stuttered every few minutes. In the middle of a sentence, he would get hung up on a word and while locking eyes with us, misfire syllables in a staccatto geh-geh-geh-geh or teh-teh-teh-teh. He would be flying along and then, like an aerial barnstormer who had been doing tricks high overhead and who suddenly ran out of gas, John would drop into a sickening dive. We sat, frozen, while he sputtered and spasmed his way out of whatever mental turbulence he'd run into. Just when I thought he might be having a brain seizure, he snapped out of it and finished his sentence. John didn't acknowledge the stuttering. I'm not sure he even noticed it himself.

John was talking about how they tried to execute Rasputin ("The fucker died three times!") leading somehow to Zen Buddhism and the Tokugawa feudal regime and Japan during World War II and the Black Dragon Society and the "Zen of decapitation" (the Zen monks would teach the Japanese Imperial officers how to find transcendence by beheading their prisoners with one strike of a razor-sharp samurai sword). He was so exuberant, he made me laugh harder and harder, even though he was talking about blood and death and horror. I stopped to catch my breath when a chasm of panic opened beneath my feet. It was as if I were on a high wire a thousand feet above the ground and John in his stuttering mental aeroplane was flying circles around my head. This cherubic, laughing weed-brain was starting to freak me out.

I focused on the coffee table.

It looked like an ancient door, stolen from a Moroccan mosque, its dark brown timbers strapped one to the other with lengths of beaten black iron. It was heaped high with all kinds of stuff. At first all I could register was a disorganized pile of books, but then I noticed that the books (one title: *Paris Sewers and Sewermen*, another: *Sexuality, Magic and Perversion*) were only part of the rubble. Mixed into this slush of printed matter were ancient *Life* magazines featuring black and white portraits of Hitler and Churchill; faded "naturalist" (nudist) journals celebrating toothy sun-drenched Scandinavians all bushy and flaccid tossing beach balls; luridly multicolored *Tales from the Crypt* comic books and vintage *Mad* magazines.

There were dog-eared phone books from places like Moscow and Melbourne. Glossy 8 x 10 photographs of anonymous actors and ac-

tresses, Polaroids of prize-winning farm animals, yellow pamphlets au-
thored by the Pope, and bound manuscripts (one which was labeled
"EYES ONLY!") which might have been screenplays or novellas or top
secret government documents.

Mixed in were generous Baggies of marijuana buds, prescription drug
vials, dried-out oranges and lemons and limes, spent machine gun shell
casings, loose Oreos, engine parts, miniature Buddhas and an assortment
of tiny black dolls made of cloth. A huge twisted ram's horn the size of
my forearm, a mean-ass bone-handled Bowie knife and a cruel-looking
rust-smeared hatchet with feathers bound to its haft. A genuine glass eye-
ball, watching me. This last item transformed the pile into a living thing.
An archaeological puddle of quicksand in which floated a chunk of every
aspect of humanity, alive and waiting to pull me into it.

I picked up a miniature metal statuette, green with patina. I didn't
think John would notice because at that moment he was demonstrat-
ing the correct way to hold a samurai sword. But I guess nothing gets
past John. He halted in mid-sentence, pointed at the statuette and said,
"You are familiar, of course, with the great Lisbon earthquake of 1755?
Destroyed the whole city. Killed a hundred thousand people. Never been
anything like it. Shook people's faith in God. Everyone thought it was the
end of the world. The king lived in a tent for the rest of his life. Never set
foot in a real building again. But that's human nature. Always think it's
the end of the world. But usually, it isn't." John took a hit from the pipe
and coughed, then his eyes grew moist. I thought he might start stuttering but he continued. "That figurine is from the Archbishop's bedroom.
Tomás Torquemada's great-great-nephew. You know Torquemada, right?
He was the Grand Inquisitor during the Inquisition. Skinned people alive.
Stretched 'em on racks, drove nails into their skulls. You ever read Edgar
Allan Poe? 'The Pit and the Pendulum'? If you haven't you should. Poe
was the real deal. Was one of the great navigators of the mind's oceans.
Big gambler, married his cousin when she was thirteen. Was addicted to

absinthe. And wrote like a demon, invented the mystery story. People were much more interesting in those days."

I gently placed the little sculpture back on the table. Jack's eyes were closed and he was nodding his head as if listening to some music very far away.

That was when 'Gitte entered the room. She floated along the periphery of the available light so I couldn't quite discern her features. I was so wasted, I wasn't sure if she was an apparition. She slipped up alongside John and laid one delicate white hand on his head while he circled her waist with his powerful arm.

Her hair was flaxen and parted down the middle, falling to her shoulders. She wore no makeup. Easy, lovely lips. About medium height. A peasant blouse. Some simple silver jewelry graced her lithe throat. That's all. 'Gitte's only defect, if you can call this a defect, was that her body did not conform to the Hollywood norm. Her rib cage was smallish, though her breasts, if not large, were not small either. Her hips were slightly wide for a woman with such a slight frame. She projected a girlish fertility.

'Gitte's face came into focus. I don't think I've ever been that close to true beauty before. Her eyes met mine and an enormous charge ripped through my gut. I was paralyzed with love. In that one glance, all the promise, all the possiblities of insane bliss hit me. Not that she was promising any of that to *me*, but I understood in the most concrete way, in that one moment, that bliss was actually *possible*. This truth entered me and this truth rocked me. In that half-second when our eyes met, a massive flood of love and blood and happiness and sadness and the future and the past and everything that I had ever desired in the world and the reason for that desire poured into me. A shiver ran across my chest. I don't think anyone noticed, and then 'Gitte whispered something in John's ear, he smiled and she slipped out of the room as smoothly as she had sailed into it.

What did she say that made John smile? That she loved him? That she was waiting for him? That she was going to make him feel good? What a prize, what a gift to have a woman like 'Gitte whisper in your ear! All the treasure in the world couldn't buy it.

Where was she going? Maybe she was returning to the perfumed bedroom where she and this gregarious pot dealer spent their private time together. Or maybe a study where she could continue reading philosophy, or a studio, where she would resume her oil painting. The loft was so spacious, she might as well have been leaving the city. I wanted to join her, wherever she was going. But I wasn't even sure she had seen me.

John continued his narrative without acknowledging that his lady had just visited. I was now completely in his thrall, because a new fact about this man had been added to the equation. I knew that he was loved by an unbelievably beautiful creature. And obviously any man who could be loved by such a woman must be a man of great wisdom and substance.

After we left the loft and were making our way down the deserted Brooklyn streets, a radiant sky brightening overhead, I asked Jack, "Who is Big John? Where'd he come from?"

Jack said he was pretty sure that John was an ex-professor of literature from some Ivy League school and that Brigitte had been his student and they had been thrown out together sometime in the sixties. Which made sense to me. Then Jack added that there were conflicting theories. It was also rumored that John was actually a disgruntled ex-CIA agent who left the Agency when he discovered all the nasty shit they were doing. Another theory was that he had been a banker who had become wealthy selling counterfeit bonds for the Mafia before he ate some peyote and "dropped out." Jack said he also knew someone who knew someone who claimed to have known John in Vietnam when John was a gonzo journalist for Reuters. And someone else who said he saw John get run out of Vegas for counting cards at the blackjack tables.

Finally, Jack also heard of someone whose brother-in-law served time in Attica who swore that John was an ex–Hell's Angel motor captain from Oakland, California, where he served ten years for killing a man with an axe. Over a woman.

I liked the guy. I want to go over to his place again sometime.

March 1, 2006

I can't escape my dark, dark discouragement. I sit by the window watching the clouds and cry. I wander the house, touch things that Elizabeth once touched and think, "This was my life. It happened. It is behind me now. What did I do?"

Am I famous? I guess I am to the degree that I have made a big enough impression that someone, perhaps hundreds or thousands of people are meditating on my simulacrum, i.e., my writing. They think they "know" me. What do they know? Words. What does anyone know of any author? Virgil, Goethe, Mann, Nabokov, Mailer. "Advertisements for Myself." "Pay no attention to the man behind the curtain." Etc. Words. Not reality. Words.

Of course my fame is not like real fame, real "stardom." I've never achieved that. I can see the peak, but I've never stood upon it. Elizabeth was/is genuinely famous. She'll always be famous. She's *tattooed* with fame. Probably even when she's aged, she'll be famous. Like Brigitte Bardot or Lauren Bacall. In the nursing home, the children of her fellow patients will approach her, hat in hand. "I don't want to bother you, but my mother was a huge fan of yours. It would make her *so* happy if you could sign this napkin. Do you need help with your wheelchair?"

For a while, I shared her fame. I'd be traveling on a six-city book tour and would catch up with Elizabeth in Seattle or Toronto, where she would be shooting. Once I messengered a freshly completed manuscript to Leon, called a car service, hit the airport and grabbed a seat on the Concorde so I could attend her SRO play in the West End. The Claridge's hotel suite in which we romped was bigger than most New York City apartments. Room service would knock on our door and we would shout out, "Come on in!" Happy, half-naked, damp with fuck-sweat, I wouldn't even bother to leave the bed to sign the check. Entwined in our sheets, we would pick at breakfast while watching ourselves being interviewed on the boob tube.

We both got sacks of fan mail. Our names appeared in crossword puzzles. We made more money than we could spend. Who could touch us? We were golden. We laughed at a world of nobodies swarming fruitlessly far beneath our feet. We were the kind of duo that seizes the public imagination: a star of stage and screen and a cynical author who would entertain his beautiful Juliet forever with his stories. What a great combo we were.

And I had special access, I knew Elizabeth's secrets. I knew about her bouts with bulimia. I knew about her bizarre relationship with her father. I knew how hard she worked to gain the appearance of effortlessness because, in fact, she was deathly afraid of cameras and audiences. I would watch from my orchestra seat, hundreds of people seated behind me, and think, "That woman up there doesn't belong to you, she belongs to me. Because I know her in a way you can never know her." The ultimate transaction had been struck between us. She loved it as much as I did.

Reading my ridiculous journals depresses me. To relieve my mood, I uncorked a bottle of Bordeaux and organized my stock portfolios. There are two things in this world that cheer me up: my library and my money. If inflation doesn't eat it all up, I should be pretty comfortable in my old age. In fact my CPA called last week and informed me that he liquidated a "basket" of investments we bought ten years ago. I made something like forty percent on the transaction. So I'm financially comfortable enough to never write again, to sit and read all the Henry James and Kierkegaard I never got to first time around. Maybe I should move to someplace exotic to do my reading. Amsterdam? Bangkok? Tangier? And what would change?

March 4, 2006

Sarah arrived at noon. My only warning was a ten-second cell call from the interstate highway. She bushwhacked me. I had forgotten it was my birthday.

She brought lunch along, of course. A crisp green pea soup from Bouley and an assortment of smoked fish from Russ & Daughters. Small white paper bags of dried fruit. A miniature crate of clementines. Organic cashews. A freshly baked strudel. A bottle of New Zealand sauvignon blanc. And her lovely self.

She smelled of flowers, and her skin was still flush from her morning Pilates class. Probably spent the entire previous day in the spa tenderizing herself for me. She curled up in my ancient leather armchair scanning copies of *The Paris Review* while I noshed. She knew better than to rush things and kept her distance. Then, restless, I found myself leading her over to the couch, stroking her, the warmth of her body soothing me. She makes it so easy. She asks for nothing. The cuddling morphed into smooching which led to a trip to the bedroom. I'm a slow starter now, but it's all still there. As I orgasmed, strong ripples of intense euphoria ran over me, and for a moment, I thought, if this is it, it's over. This is the way I leave the world.

While I lay unstrung aside her long body, I fell into an empty dream. The house finches twittered outside. Sun-warmed air blended with the last cool northern breezes wafting in through an open window. I opened my eyes to find Sarah nuzzling my neck, one breast heavy on my ribs.

How can I expect her to back off? Especially since that's not precisely what I want. I like talking to her. I like having sex with her. I like her taste in clothes. Plus she keeps me organized. No question, Sarah slipping into my life once every two weeks is good for me. In a "rehab" sense of good.

When Sarah and I started up, I didn't make any promises. The autonomy made the relationship function well. I showered her with praise, she felt good about herself and we fucked. She always knew to make a large detour around the subject of commitment or "living together" and not to label what we had as a "relationship." I thought, she's younger, she's more open-minded, she *likes* the flexibility. This is what she *wants*. She sees all this noncommitment as a *positive*. She's a freethinker. A graduate student having a fling.

The problem is that though she is all those things, she's also a woman and proximity is never enough for her. Like a boa constrictor, she gets closer and closer and then too close. Maybe I could do this with someone who is more of a sterile goddess. Is it because Sarah was my student that things are both easier and more difficult with her? She never dares to lock horns with me. Is that a problem? Or is it that she is so damn fertile? The girl is aching to be pregnant, whether she knows it or not.

In fact, one of our favorite topics of discussion was the straitjacket of marriage! We would lie next to one another after sex, stare at the ceiling, and share banal anecdotes culled from the lives of our happily married sisters, brothers, best friends, etc. I thought we were completely agreed that one of the greatest enemies of artistic endeavor is familial comfort. It's all about priorities, isn't it? You either want to make art or you want to make babies. With babies comes nursing and protecting and schooling and worrying and God knows what else. How can one make art when new problems and crises burst from the family corpus like mushrooms off a rotting log? I made it clear to Sarah, this was something I could not and would not do. I'm *fixed* for God's sake! I thought she felt the same way. I thought she was committed.

After dinner I drank an espresso and feigned exhaustion. We hit the sack, no sex, no nothing. Once she was knocked out next to me, I limboed myself out from between the sheets, and out the door.

She's in the adjoining room as I write this. Sleeping like an innocent. What's wrong with that? That's good, right? I should be happy to have such a beautiful girl under my roof. Tonight I'd rather sleep on the couch, tonight I need isolation. And even though that is what I *want*, some perverse streak of responsibility will take control, and I will do what *she* wants and needs. I will *return* to the bed and lie next to her and hold her in my arms. And I will probably "make love" to her before she leaves tomorrow. (She is leaving tomorrow. No question about that.) Of course, no child will ever come of our union. At least I've been honest.

What possible motive could there be for me to try to make Sarah happy? So she will like me even more? Because it's the "right thing to do"? So that when she discusses me with her friends, which I'm sure she does, she will say nice things? Because I actually *do* care about her? No, it's none of that, it's because I'm weak.

The world continues apace. A hurricane almost destroyed New Orleans six months ago. Last week they celebrated Mardi Gras anyway. Nothing stops humanity.

Also Elizabeth called. Says if she doesn't hear from me in two weeks Russell will file papers in court and get an injunction against the book. I asked her if she was going to wish me a happy birthday and she hung up on me.

February 10, 1977

Huge snowstorm. Turned the roaring city into a fluffy white kitten.

I am making tape recordings of random people I meet. I hung out with this raggedy but dapper guy for two hours yesterday. He wore a fake leather coat and very shiny shoes, his brilliantined hair was slicked straight back. I bought him an egg salad sandwich and a coffee and let him jabber while I smoked cigarettes and kept my mouth shut. This is the transcription of his "monologue" (which I "improved" in places):

Damn. All right? So I ... so what happened was, wait a minute, so I gets my ass down to Welfare, right? And I gets my check. And then I scores my methadone, right? Planning ahead, 'cause I'm that kind of person, a planner. I say to myself I'll pick up a carton of Benson & Hedges, go home, drink my zombie juice, space, then I'll order up some chicken wings and shrimp balls. I love my shrimp balls. Maybe take a bath, watch a little Donahue with Snowball on my lap. I deserve it. I deserve it. I've been very stressed lately. What with my old lady calling me night and day. She never gives it a rest. Always bitchin' about the kid. (coughing) (inaudible) ... in college now.

Oh yeah. Oh, she calls me wantin' money, you know? And I say to her, Sondra, if I had the money I'd send you the money. I love my kid, you know? Fucking flesh and blood, right? My leg, shit. They give me these bandages but they're no fucking good.

So I gets home, I'm waitin' for the Chinaman to deliver the goods and I'm catchin' my breath, got Snowball next to me on the couch and for two seconds I'm happy. This is my life, for two seconds, maybe three, I enjoy happiness. That's it. That's the limit, three seconds, max. Then the phone rings. It's the bitch. Like she's got special radar. She's like the Wicked Witch, with the crystal ball, she can see me, no matter where I am. She sees me happy and she says to herself "He's in a good place, why don't I give him a call and fuck up his day?" And she starts with the money. And what can I say? I wish I had the money. I play the scratch-offs every chance I can, trying to do the best of my ability to get some currency together for my kid, to send to my kid. But the odds, my friend, the odds are stacked against me, always have been, always will be. So I hangs up on her bitchin' and moanin' and I'm so pissed off, I yank the phone outta the wall. That does it. Fuck the food. I'm doin' the methadone now. So I gets out the bottle and right then, there's a knock on the door. Knockedy-knock-knock.

Who is it? Bet you can't guess. Well, you wouldn't be able to guess 'cause you don't know my acquaintances, I won't say "friends" because these are not friends. These are parasital leechlike aliens. Carol, another witch from another corner of my fucked-up life. She just copped some smokin' smack, right? So she's lookin' for a place to fix and catch a nod, right? So she's making me an offer, like gonna lay a Jackson on me so she can park herself in my place, shoot up, catch a nod and drool all over my couch, right? So I go along with it. First mistake. I'm sittin' there, trying to stay calm, watchin' her amateurish attempts to hit a good vein, gettin' blood all over my furniture, finally I say, "Here let me do that!" and I find a spot in the back of her arm, hit her good. Man, she's out so fast, she practically collapses onto the floor, but I'm bootin' her 'cause you know if I take that spike out, and she wakes up, she's gonna be pissed. Right? Plus I'm kind of into it. Pumping that spike. Which wakes up Mr. Jones. You know Mr. Jones? He's a monkey. Lives right here. (pats his shoulder) And so I'm gone to the races. What else could I do? I can taste the junk in the back a my mouth. (inaudible) I mean I'm watching Carol nodding out with the cigarette burning her fingers, the needle hanging outta her vein and this whole scenario is pushin' all my buttons, you dig? I'm thinkin' a nod would feel real good right now, after all the stress I been through this morning. And this is after making such an effort to be good, you know? Just having her around defeats its own purpose. So I say, wake up Carol, you win, forget it with the twenty bucks, just lay a bag on me.

Just then the chink food shows up. And you know the way those guys are, givin' you that Asiatic fish eye when you ask 'em if it's all in there, and I'm just like cool, cool, here's the money for the food, get on your merry way, you know? I had completely lost my appetite. Guy's standin' in the door countin' his money, Snowball's barkin' at 'im, she hates Orientals, don't ask me why. Carol's wiping drops of blood off those black leather pants a hers she's so proud of. I'm thinkin' "People are fuckin' weird."

Anyway, I finally gets rid of the coolie, sticks the wings and the rice balls in the fridge so the roaches won't devour 'em, although I should point out I once found a roach frozen into an ice cube, don't ask me how it got there. And Carol says: "I don't got no more. We gotta go cop."

And you know how it is, my friend, when that monkey wakes up. He don't just wake up, he's speedin', he's shootin' pure crank. Jumping up and down on my back like he's on a pogo stick. So I say, "Fine, let's go take a walk. I had this C-note stashed away, there's people I owe it to, but they can wait, if you catch my drift."

We go cop. And, of course, we get beat. You know how it is, whenever you're desperate, you get ripped off. It's like life man. It's like fuckin' life. So there you go, a C-note down the drain. Then I remember, I didn't drink my methadone yet. So me and Carol hike back to my place, when we get there, Snowball is completely confused, we grab the 'done and go back to the corner where my usual guy is, and we sell the shit and I buy eight bags.

And we come back to my place and she says "You owe me two bags." And I says "Why, bitch?" And she says "'Cause I took you to my secret cop spot." And I said "I got beat at your secret cop spot, you fuckin beat-artist." And she starts yelling at me and shit, but man, fuck me if I'm going to lay two bags on her ass for gettin' my ass ripped off. Which she probably had something to do with. Plus, she never paid me for hanging out in my pad.

Suddenly she gets real sweet on me and says okay, just gimme one. So I do. And then I bang the shit and it's not as good as what she had before, but it's gonna do the trick on account of my dealer knows I'm trying to get straight so he wants me to have a good taste. "Your ex wants you back," that kind a thing, you know? So I shut my eyes for two seconds, next thing I know, the front door's open, Snowball's out on the landing barking her doggie brains out and Carol's gone. So I'm pretty high but I'm also pissed, so I jump up like I'm the Lone Ranger and run to the door to get the dog back inside 'fore she gets kidnapped or some shit like that, but I'm running so fast (plus I'm more fucked up than I realized) that when I blast out my front door a my apartment, I keep going like the Wile E. Coyote, hit pure air and somersaults right down the stairs all the way down by where the mailboxes are.

And Snowball's standing at the top of the stairs kind a staring at me with incomprehension, she's not barkin' anymore she's just giving me this look like "How'd you do that?" Right? Or maybe "WHY did you do that?" Because I try to move but I can't so I figure something must be broken. Hopefully not my back. Hopefully I'm not going to be paralyzed in a wheelchair for the rest of my life. The horror of that particular outcome enters my brain, but I'm actually too stoned to care.

And the whatchamacallit, "gentrified" assholes who live in my building are going to and fro and stepping OVER me and shit, like checking their mail and stepping OVER me. Even walking their fucking Labrador retrievers over me. The dogs are even sniffin' me and shit. I'm lucky I didn't get pissed on. (inaudible) No one's helping me up. And I'm yelling. Somebody must a called EMS, 'cause about forty-five minutes later these two spades show up and toss me into the back of this stinking van somebody must a died in there. Lots a people probably died in there come to think of it.

So they like take me to Emergency. Kind a drop me off on account of I could walk on one leg. I guess they don't actually bring you in on a stretcher unless you've got uncontrollable bleeding from an eye socket or some shit like that, then they give you the helping hand of mercy. Me, they just dumped.

So I'm in the ER and they're cutting my pants off, good fucking pants from this Hasid over on Orchard Street, but man they just cut 'em off. And I'm still pretty high so I'm trying to tell 'em to gimme my wallet but no one's listening to me they're just like dressing me up in these blue hospital pants I got on now and they're saying shit like, "Why did you break your leg? Why did you break your leg? Don't you know you could've gotten a life-threatening infection?" Like I do it all the time. Like it's my fuckin' hobby to throw myself down stairs.

And this doctor comes in. Probably right out a med school has this gig as some kind of rite of passage/gauntlet thing, you know, work with the Untouchables down in Slimeballville for six months until he can get his Park Avenue shit together. Clean, you know the type, young, serious. Very black hair. Plays a mean game a handball. Smells like a good cigar. And he checks out my chart and says "Why did you break your leg?" Like this is the fourth person to ask me this stupid question. So I get a little animated you know. And then he says "Calm down, I know how you feel."

I says "Hey, slick. You don't know how I feel. I'm a dual-addicted handicapped person living on welfare. I got hepatitis and sugar in my blood. So you don't know how I fucking feel." And he says "There's no reason to get excited." And I say "Yes there fucking is." And he says "Please calm down, it's not that bad." And I lose it. I start yelling and I try to get off the gurney, and somebody pushes me back down and I push them away and I threw this roll of bandages and uh . . . anyway, long story short, they got these bouncers at St. Vincents now.

And they threw me out on the street, would not let me back in. And I'm standing there out in the snow, blue pants, this walking cast thing on my foot. I don't have my wallet, I don't have nothing, I'm just standin' there and this little old lady, she sees me standin' there. Next thing I know she's laying a fiver on me.

So that's the situation. I'm five short. If you could see giving me a five in exchange for this interview, that would set me straight I could get my head clear and go feed Snowball.

(I will use some of this material in my book. I'm planning on a collage of "voices" gleaned from the streets. I will create a montage so that the characters will interface in a way that builds a tension up between them. I don't want to be obvious. I want the fact that the "real" has been converted to "prose" to be the "frame.")

After I paid the guy, we walked over to the place where he buys his drugs. We climbed a dilapidated staircase up to a urine-stinking tenement hallway on the Lower East Side. He shoved some folded-up bills into a hole in an apartment door and someone inside pushed little packets of heroin back out. He persuaded me to buy two more bags, one which I brought home to try. I've smoked opium, so it can't be that different.

When I got home, I locked myself in the bathroom and took about half of what was in the little envelope, which wasn't much, and snorted it. Nothing happened. I made myself some tea. While I was making the tea I realized I was getting into a very pleasant mood. I also figured that the heroin must have been very diluted, so I sniffed the rest. I finished brewing my tea, went into the living room, put some music on and gazed out the window. From where we live you can see a long distance. We face north so the planes taking off from La Guardia cross the line of vision. I sat and drank the tea until I felt sleepy and then I lay down on my bed.

I fell out, dreaming, but remembering it all. Glowing sunsets of orange and gold and purple filled me with a tremendous sense of well-being. I understood that everything is right in my life, that there isn't anything to worry about. Then I fell into a deeper sleep and didn't wake up until I heard Haim and Dagmara coming in the door. I got up to pee. But when I was in the bathroom, I was so high, I couldn't focus enough to let loose. Just stood there with my dick out. After like five minutes I finally mustered enough concentration to pee.

Haim had brought home a typical kosher dinner: egg rolls, roast pork, shrimp lo mein, the usual. Watching him ram the food down his maw made me nauseous. I spaced out in front of the TV while Dag and Haim finished eating, then ended up falling asleep again.

I woke up to find Dagmara gently shaking me. She asked me if I was sick. I said no, I felt fine. Which was the truth. I went to bed and had a great night's sleep. And today, I got up, had two espressos and started writing all this. I feel good and productive. Like I've been on a wonderful vacation. Heroin is really a kind of medicine. Maybe not something the average person should fool around with, but if you're a creative person like me, maybe it works differently on the metabolism. No wonder the powers that be want to keep this stuff away from the people, especially if it unleashes the soul. I'm not saying this is something I'm going to do again soon, but I wouldn't say no to it either. You only live once.

March 10, 2006

Long week of nothing. I take lengthy walks through the gray bare woodland, return home exhausted, lie down for a nap only to wake in the grip of almost total amnesia. Groggy, seconds float by before I can piece together who I am. I know that I'm in Connecticut, that I've just turned fifty-seven years of age, that I write. But nothing kindles within me, no sense of purpose, of why I should bother going on.

This must be happening because of my fucked-up heart. (And a Chinese doctor would say that my fucked-up heart is a result of my spiritual state.) But there's no way around it. I am caught in the web of my physical self. Inescapable. My body is a prison. Skinsack of water, minerals and protein. I feel good. I feel bad. All contingent on what? Some chemicals washing over my brain? It all makes sense, until I discover I have cancer. Or a bad heart. I am only a man. Death is guaranteed.

I tell myself I can change, but I can't change what I am. Go on a diet, jog, eat more green leafy vegetables. That's nothing more than self-deception. Even the *urge* to do all that, where does the urge come from, let alone the ability? Where does the orignal *thought* come from? Isn't it all hardwired from the beginning? I'm the kind of person who gnaws this particular bone. Of what? Dissatisfaction. I can't change that. I was born that way. There are biological terms for this and there are philosophical terms for this, but the best word is "Fate." One can't change one's attitude, or height. Or mental capacity. Or skin color. Or age. Fate.

"Live by the sword, die by the sword." As long as you have a body, you're stuck with it. There are only two solutions to physical existence. Art and money.

So alone. Me and my heart. And the flitting birds outside my window.

February 16, 1977

Ran into Zim at the bookstore on Spring Street. Told him about the heroin cop spot. He was curious so we took a walk over to the Lower East Side and ended up buying four bags of dope from a guy on the street. Then we went over to Zim's apartment in Chinatown and did the shit. Spent the afternoon nodding off and talking and throwing up. Zim went into a long exposition about Kenneth Patchen and Hubert Selby Jr. and Charles Bukowski. There's nothing finer in life than smoking cigarettes, sniffing smack and discussing literature.

Zim lent me his copy of *Last Exit to Brooklyn*. Shit's amazing.

April 2, 2006

Book signing in Cambridge, Mass. I felt healthy enough to do this one. A "mini-tour." Fans and old friends showed up. I didn't recognize the high school chums until they introduced themselves.

After the reading, one earnest fellow in a hooded sweatshirt had a question about the original short story collection ("We studied them in college."). A middle-aged woman wanted to know when I'm coming out with another collection. I told her that I published a new collection of short stories only five years ago. She replied without missing a beat, "I missed that one." One person asked me about the "Jan" character (John) from the first collection and the first novel. No one seemed to have any interest in my more recent work, especially *A Gentle Death* even though I had only finished reading from the book minutes before. It was as if I were there as a representative of my former self.

Who are fans? Why do they bother coming?

February 27, 1977

Jack is in the hospital. He got hit by a motorcycle while crossing Broome Street. He'll live but every bone in his body is cracked. He can't eat solid food because his jaw is broken. I snuck him cigarettes. He's got plenty of pain pills. I guess we're not barhopping anytime soon.

Been spending more time at Big John's. John knows everything. You can bring up any subject at all and the guy can give a lecture about it. Like I didn't know that Haydn was Beethoven's teacher or that the Mosuo women of China don't live with the fathers of their children. I didn't know that Sirhan Sirhan wasn't the guy who killed Robert Kennedy. I didn't know that zebras can't be domesticated. And I didn't know that the Masons are the largest secret society in the world. I had never even heard of them.

Last night he was talking about this Jewish guy named Levi who claimed to be the Messiah and started a whole new religion during the Middle Ages. This topic got John started on Genghis Khan, who had so many children that today something like a tenth of the world's population carries his DNA. Which got him on the subject of the Mongols and how they would kill every living thing in their path as they rode across the steppes and how this guy Tamerlane killed so many people he made mountainous piles out of skulls and how the ancient Incas would cut the still beating hearts out of their sacrificial victims. Said that the Incas were *communists*! On the topic of communists John launched into a story about Clifford Odets and the Federal Theater Project and how they were shut down by the House Un-American Activities Committee when they produced a play about beavers building a dam (interpreted as left-wing propaganda). Which led to the hunting down and blacklisting of all sorts of people in the arts, including the guy who wrote the movie *Midnight Cowboy* and *Serpico* (which starred Al Pacino). Then John backtracked to the beavers and informed us that beavers often drown when they get stuck underwater. But he said they deserve it because beavers contaminate streams with their bacteria-filled shit and that bacteria poisons cattle when they drink the bacteria but that that's not as bad as these tiny Amazonian barbed fish that are so tiny they can swim up your piss like a trout swims up waterfalls. Once these tiny fish are up inside your dick they get stuck there because of their spines and there's no way to get them out.

When I asked John if he knew anyone who had had any of these fish stuck in his dick, he turned very solemn and said, "I'm not going to discuss South America." And then, without missing a beat, said the flu and smallpox killed most of the Indians living in America long before Columbus arrived, which was news to me, and that the wheel didn't exist in the New World, and how the horseshoe led to the Roman Empire, and I think I fell asleep during that part. When I woke John was describing how the ancient Romans would parade enormous eighty-foot-long penis statues down the avenue before cheering crowds.

'Gitte passed through the room. She never says much. She usually comes in, rubs John's shoulders or brings him a beer and then drifts out again. I think of her before I fall asleep at night. Of all the women in the world, I want her most of all.

I read in the paper that the government is working on a "neutron bomb" that will kill people but will leave all the buildings standing. This is reassuring. Reading *Dog Soldiers* by Robert Stone. Really great.

I'm fucked up.

April 22, 2006

I received a letter today from Sarah ending our "relationship." She wrote that she didn't want to "argue." Wrote that I am "duplicitous." I screamed at the notepaper clutched in my hand: "When did I lie to you, Sarah? When?" So that was it, I guess. Finished. Alone.

I think I'll develop a functional relationship with an escort service and a maid. I'm sure I can find a couple of women who would be happy to fuck and cook for me. Pay the women, that's what they understand. No strings. An up-front transaction.

I have money and so I will have the sex in the way I want it.

But sex alone, what is that? I want companionship. Right? "Love."

I don't mind the underlying notion of a "relationship." So, if I want to continue this, I will have to "win" Sarah back. How hard would that be? She's the one good thing in my life. Also she has amazing breasts. She loves me. I should preserve this. I'll call her tonight.

April 24, 2006

Sarah informed me that she's not interested in any renewal. This made no sense because I know she doesn't have the guts to choose solitude. After an hour on the phone, I extracted the truth: There was another man in her life. Of course. I felt better knowing the facts. Fuck her.

April 25, 2006

Drove into town to see Leon. We had lunch at Jean Georges. Waded into a quick summation of how I was recovering. He lost interest and began to scan the room for VIPs. I raised the stakes and confessed my new fear of orgasm. *That* got his attention. Anything having to do with sex interests Leon. He is under the impression that I have this tremendously active sex life and he is always trying to pry details out of me. He quoted something in Latin from his school days. It sounded like "agreeskeet medendo," would have to look it up at the library. Eventually his tarragon artichoke and my mesclun salad (strewn with saffron and gold leaf) arrived. He troweled his bread with French butter, snapping it up like a trained seal. I imagined the butter lining the inner surfaces of his cardiac chambers, slowly occluding his life force, strangling him, bringing him to his knees, his face ruddy with pain, crumpling down before me, bowing before me, admitting he's been wrong about my work, has always been wrong, and now, with his final breath, begging forgiveness.

Leon prattled on about himself until dessert was cleared away. From what he told me I gathered he's sitting pretty because he has signed this new kid, Joe Versa. Four hundred thousand copies of the second novel are on order. There's a movie deal. Etc. Etc. Blah-blah-blah. Not once did he describe the book itself. Obviously, the writing qua writing is of no interest to Leon.

That is, until I opined that Versa's first-person confessional novel was obviously a pack of lies. This is the current fad, "truth." I lectured Leon, "It's too easy, this writing. Leon, I'm warning you, break your addiction to this loathsome shit now before it's too late. This fake literature will destroy publishing and sooner or later destroy you. And me."

Leon's eyelids drooped with anger. I was spoiling his party. He was making money and I wasn't big enough to congratulate him. I read his mind: By not accepting money as the final arbiter of worth, I was implying that there is some *other* yardstick by which to measure literature. And to defend that "other" yardstick is to defend what? "Good writing"? "Come on," Leon would argue, "what's that?"

Leon's the big dog now and wants to piss on every tree. This translates into a mini-revolution. The artist is no longer on top, Leon is. I wanted to say "MONEY? I MADE YOU PLENTY OF MONEY, YOU ASSHOLE, BY WRITING GOOD BOOKS." But that would sound desperate, wouldn't it? Never show a hand until you're ready to play it.

I noted an oil stain on Leon's necktie. He's not my friend and yet he's the best friend I've got. The others. Where have the others gone? Only Leon and Sarah are left. And Elizabeth, maybe. Here are my friends as I enter midlife, an editor who is indifferent to my writing and two women who hate me.

Later I spoke with my father on the phone. His depression is widening, threatening to suck me in like an intergalactic black hole. I called him thinking I could gleen a droplet of pseudo-empathy. If not your own family, who? Papa, throw me a lifeline here! But every lifeline drags both ways. He's stuck in his own dark, cold, bottomless-pit quagmire. He needs companionship too. I hung up the phone and let go my hold on the rope before he could pull me under.

All of this—the failure of the book, Sarah's abandonment, Elizabeth's threats, Leon's indifference—conspires to defeat me. But they all underestimate me and my feeble, scarred heart. The mistake is presuming that I am close to death. Fuck my heart. I don't need a heart. My next book will set them all straight. Leon will be wetting himself to get his paws on it. He has no idea what I am made of.

April 26, 2006

I looked up Leon's Latin phrase. *Aegrescit medendo.* It means, "it grows worse by the remedy." Now I can't rememeber the context.

I called Elizabeth and insisted that she had to come see me at the apartment immediately. That it was an emergency. The line seemed to go dead and then I heard a soft "Okay," and a click. I fretted for an hour, waiting for her to materialize. If she didn't show up, then the tectonic plates of my emotional life were moving in all the wrong directions. It is true Elizabeth and I are no longer a couple, but we have a bond built from our past couple-dom. And that should have been enough, more than enough, to have compelled her to my home. In an attempt to stave off my anxiety, I sorted new books into my library.

She arrived an hour after my call. Burst through the door all blushing and breathless as if she'd torn herself away from a sexual tryst. Or was it merely a lonely session of drunken isolation? Who knows with her? She was probably my most opaque lover. Or was it possible that Elizabeth derived excitement, even pleasure, from racing to my aid? I'd never noticed this side of her before but people change.

I sat her down, made her tea. Her hand shook when she brought the teacup to her beautiful mouth. I outlined my spiritual crisis. I painted my despair in bold strokes. I implied that if she didn't soothe me, didn't touch me, I would fall apart completely. I told her that if she was ever my friend, ever, she had to stay with me. I implied that it was a matter of life and death because I had plenty of pills and did consider suicide an option. I was ready.

I couldn't read her. She had loved me once, certainly she would come to my aid now?

She said, "Your lawyer has not returned one of our calls."

Why was she bringing all that up now? It's true, I had told my guy to put it on the back burner, but what did that have to do with what I was asking for right at that moment? What was important was that I needed her to be there for me. Instead she insisted on nagging me.

I heard myself say, "I thought I should do more research. Get to know you better. For my *next* book."

Her neck flushed pink. Honestly, I wasn't saying any of this to make her angry. It was more like an exploration. I was sincere.

Why did she insist on being so difficult? Why couldn't things be as they once were, if for only ten minutes or so? All I needed was her warm skin pressed against my dying husk. I wanted to be reenlivened by her pulse, by the heat of her blood. Would it be that difficult for Elizabeth to gather me up in her arms and soothe me, if for no reason than to plan a getaway from me? But she didn't take me in her arms. Instead she snarled, "You fucker, Richard!," grabbed her jacket and was gone as quickly as she arrived.

I shuffled into the bedroom and lay on the bed. Seeking some relief, I masturbated like a traumatized high school senior who has just learned his girlfriend is going to the prom with his best friend. As I played with myself, profoundly clear recollections of my Elizabeth of twenty years ago danced through my mind. She was so lovely, so fierce. I mused on how, when we made love, she would transform once I was inside her. Tossing her head, clenching her jaw, her breath sucking at my shoulder. I would inhale her hair, loving her slick and vibrant beneath me. We would both holler as we came, momentarily freed from our horribly self-involved selves. Those were tremendous times for us. Perhaps she was like this with everyone she slept with? I couldn't know. But she was like this with me once upon a time and that was enough. Afterward, we would lie there in peace, our hearts drumming with love. Twenty minutes later we would be fighting again.

After jerking off, I lay still, pulsing, per the usual routine, as my heart caught up. In the adjacent apartment someone was practicing Beethoven's "Für Elise." The performance was tentative, garnished with charming blunders. I assumed it was one of the shiny, perfect children who live next door, perhaps alone, practicing out of some sense of duty to an absent parent. On the avenue, a horn commenced to honk angrily, obviously mired in the traffic beneath my window. The sound of the piano player mingled with the equally anonymous horn honker. Only a minute or two had elapsed. I was achingly aware of two humans out there, crawling through life, vulnerable in the pointlessness of the effort. And they had no idea that I was absorbing them into myself.

Satisfied with proof that I was still alive, I jiggled a leg. I was animate. I changed my clothes and then, feeling frail, crept down to the parking garage, slipped into my car, the only reliably virile extension of myself, and entered the thick traffic aimed for Connecticut. For much of the ride I fantasized jumping the divider. Leon would be happy. He would publish my unpublished short stories in time for the Christmas rush.

As I rolled up the gravel drive of my country home, I spied a comical raccoon waddling toward the barn. Little fucker. Probably digging up the flowerbeds or tossing garbage. I leapt out in hot pursuit. The animal vanished as soon as my foot touched the ground. I sprinted, something I rarely do, and as I rounded the barn, I slipped on the damp grass and with an awkward hop landed sideways. A hot punji spike of pain lanced my ankle. I sat up. I tried to stand. I couldn't.

I remained on the icy spring turf for ten minutes before attempting to raise myself, then limped toward the house. The seat of my pants was shredded and damp. I was trembling. As I unlatched the back door, moved through the mud room and into the kitchen I realized that *had* I broken something, my cell phone was still in the car, out of reach. Or if I had had a heart attack out on the lawn, I'd have been stuck there for days. Given the time of year, it would have been at least a week before anyone would have found my corpse. The possums and crows would have gnawed into my gut, sucked out my eyes.

I spent the remainder of the darkening day laid out before the fireplace reading my damned journals, the sustained notes of Verdi's *Requiem* my only companion. I'm stuck in this house, the house that Elizabeth and I shared. It is filled with antiques and meaningless appliances, things that to this day radiate her personality, make her continually present in my life. As the fire in the hearth burns down to embers and the shadows draw a veil over the familiar shapes of the life we had, I understand that Elizabeth is not here in the house with me, is never here and that I am alone.

March 22, 1977

I have hepatitis, not the dangerous kind. I guess I caught it from Haim because we share plates and eating utensils in the apartment. He must have become infected hanging out in the filthy strip clubs he loves. Of course, he's such a bull, it hardly affects him, while staining my skin parchment yellow and my piss the color of Coke. I can barely move. The doctor (a wrinkly old New Yorker who chain-smokes) told me to "keep my distance" from alcohol. Not that I have any desire to drink. Or eat. Dagmara's been deriving great pleasure from nursing both of us back to health.

The lack of alcohol in my system seems to have improved my discipline. Even though I'm physically tired, I eked out a short story based on that guy I interviewed. Titled it "My Lucky Day." A small magazine that publishes new writers has said they're going to print it. I'm getting a hundred bucks which is pretty amazing.

No girlfriend at the moment. Dagmara has zero interest in me that way now. Dagmara's friend Anita doesn't come by anymore, probably because I had sex with her. I'm so tired I'm not sure I can get it up anyway. Been reading this guy Philip K. Dick. *Do Androids Dream of Electric Sheep.* More Henry Miller. Keeping a list of vocabulary words. And a list of books read.

May 5, 2006

Drove into the city, traffic was very light, even found a parking meter downtown. The afternoon unwound while I roamed the aisles of Coliseum Books (rumored to be closing soon) and the Strand. Sold a pile of review copies Leon's secretary sent me. Then found most of what I "needed": *The Return of Martin Guerre*, Schopenhauer, Kolakowski's *Main Currents of Marxism*, Murakami's *Norwegian Wood*. Could have bought it all online, but it's important to support the bookstores. Only a bookstore provides the serendipity of looking for one thing and finding another.

Sarah agreed to share a meal with me. She seemed deeply guarded and, at her core, depressed. I don't think she can handle the truth, which is that I never lied to her. I got her to admit that she was the one who had been "lying" because she'd wanted more than I had ever promised her but had pretended that she didn't.

The slow accretion of time we spent together forced the inevitable question, "But will it be forever?" But that wasn't my fault and she knew it. She seemed genuinely frightened when I cornered her. I simply wanted her to admit that the fault was not mine, but *hers*. I had done nothing "wrong." She tearfully confessed that she wants kids. *My* kids.

I told her she had the wrong guy. Furthermore she had always known who I was. So who was at fault here? Who had led who on? I pointed out that she shouldn't have entered into a contract she had no intention of sticking to. *She* hurt *me*. I was the one who was wronged. I was the one left holding the bag. I was the one who was abandoned!

Her admission of wrongdoing was small consolation for the fact that what's done is done. Once all of this was aired, there wasn't much else to talk about. I sucked the dregs of my cappuccino and claimed I had an appointment with Leon. We went our separate ways amicably around nine.

By ten, I had found myself in Times Square. I was jostled by tourists munching kosher hot dogs, their souvenir *Playbill*s clenched in pale Midwestern fists. They took pictures of one another. They gathered in teeming clusters at the crosswalks. They gaped at the shimmering, multicolored electric billboards looming high above. People get a certain reassurance by being small. They come to my city to be awed.

A spitting rain drifted in with the evening's breezes. Theaters disgorged their occupants. The crowd thickened as the parasitic vendors and hawkers stirred the throng into confusion. Swarthy men sold umbrellas. Flyer flippers, pretzel men, smokers and spitters and cops. A fearful, excited energy rippled through the mob and the air was peppered with shouts and nervous laughter.

Thirty years ago, these same darkened doorways framed girls who chanted, "Wanna go out?" "Wanna party?" Prostitutes, drug dealers, pickpockets. Where are those wonderful folks now? Grown old. At home with their grandkids, or in a drug rehab or in prison or pushing up daisies.

I found myself tracking a woman who had passed me only minutes before. A thirty-something ingenue with a distinctive blue and white umbrella.

She paused when she got to the corner. I expected her to hail a cab, but she didn't. I lay back, observing her, when she made an abrupt reversal and stepped into the southward flow of pedestrians and then, as if window-shopping, began to wander along the lighted storefronts. She scanned the confusing displays of the discount electronics shops giving me a chance to analyze her more fully. What was she doing?

She possessed a classic profile and her clothing betrayed a certain suburban cutting-edge style. Doubtless she had arrived from parts west only that afternoon and, bored, had managed to escape from her charter group of single secretaries from Minneapolis. I sensed her appetite for adventure. I was ready to provide it. I ambled up alongside her and feigned interest in a display of nasty green Statue of Liberty replicas. I began with a question (the standard ploy of every hustler), "Who buys all this stuff?" It startled her.

Doelike, she said, "I'm sorry, are you speaking to me?"

I said, "I'm curious. Why would anyone as sophisticated as you waste her time checking out tourist knickknacks? What happened? Had a fight with your boyfriend? Slammed the door and went for a stroll?"

At that moment, a well-built black kid wedged himself between us and said, "Good evening young lady. How'd you like a free CD?" He handed a CD jewel case to my new friend. Gangsta rap, no doubt. As expected, Miss Minnesota took the CD. The kid grinned and says, "That'll be five dollars postage and handling." I snatched the disc and handed it back to the kid.

"That's okay, pal. We already have this one." I took her by the elbow and steered her away from danger. Maybe not danger exactly, but certainly attention other than my own. I smiled. "He knows you're not from around here." We moved purposefully along with the flowing throng.

She did not scream, "Let go of my arm!" or "Who the fuck do you think you are?" She was ready, for anything. I said, "How 'bout a drink?"

At the Café des Artistes we shared a glass of pinot grigio. There I convinced her to join me in a cab ride and proceeded to entertain her with a guided tour of Central Park, Fifth Avenue, SoHo and Ground Zero. Near City Hall, the sky cleared and we hopped out and strolled the Brooklyn Bridge. She was, of course, enthralled by my expertise on all that is New York City.

In return for my seminar on the Big Apple, I got a short seminar on her world: her job as teacher at a Montessori preschool in Ohio; her brother and sister-in-law with whom she is traveling; some details on her father's recent retirement from his job as an oil refinery engineer. We even discussed her wire-haired terrier, Alfie, who was back home with friends. After accepting my invite earlier to show her around, she had called her brother to inform him she had "run into an old friend from high school." Her deception kindled hope. If she could lie to her brother this meant she was naturally devious. If she was devious, perhaps she was audacious as well. (This could be the start of something! I pictured quick trips out to the Buckeye State for trysts in the local Marriott. Wouldn't even cost much. I could use my Marriott points!)

Eventually, believe it or not, my new friend joined me in my apartment "for a nightcap." When I finally told her who her companion for the evening was, turned out she'd never heard of me! Nor was she impressed! Hmmmm! This independence made her more not less interesting to me. She was not a run-of-the-mill suburbanite. No, she was a diamond-in-the-rough. An enchantress with clear skin and great bones. Not very young, but not old either. Mid-thirties? Single. An American beauty.

But as soon as I began the physical overture, I became a China-man speaking Mandarin! She missed every hint. Apparently in Cincinnati strangers don't have sex. Ever. Not only do strangers not have sex, strangers don't *want* to have sex with anyone other than their spouse. It would never cross their mind. Where she came from, men and women enjoy each other's company simply because it is enjoyable. There are no ulterior motives in Ohio.

As the evening wore on (and my initial surprise that this young woman was willing to trust a stranger wore off), impatience replaced curiosity. Impatience and irritation. Not only did I want to get on with it, I resented the fact that she saw me as so safe that she could walk off into the night with me and remain unmolested.

I was determined to give her an experience she would be afraid to confess to her beloved brother and dog.

But first things first. The ice needed to be broken. I had to make her understand that this adventure was going to bring her manifold pleasures. I pretended to be intoxicated with her charm. I popped bottles of vintage champagne, called in caviar sushi from the new, very expensive, Japanese place near the park. As we drank and noshed, I read her passages from my work. She sipped from her champagne flute as I massaged her shoulders, her bare feet. How could she resist me? I was the maestro.

But when I moved to kiss her on the mouth, she ducked her head and smiled like she was embarrassed for both of us. (She'd probably been warned about the voracious sexual appetites of East Coast Jews. I could imagine her telling her friends: "Well he was a very interesting man, despite, you know, his perversions.") My lips grazed her bare shoulder and she separated from me and stood up.

Every woman has a key, you only have to find it. I baldly confessed to her of my past love affairs, and she admitted to her own disappointments in love. We retrenched and, with relief, blabbed on about sex and adventures and life and opportunities missed and . . . on and on and on. Plato never wrote more thorough dialogues.

I hung in there, determined to see it through. But after two hours of this circular seduction ad absurdum, I tired. It was obvious that since I had forgotten to refill my monthly supply of date-rape potions, I could confess and connive and debate this lovely young woman (not that young, not that lovely) until dawn and I would not so much as lick a nipple, nor touch a hair on her head. My icy resolve melted into a puddle of soggy frustration.

When the evening finally died a natural death, I lied and claimed that I'd had a great time with her. In a way perhaps I did. It was something different. And clearly she had not been offended by my siege. She was delighted by everything, every distraction. Finally, she threw me a bone and admitted to having been tempted, but added, "I know my boundaries."

You can't buy the tour of New York City I gave her. The cab ride, champagne and food set me back two hundred and fifty-six dollars. I gave her a precious evening of my time. It was annoying to have generosity left unanswered.

Exhausted and witless, I packed her into a cab and said adieu. She promised to write me, her new (Jewish) friend, the New York author ("He has books on Amazon!"). I promised to send her my most recent published work. Of course I had dozens of copies in the apartment. But I couldn't stomach the thought of her reading my words.

Her car merged with the downtown traffic, and I headed upstairs. I finished the bottle of champage on my own, and fell into bed. So what? That's life.

May 12, 1977

Gave a reading of my story "My Lucky Day" with a bunch of new writers at the St. Mark's Church Poetry Project. This is a famous place. Allen Ginsberg reads there. Also Patti Smith, who is this amazing new poet.

Didn't pay much attention to what the other people were reading. Except this one skinny guy, Jim Carroll, who was pretty cool (he's famous for being a heroin addict). Most of them just seemed stoned. I was fifth on the bill. As soon as I stepped up to the podium, I could see that no one had ever heard of me, didn't know me at all, and so they weren't going to like what I read, no matter how well written it was.

Overall I'd say that what I read was mostly misunderstood. On the other hand, I actually got up there and did it. I give myself that credit. I transferred the story from an idea to a tape recording of the junkie to writing it all down to actually producing a written piece. Something I originated as a concept became something that existed within the coordinates of TIME and SPACE. Out there in the world. This is the beginning. Even if no one got what I was doing, I get what I'm doing.

Afterward went out with Dagmara and some friends of hers she had dragged along to my reading. We took over a booth at one of the Slavic restaurants over on Second Avenue. Dagmara ordered in Polish. Her friends were incredibly square girls. All giggly and weird. As a group, they had a certain appeal, but individually they fell flat. Each one had a defect of some sort, one was too heavy, one had horribly pale skin, like she was dying. I drank two bottles of beer while they devoured Polish sausage and pierogis. The beer loosened me up and I flirted with the almost pretty one, but then Dag shot me the Gypsy evil eye and I realized no way was I gonna pull that off.

Worst of all, I don't think they got my writing at all. They kept saying how "funny" it was. But they also agreed that it was "depressing" and "negative." On the other hand, they fell in love with some coy crap that this overweight, incredibly homely poet wrote. He was describing the hair on his stomach and they loved that. I ended up taking the subway uptown with Dagmara. It's hard to go home with someone who you're not actually sleeping with. Especially after a big night and a couple of beers.

Haim wasn't there when we got home, so we started fooling around in the kitchen but she stopped me when I slipped my hand under her cashmere sweater and fondled her brassiered breasts. She has this weird Eastern European Catholic mystery about her. She brought out a bottle of port wine. We got real drunk and I woke up around three A.M. Dagmara had already gone to bed. No idea where Haim was.

I split the apartment and trooped across Central Park. I sat on a bench in the dark for almost an hour watching anonymous figures moving through the glow of the old-fashioned streetlamps. I realized that I need a level of intensity beyond anything that's in my life right now. I need to get as close to madness as I can. I thought, this is my life. Right now. Sometimes I am so alone.

May 12, 2006

Visited Tullio Lombardo's *Adam* at the Met. A perfect artifact. The Renaissance at its best. Locked into that sculpture is a moment from four centuries ago. Art as time machine.

The quiet crowds and hallways of the vaulted airy building calmed me. Visiting the *Adam* put my troubles in perspective. I sipped an espresso in the little café, pondered the families and tourists around me. As I left, I felt joyous.

I descended the marble steps and noted the freshness of the air, so I took a sharp turn 'round the building aiming for the park. On the asphalt pathway just south of the museum, I passed an ice cream vendor.

For some reason, I glanced at him as I passed and he, in response, nodded. I nodded back in turn.

The moment meant nothing to me. On the street, the city people often meet my eye and since there's always the possibility that they know me from the dust cover of my books or an appearance on Charlie Rose, I make it a habit to greet people with a small nod. There's also always the possibility they are an acquaintance I don't recognize. So for insurance I nod as if to a friend. I do this without thinking. It's a reflex action.

But yesterday, as I moved on, I had an urge to take another look at this ice cream vendor. He had his eye on me too. Our gaze met once more. And this time there was a genuine spark of recognition.

I said, "Do I know you?"

He said, "Of course."

I said, "How?"

He said, "Haim."

Tony the ice cream guy snapped into focus. Thirty years later. How old was Haim when I lived in that apartment? Thirty? So this guy, his peer, would be what? Sixty? Not that old. Not retired yet, probably has no choice but to work.

I said, "You're Tony."

He said, "I know."

A tourist came up and bought a King Kone from Tony. After he had pocketed the two bucks, I learned that Haim had abandoned New York fifteen years ago, reluctantly returning to Tel Aviv. The ice cream man produced a folded piece of paper from his wallet upon which was scrawled a fourteen-digit phone number. I copied it onto the margins of a Met floor plan.

As I reentered the sun-dappled park, I was struck by the coincidence. Only days before, I had been reading in my journals about this ice cream guy. Here he was in the flesh. I never would have recognized him if I hadn't been reading about him. I had memorialized him into existence.

I passed one of the ornate black iron streetlamps that decorate the pathways throughout the park. I checked the small stamped aluminum tag riveted to its base. A four-digit number, which I knew was code for the cross street corresponding to this latitude of the park. 8803. Eighty-eighth Street. I smiled to myself, feeling privy to a New York secret only real New Yorkers know. "I am a New Yorker," I thought. It's taken thirty years to become one, but I am one now, for better or for worse. I have walked this path many times with no inkling of what the future held for me. As a young man, could I have imagined that someday I would be standing here, published, celebrated, rich and . . . old? Or perhaps I *did* have an idea of that. And the idea became who I am now.

Around me park visitors pushed prams, blabbed on cell phones and bagged canine feces. On the main road, blinkered horses hitched to hackney coaches passed, the Rollerbladers pumped by with ease, the parksmen raked old leaves from the fresh grass. A lazy river of humanity. I was but a leaf adrift upon it.

June 1, 1977

A couple of weeks ago, five people were killed when a helicopter flipped off the Pan Am Building. Then last week, a guy climbed the South Tower of the World Trade Center. Made it all the way to the top. New York is about buildings. We are small compared to buildings. But we build the buildings.

Dag isn't speaking to me for some reason.

June 8, 1977

(written June 9)
What would it be like to be extremely famous and celebrated and rich?

To have that kind of total and absolute power? Especially in the arts? To have everyone begging to do whatever you wanted them to do *whenever* you wanted them to do it? There are people who have that. I've seen it with my own eyes.

Last night MOMA held a special "professionals night" in which they opened the museum to people who work in the arts. Jonathan has access to special events there because we're a nonprofit arts organization. So he laid a pair of tickets on me. The Cézanne show has been a big hit and this was an opportunity to go see it without standing in line or enduring the crowds. A highlight in my boring life.

Katie seemed like the right person to invite. The ticket is almost impossible to get and she's an artist so I figured she would say yes and she did. We met at the museum. The thing about Katie is she's very, very attractive and she knows it. Curly blond hair, blue eyes. Highly intelligent and sarcastic. Definitely someone I would like to have an ongoing sexual relationship with, maybe fall in love with.

So we went. And the show was magnificent. The walls were hung with canvas after canvas of blazing chips and chunks of color. As we worked our way around the spacious gallery, from one pile of green apples to a poplar-strewn landscape to the next set of orange rooftops, I was in visual ecstasy. I assumed Katie was sharing my experience. I thought, we're bonding. I checked her reaction. But her focus was not on the paintings, it was elsewhere. She smiled brightly and said, "See that guy over there?" As she asked her innocent question, I thought, this girl is really beautiful. But she'd already turned away from me, lifting her chin in the direction of the middle of the room, where a disheveled man in an oversized trench coat stood looking lost. He wasn't viewing the exhibition, he seemed to be simply hanging out with his buddies. None of them paid any attention to the paintings.

Katie continued, "The guy in the middle. That's Al Pacino!"

I said, "Really?" Whatever this man, this movie star, was in my imagination, in real life he was only a man in a coat that was too big for him. I didn't want Katie to know that I thought he was one of the greatest actors of our time. I was hoping my disinterest would inspire Katie to cool down and refocus on more important things, like the lifework of Cézanne, or me.

Katie was not the only one interested in this man—the entire room was roiling with restless energy. All these art world folks, people who supposedly were drawn to a more complete engagement with life, were all, like my date, riveted. Al Pacino was the work of art on display. An unremarkable man in a scruffy trench coat was more visually interesting than the greatest paintings of all time.

Katie was practically panting with excitement. With perfect aplomb she stage-whispered, "If I offered Al Pacino a blow job, do you think he'd let me?"

I thought, it's such a lovely question. It accomplishes so much with so few words!

I said, "You want me to ask him?" But of course, she didn't, which proved this was nothing more than viciousness aimed at me. Eventually Al Pacino wandered off with his entourage. Everyone in the room exhaled.

Later I lied to Katie and told her I lived in Brooklyn so that I could tag along on her train downtown. At Prince Street, her stop, I asked, "Maybe I should come up for some coffee?"

Katie replied sweetly and clearly, "I've stopped drinking coffee." And exited the train. No kiss. No thank you. Probably in a rush to get up to her place so she could plug in the vibrator and fantasize about Al Pacino. Probably.

I rode the train down to the City Hall station and walked the Brooklyn Bridge. I considered jumping off, didn't, turned around, made my way up the Bowery, found a bar that Jack and I sometimes hung out in, got drunk on boilermakers and had a long conversation with a pimply punk rocker named Bobby Battery. He works at CBGB tuning guitars, setting out mike stands and rolling up cable. Bobby claimed to have done drugs with Sid Vicious, the bass player with the Sex Pistols. Bobby is from Brooklyn, dyes his hair black and has terrible skin.

I got home at three. Haim was watching TV in the living room while gobbling whole peaches and spitting the pits onto a copy of the *Daily News*. I gave him a summation of the evening, and in my retelling, gained his opinion that Katie is a fucked-up bitch and that I am a great man for loving Cézanne. We smoked a joint and drank some kind of vicious Israeli brandy that seared the lining of my throat. I woke from a blackout three hours later, Haim splayed out beside me, the TV gurgling like a pebbly brook. Mary Tyler Moore was on the little screen crowing about something while the audience screamed with laughter. Mary Tyler Moore looked a little like Katie and I hated her for it. I crawled to my bed in the dinette area and passed out.

June 11, 1977

I'm not supposed to be drinking but every now and then I allow myself a beer. I ran into that writer Zim. We spent the afternoon in a bar discussing Philip K. Dick. He laid more cocaine on me. Then when I left, he laid a half-gram on me and said I could pay him when I had the money.

When I'm working in the library, I sniff a line in the bathroom and can focus nonstop for hours. The coke definitely helps me write. Also I've been hanging around John's. I try to listen carefully because he says interesting things. I wouldn't dare tape-record him, so it's difficult to get it all down exactly. Is it possible you can be in the presence of a great man who lives outside of history altogether. I mean, no one knows him, but he's great all the same?

I arrived at John's loft about one A.M. last Thursday night. I had been writing in the library, but I got tired and restless. I needed something. I

needed John, so I caught a train out to Brooklyn. Some gang kids shuffled onto the car with me. They gave me the once-over, but they knew I
had nothing, so they left me alone.

John was hanging out with two men who didn't seem like Americans. Perhaps they were from South America or the Middle East. Maybe
they were his connection. I don't know. John seemed happy to see me
when I walked in.

Big John was his usual self, tilted back in his chair, stoned. His hair
was all tufted up and he was red in the face as if he had been wres-
tling with these strangers just before I came in. Clearly he wasn't into
anything physical now. They were passing around an enormous pipe of
weed mixed with hash. I found my usual spot on the couch and confis-
cated the pipe.

When I finally stopped coughing, I asked, "How's it going, John?"

He said, "We are revisiting the debate over the body-mind duality."
The two foreign-looking guys looked pretty blown out. I think one was
asleep. As far as I could tell, no one was debating anybody. When I passed
the pipe to the one who was awake, he snatched it without meeting my
eyes. His fingers were encased in enormous carved silver rings, the kind
that act like brass knuckles in a fight. Not only did he not appear to be
debating with John, he did not appear to be listening to John at all.

I said, "Really?" as if I had any idea what John meant. I wanted these
thugs to go away.

John released a long stream of white smoke from his cherubic
lips. He addressed the ceiling, "Of course it goes beyond the Cartesian
problem, is pain 'real,' is intention 'real'? These philosopher guys got so
wrapped up in God. Like God requires thought. He doesn't. That was
what the Meister was getting at. God is a City on the Hill and we're a
dog running around in His city, pissing on His fire hydrants. We have
no way to see the big picture. We're just dumb dogs. Fuck Leibniz and
his clocks!"

John shot me a threatening, red-eyed stare. "You know what causes the most complications for humanity? The fact that everyone is walking around thinking they can read each other's minds! 'I know what he thinks about me!'—But you don't have a fucking clue. You don't know what people think of you and more than that, it is *impossible* to control what people think of you. You think you can affect their thoughts about you, but you can't. All the same, you and me and everybody tries to be special, we dress a certain way, we achieve, we behave. Why? To make a good impression on everyone 'out there' in reality. But that's impossible! Even do-gooders do good because they want to make an impression. Right? But you never know what the outcome of any action might be. You *can't* know. All you can know is what you *think* you know and you don't even know that for certain. It's like poker. You can bluff some of the time, but not all of the time. Everyone *conceptuates* differently about everyone else. SO THERE CAN'T BE CONSENSUS. Can't be. Each mind has its own unique pespective. Obviously. And no mind can see from the perspective of another mind!"

I wanted to say, "There is no such word as 'conceptuate.'" But I wasn't sure. So I kept my mouth shut.

John added that celebrities and other famous people who we see on TV and in magazines are not people "per se," but *representations* of people. Then John said something about "That's how Hitler took over so many people's minds."

We passed the pipe. I was très stoned and had completely lost track of what John was talking about. I thought I was following, then I'd realize I was only watching his lips move. (That's why I'm writing this all down now, to try to remember as much as I can. What's the point of hearing it if I don't remember it?) As the night wore on, John got into discussing death more and more. He likes to say that death is the "great equalizer," that "no one gets out of here alive" and that death is part of "God's plan." He claims that not only can no one beat this rap, which makes us all equal, but that humans, unlike all animals, *know* that someday they will die and that being aware of your own death, that one day you're not going to exist, changes everything, actually *creates* consciousness. (Not sure why that is.) John loves to quote stuff in Latin. He'll stop talking, get quiet, stare at me and say something like "Memento mori."

I woke up on the couch and John was describing the enormous catapults the Kaffa Tartars used to heave plague-infested bodies over city walls to infect the inhabitants. The silent men were gone. Everything was quiet.

On the train home, another gang of black kids got on. I was all alone in the car. But as usual, they didn't bother me. They knew I was on their side.

May 15, 2006

I can't write. I can't move. What's the point of writing? To preserve my reputation? To make money? I have plenty of money. Plenty of reputation. The problem is that my reputation will wither and die if I don't come up with new work. I have to generate new writing to keep the old writing alive. Like children working for their father. One needs many children to survive. Even if the children will never be as great as the father.

I guess my first book of short stories will live on no matter what. A task completed over twenty years ago, when I didn't know my ass from my elbow. Now that I know how to write, now that I have something interesting to say, no one cares. Or the critics completely misunderstand. The irony is that I am the caretaker of the young man I once was. He's my responsibility.

June 20, 1977

I've just slept for two days. Been kind of sick. But also hungover.

Went out to John's and found him all alone. Even 'Gitte was out. It was like it was a special occasion. He produced this little envelope of white powder and we each sniffed a couple of harsh lines and then he carefully put it away. I was surprised that he did that because I've never seen John do coke. After I snorted it, I didn't get the usual numbing sensation. Nothing happened at all. I figured the stuff was no good, or that I was used to Zim's shit. Then about five minutes later this little explosion erupted in the back of my brainpan and a thrill raced up my spine. John gave me a knowing look, produced a joint and we smoked it. I felt sexy and ticklish and powerful all at the same time. I asked John if it was a new kind of cocaine.

He chuckled and said, "Young scholar, that wasn't no coke, that was pure unadulterated *crank*." Methamphetamine sulfate. Speed. Crystal. My jaw clenched and surges of physical rapture flowed over my loins, poured into the pit of my stomach, tore through my heart and dried out every mucous membrane in my body.

The walls shimmered. The air grew hot and electric. Colors swam. I felt very, very good. I could feel my heart beat, hear my breath. I could even hear John's breath. I could hear *everything*. I stood up. John said, "Sit down." Then he passed me a bowl of hash.

John began to talk. But this time, I started talking too. We were talking simultaneously, perfectly and with no effort at all filling in the gaps of each other's logic. Like this mighty jazz duo, but instead of instruments, we were playing our *brains*. Even when John began to stutter, it made sense and I talked through it, around it. We were seated side by side at a magnificent conceptual loom weaving these infinitely complex idea-tapestries. We were figuring everything out, the structure of the universe, the exact nature of the soul and of God (John said "God invented time so things wouldn't happen all at once.") but transcended even that as we went further and further out to the farthest reaches of space, time and thought, and then back again.

John outlined my future career as a writer. He explained to me how I would conquer the literary world with my words, words exactly like the ones I was speaking *at that very moment!* He informed me that my words were the foot soldiers in my army, fighting for me, capturing territory, defeating my enemies. He said I had to train my army to be the *best* army. He announced that I would be a Napoleon of literature. And something in my gut told me he was right.

Hours passed. John left the room and I tried to organize the junk on his coffee table. But every time I had it all straightened out, there would be a new angle I hadn't thought of. (Organize by subject matter? Size? Type of publication?) I couldn't get it right. I began to lose my ability to string thoughts together in coherent succession. I was forced to retrace the steps of my thinking. As soon as one brilliant thought entered my head, it would be replaced by another and I would forget the first.

The ideas blossomed faster and faster, but so did the empty spots between them. I felt like I was traveling through my thoughts the way a spaceship slices through space, effortlessly, but surrounded by a total vacuum. I would pass a solar system, then a huge void. Then a star nebula. A galaxy, then more limitless space. I entered a mental black hole and couldn't get out. My thoughts lost their way. I was becalmed in my spaceship, stuck in the middle of nowhere, drifting.

Anxiety sparked and ignited all the clutter in my head and before I knew it a firestorm of panic was raging through my skull. I became deathly fearful that John had abandoned me. Perhaps left the building for good. Maybe he knew something that I didn't know. Knew he had to get away. Before the "bad thing" happened. I became obsessed with the bad thing and anticipated the arrival of police. I had this crazy idea that John had been busted by narcotics agents somewhere in the loft and now they were watching *me*, waiting for me to trip up so they could make their move. I tried to remain as still as possible. If I didn't move, maybe they wouldn't see me.

Then John returned with a plastic bottle of liquid. He was half-naked and barefoot, wearing only drawstring pants. A thin strand of beads lay over his hairy barrel chest. Overweight, he almost had breasts. Despite his pale bare skin, he looked fierce. He handed me the bottle and commanded me to drink from it.

We passed the jug back and forth, taking sips. It looked like tea but it tasted old and musty and bitter. I assumed it was some kind of alcohol, but it had no alcohol sting. Still, it got me drunk real fast, or what felt like drunk. I was speeding and stoned, my mind had nowhere to go, so I just got that much higher. John said it was 'shroom juice made from powder a Yaqui Indian had given him. That he kept it for special occassions. My mind finally began to quiet down. A faint peacefulness replaced the anxiety. I was conceptualizing in great, ephemeral blobs of color. I lay back and listened. John was talking about Antarctica, then about whaling (*Moby-Dick* is his favorite book), then about icebergs and massiveness and coldness and then finally about stillness.

'Gitte arrived. She whispered in John's ear and led him into another room. As they left, John passed me a little pink pill. He said it would relax me. They never came back. I took the pill with more of the juice and after a while I did feel much calmer. Calm enough to leave the loft.

When I stepped out onto the street the sky was much higher than usual, tinted an awesome robin's egg blue striped with long pink clouds. If there is such a thing as a spiritual experience, it is walking across the Brooklyn Bridge at dawn as the sun burns its way into the city of New York.

Exhausted and speeding at the same time, the tranquillity in my heart grew into elation. Little bursts of light flashed at the periphery of my vision. The speed was strong. It torched the hash high and the 'shroom high. But the little pill, whatever it was, took away the crispy feeling, exterminated the ants crawling all over my skin. I felt good and powerful and full of energy. I could see everything and be everything. Potential became equal to manifestation.

As if I were standing on a huge conveyor belt, my legs moved me without my will. So I let them do what they wanted and I was propelled across the bridge, up through Chinatown. So much early morning bustle in Chinatown: people yelling in dialect, trash cans smashing and clanging, trucks honking their way through the narrow streets, stray cats mewing, sooty bums panhandling. The stink of fish stalls and fried dough hung over the shoving and jostling on the sidewalks as the harried Chinese squeezed past vendors selling dozens of different newspapers, lotto tickets, globs of food. Someone spat and the spit was trampled in seconds. Further north I passed by the white-bearded Bowery men in their overcoats (they don't strip down until July) shoving broken wooden pallets into flaming barrels (also past the guys lying on the pavement, bruised faces crushed into last night's vomit). Gray-faced junkies migrating toward the shitty little park, zeroing in on a fix. The ever-present hookers doling out their morning wake-me-up blow jobs in doorways and parked cars.

I surfed through the East Village, which was pretty quiet, passing an area I don't know the name of where old Polish guys stood in clusters, hands on hips, smoking and watching the passing traffic while muttering in dialect. Then past the Empire State Building, gleaming like a brilliant futuristic rocket waiting for lift-off. I banged a left and detoured through Times Square. Almost nothing was going on there, street sweepers, cops, more bums, then on up into Central Park, blissfully natural and verdant. By this time, the day had broken open, all breezy and hopeful, so there were dozens of people out in the bright sunshine walking their dogs, jogging, zipping along toward the next moment in their personal history.

I made it as far as the reservoir, turned right and trotted the last few blocks to our building. I could feel my blood growing thinner and thinner. A slight dizziness strobed inside my skull. The elevator ride took forever—Latina house cleaners eyeing me with suspicion and more dog people. I danced in the front door just as Dagmara finished her morning powder and perfumage. She furrowed her brow when she saw me, said nothing, then split for her real estate job. I realized I had forgotten about my own employment. Haim was sleeping.

Once Dag was gone, I sat down to write. I wrote and wrote and wrote. I've been reading this Raymond Carver short story book, *Will You Please Be Quiet, Please?* It has inspired me. Describing what's really there right under my nose. The plain, the unadorned. Carver understands that we never really know where we're going, we just go. Go-go-go. It doesn't matter what a person thinks. There is no interior "self," there are only the facts of our existence.

I wrote about my walk. I wrote about John. I wrote about the bums and Dagmara's perfume. I wrote about fucking and eating and smoking cigarettes and drinking Little Italy espresso. Haim roused himself around noon. When he saw that I was writing he kept his distance. Anytime he sees me at my desk, he's respectful, as if I were a rabbi at prayer. By three, I got restless and left the apartment. Dropped into a neighborhood bar and sucked down three cold beers. I had no appetite, but beer seemed to make sense. Calories. Vitamins. Again my brain began to drift into black holes and I caught myself staring into space, my head completely empty. But good empty, not scary empty.

I went to a movie, *Star Wars*, and fell asleep and then woke up during this unbelievable interspace war scene. Very loud and fast. The action on the screen turned me on and the speed kicked in again. My heart was racing. My eyes popping out of my head. Also I was sitting in the second row, that might have had something to do with it.

It was dark when I left the movie theater. I grabbed the IRT subway out to John's place. He was kicked back on his Barcalounger watching

TV with the sound off. Said he was meditating. We got pretty stoned and I fell asleep on the couch. I woke up around midnight and finally, exhausted, struggled back to my apartment. On the way I got slices of pizza at Ray's. Every forty-eight hours should be like this.

June 3, 2006

I'm at the apogee of my life. Everything that I ever looked forward to has either happened or I'm in it now. So it's all downhill from here. What am I supposed to do for excitement for the next twenty or so years? I can reminisce about the good old days I guess. I can ponder death. I can write my memoirs.

I have a good life. No real pain yet. But pain is inevitable, right? Sooner or later I will begin to die and that will be painful.

A turning point, twenty-five years ago. A dumb young writer, me, writes boldly with rash impudence and scores big time. Makes a million. This kid gives birth to the man I am now. One false move, one slip of chance, I'd still be an unknown scrabbler. Like all the other writers, all the other artists. Stuck and fucked in some vermin-infested Lower East Side railroad flat, still committed to the illusion that someday I might be discovered. But that's not what happened. I *was* discovered. I *had* my day. Perhaps it's better to never have had that consummation. To never know that being a big deal author isn't everything it's cracked up to be.

For years, I've enjoyed the certitude that all I have is the product of my efforts. "I" did this. But "I" did not do this. Not the "I" that I am now. No. The "I" I was then, that's who laid the foundation for this life I have now. I am a guest in someone else's house. The house belongs to the stupid "me." The child "me." The one who had no idea how reckless "I/he" was.

June 5, 2006

With perverse curiosity, I tried to find John and 'Gitte today. Yes, things hadn't ended so well between us. In fact, threats had been made. But it couldn't hurt to take a look at the old stomping grounds.

I retraced my old route on the subway out to Brooklyn. I found the right stop, but when I emerged from underground I got lost immediately. The first obstacle was that the sun was shining. I had never visited John during the day. But more confusing was the fact that the neighborhood had no semblance to the broken warehouse district I used to frequent.

Where the buildings once stood sealed and dark, probably not functioning for decades, now every exterior was newly sandblasted, every window lit up. The neighborhood, for it has become a neighborhood, teemed with a happy population of young upwardly mobile et ceteras. The once empty ground floors of the stolid nineteenth-century structures were now grocery stores, coffee shops and boutiques specializing in infant sundresses, handmade organic candles and decorative pillows. I spied a furniture shop, an upscale hair salon and a French dry cleaners.

Eventually I came upon the massive bulwarks of the bridges spanning the East River. These had not altered in thirty years, probably not in a hundred. From these I finally established my bearings. I recalled a couple of street names. I found myself standing before a gleaming lobby fitted with marble floors and a doorman. I was sure. This was once John's building.

It was a handsome red sandstone affair, freshly scrubbed clean of graffiti and posterage. It squatted in the middle of the block like old royalty. Every building in the row had been refurbished. Next door, a small billboard announced condos for sale "starting in the low 800s."

I entered. The doorman sat at his desk, perfectly lit by recessed fix-tures. An elegant potted fig stood behind him. He paused writing in his journal and spoke before looking up. "Yessir, how may I help you?"

"A friend of mine once lived here. Years ago." My voice was a squeaky croak.

"Does he live here now?" This doorman was almost certainly an ex-cop.

"No, as I said, he lived here years ago." My voice found its proper register. I wanted him to know I was not afraid of his ersatz authority.

"So how can I help you, sir?"

"Would you have any records of the people who once lived here?" I smiled. I wanted him to know I meant no harm. I was his friend.

"No, sir." He turned his attention to his multi-buttoned phone con-sole. He picked up the handset. "Yes? Yes, in about ten minutes. Yes, sir." He hung up and returned to his writing, no longer interested in me.

"Do you know who would?" The guy was a doorman. His job was to meet the needs of people coming through that front door. On the other hand, he was a modern man and resented his job. And so, in a perfect Sartrean exercise, he turned the tables whenever he could, to show peo-ple like me who was boss.

Looking up, he seemed to be surprised to find me still standing be-fore him. He said, "Excuse me?"

"Do you know who would?" I repeated.

"Would what?" His face betrayed nothing of the aggression he was aiming my way.

"Have records of who might have once lived here." I met his passive aggression with a potent combination of stubbornness and false sweet-ness.

"No, sir." Back to the journal.

"Who's the managing agent?" A degree of officiousness usually gets results. He replied by pointing his chin toward a bronze plaque attached to the wall. I recognized the name of one of the larger developers in the city. Stalemate.

Finally, probably for no other reason than to send me on my way, the doorman offered a smidgen. "This building was completely gutted and the lofts were sold before renovation was finished. That was three years ago. When did your friend live here?"

"The seventies. Thirty years ago, I guess."

"Are you kidding me? Those jokers are long gone. The contractor chased all of them out of here ten years ago before the C of O."

I couldn't remember if John owned or rented his loft. People didn't discuss real estate in those days. People who lived in lofts had a squatter mentality. Only frontiersmen lived in lofts. I did know that John was proud of having an unlisted phone number, so digging up old phone books would do no good.

I returned to the subway, to the Upper West Side and my apartment. In my mail was an official-looking letter from a law firm informing me that Elizabeth would be proceeding with her lawsuit. I tossed the letter into the trash.

I went online and browsed the name "John Davis." Pretty useless. In New York state there are over a hundred John Davises. And who knew if he lived in New York state any longer? Or if he was alive at all? Who knew if John Davis was his legal name. I punched in Brigitte Davis. Nothing came up.

The puzzle gave me a headache. My drinking buddy Jack introduced me to John. But I had not seen much of Jack since around the time he was hospitalized. I punched Jack's name into the browser and got similar results to the John search.

According to my journals, I met Jack through work at the video place. Jack had worked for another production house that my boss, Jonathan, had dealings with. Perhaps Jonathan could help, but where was Jonathan now? I quit working for Jonathan as soon as I started to sell my writing. No, I quit before I started to sell my writing. "The hungry years." Jonathan had graciously "laid me off" so I could collect unemployment and write.

In the eighties, Jonathan's place had lurched onward like most of the old SoHo establishments. But eventually it succumbed to the inflated leases of the nineties. All the places from that time, Anthology Film Archives, Food, The Kitchen, even Castelli were long gone. Only Ken's Broome Street Bar remained. So Jonathan, where had he moved to? Was he in the video business anymore? Was he alive? I Googled his name. Nothing. His company was also history.

Can the past disappear?

July 15, 1977

An exciting few days. Two nights ago I was sitting in our living room, twenty-three stories up, writing. I was at a small table facing the broad vista of the Bronx and Yonkers. The city lay before me like a magical dark forest embedded with sparkling jewels. Haim was in the bedroom. Dagmara was out having dinner with her irritating workmates.

I wanted to write, but instead I was daydreaming about Katie. I have slept with her one time. Was I obsessed? Did I love her? One minute I would be absolutely sure she was the one, then I would remember the bad night at the museum and then I'd start thinking and things would get confusing.

While I was busy with all this thinking, my reading lamp pulsed and died. I reflexively looked up. Of course I assumed the bulb had burned out. My eyes naturally fell upon the view out before me. A chunk of the twinkly carpet went black before my eyes. Then another. I was witnessing the domino effect of a crashing electrical system but my brain couldn't understand what was happening. Everything before me slipped into a velvet void. A distant billboard advertising Kent cigarettes was all that remained illuminated.

From the bedroom, Haim bellowed. He charged into the room brandishing a flashlight. The light bounced off the plate glass and for a second I saw a reflection of the stunned look on my face. Haim shouted, "Do you see?"

I said, "I think we blew a fuse."

Haim said, "No. Look out the window! It's a blackout. We have them in Tel Aviv all the time! Get up! Get up! We have to go!"

His eyes scanned the nothingness out past the plate glass, perhaps searching for enemy aircraft, who knows, then he turned, taking the light with him. I could hear Haim in the kitchen galley crashing through the pots and pans like a clumsy bear. Then the gush of water splashing into the bathtub.

From the bathroom Haim shouted: "We have to collect as much as we can from the pipes above us. We only have fifteen minutes before all the water drains out of the building." He burst into the kitchen again, found and lit two candles. In the candlelight his eyes danced with excitement. "And we will need food."

I found a beat-up portable radio and tuned to "1010." The announcer sounded very grave. We were in the midst of an emergency! A massive electrical failure. And I had witnessed it with my own eyes! A thrill ran through me. The man on the radio was reporting that the entire city had blacked out! His voice faded to a murmur, then total inaudiblity. The batteries were old.

The taps ran dry as Haim predicted they would. The apartment glowed with eerie waxen light. Sirens wailed twenty-three stories beneath us. I felt a lightness in the pit of my stomach, weakness in my knees. I thought, this is what fear feels like. Or life-threatening thrill. Maybe we were under attack! Haim grabbed a bottle of whiskey and a very sharp chef's knife from a kitchen drawer. "Time to go." He slugged the whiskey, slipped the knife under his belt and hustled me out of the apartment.

No elevators, of course, we had to walk down all twenty-three flights of gloomy stairwells. As we descended, we were joined by confused neighbors who were making the same exodus. Most of the emergency lighting was nonfunctional and the flashlights barely cut into the murk. We stepped carefully, moving through total coal mine blackness for two or even three flights at a time. My neighbors were bodies without faces. Groping, muttering. Every so often, someone would call out a name. "Sidney?" "Fran? Where are you?" "Up here!" "Where?" "Here!"

Emerging at ground level, we joined a parade of excited if shadowy souls thronging under the dead streetlamps as happy as clams, grinning and blabbing away as if they were off to see a county fair fireworks show or a Little League playoff, everyone moving forward with clear purpose, toward an indefinable something.

Every few minutes an echo-y loud sound (A shot? An explosion? A cherry bomb?), from maybe blocks away, ruffled the gentle crowd. Everyone stopped and craned their necks, confused. A shouted sarcasm was followed by crazy laughter. The march resumed. Haim and I passed the bottle. He guzzled the booze bottoms up, like a sailor, caught up in the spirit of revolution or anarchy or whatever this was.

We inspected the damage left by vandals preceding us. Security gates had been peeled off storefronts, trash cans overturned, the windows of cars punched out. We remained alert, especially with an eye for arson, but there was none of that, at least not in our neighborhood, only the distant police sirens.

We did see Good Samaritans directing traffic and people drinking beer openly as if they needed an excuse and folks walking arm and arm. Others sat on stoops with their miniature poodles on their laps, candles beside them, eating from containers of leftovers, watching the passing procession. One guy was in the middle of the avenue grilling hot dogs on a barbecue. The refrigerators are dead! Time to eat!

In the dark, faces were unclear and the vagueness prevented any real engagement with anyone. Young women stuck close to one another or had men by their side. I didn't see weapons, but I did see one guy carrying a nine-iron. As we made our way to the Village, Haim grew more and more discouraged. He wanted action and there was none to be had. I think he was hoping for some kind of spontaneous rioting to break out.

Eventually we grew tired of walking, abandoned the search for adventure, and headed home. Climbing back up to the apartment was like ascending a small mountain. In the glimmers of flashlight I could see Haim's perspiring brow. Entering our apartment had a weird anonymous feeling. Like this could be anyone's apartment. A vacant, abandoned atmosphere. The drapes were open and now the hushed city was laid out at our feet, still and black. I thought, this is what it would be like if civilization ended. As we shut the door behind us I was thankful that Haim saved water. With a groan, my roommate flopped onto the couch like a massive narcotized golem.

We had gas, we had water, we had a few bits of food that would begin to rot by tomorrow afternoon. Down on the street, the word was that the problem would take days if not weeks to fix. No one knew the cause. Everyone was fairly certain the Russians had nothing to do with it. I had no idea what was coming next for the first time in my life.

The ringing phone broke the silence. It was Dagmara, hysterical, saying she had been calling for hours. Without electricity our answering machine was dead and hadn't picked up her call. I don't know what she thought could have happened to us, but she finally calmed down when she realized that we were safe. She was okay also and said she was going to stay overnight with her girlfriends from work.

I phoned my father. He also had no electricity but he seemed unworried. He told me a long-winded story about the blackout in 1965.

Haim began to snore. In the candlelight, he looked so harmless. I realized I love this guy so much. The snoring built to a small roar.

I hadn't drunk as much as Haim and I wasn't tired. I tried finding Katie but her answering machine didn't pick up either. I decided to walk to Brooklyn, to John's. I found my way downtown, over the Brooklyn Bridge and eventually to John's neighborhood.

When I got there, John and a small crowd were assembled around the loading dock at the front of his building. I could smell the weed from a block away. John hailed me like a long-lost brother and handed me a warm beer, then 'Gitte emerged from the building with a bowl of hot soup (the gas was still working). John began to sing "Going Down the Road Feeling Bad." 'Gitte perched on the dock and I lay down on my back beside her, my belly full of her delicious soup. I gazed up at 'Gitte, who was laughing at John's antics. I let myself dive deeply into her shimmering beauty. The stars were out, my belly was full, I was in love. Everything inside me released and I felt weightless. I was home.

June 9, 2006

Am I wrong to assume my generation will be the last to possess a complete sense of literature and history? Is it that far-fetched to say that we, the literati of the contemporary world, are in fact the *last* of the true literates? Soon there will be no great minds. And there will be no going back. There will be no Samuel Johnson or Voltaire or Pound or Joyce with enough knowledge to make the ultimate structural connections. And *so*, no new connections, no new universal networks will be possible or created. We will become medieval, fragmented. All ideas will be equal: comic books, classical theater, advertising, nineteenth-century novels, movies, gum wrappers, the Bible.

A very thin topsoil of information (the Internet) will cover everything. A strong wind (a war, a blackout, a computer virus) will blow it all away. Chaos will enter. A new Dark Age will prevail, arriving in the breakdown lane of the "information superhighway."

As an individual, as an author, an artist and a man, I stand at the brink of this moment in history. I know what I *don't* know. Those who come after me, won't even know that.

And I only have so much time on this earth, so I am on the veritable peak of the peak. It's all downhill from here. All downhill. Gradually and inevitably I can only lose my abilities—hearing, taste, sensation (especially in the tip of my penis, the surfaces of my tongue and eardrums). I will become weaker and weaker, creep along more and more slowly, wake every morning a little groggier, breathe ever more shallow breaths.

Slowly but surely, my body will separate into its constituent parts as each organ struggles: eyes, ears, kidneys, joints, heart, even my brain. I will spin into smaller and smaller pieces, a process that will persevere even after I'm dead as I decay into a biological soup of elemental molecules. When I was a pup, I had no notion of my parts or my vulnerabilities. I thought nothing could hurt me. I bullied my way through life energized by the theme of my self-ness, my desire. But that is all past.

I've been nothing but undistinguished on every front. No friends. No family. Not even any lovers, now. Only a gallery of memory. But isn't that enough? What more can you have? So I have that. Consciousness. Soon gone.

June 10, 2006

I've spent all day burrowing through a stack of newspaper tear sheets and printouts of the better-known Internet blogs which Leon's publicity director has been kind enough to forward in a large gray envelope. Delivered by messenger, of course. Normally I don't bother reading this crap, but the wounding release of this book has metastasized into a gaping, bleeding gash. I can't help myself, I can't turn my eyes away from the torn flesh, the seeping blood, the broken sutures. I am drawn to this mess. I must probe it, mesmerized by the maggots wriggling through the rotten meat.

All self-reflexive work annoys them. They want their big dish of ice cream. They want the obvious. They want a pacifier, because they, the critics, are in the employ of the reigning academy and the academy must protect the status quo. This is all so obvious. If the status quo could see itself, it might change. No one wants that.

Also, it would never occur to the oblivious Critic that the writer is writing because he *must*. The true writer does not write out of choice but of *necessity*. Because the act of writing is an act of courage. And because the Critic himself is an employee, he assumes everyone wielding a pen is an employee.

July 23, 1977

"My Lucky Day" has been published. I ran to the Village and bought ten copies of the magazine. No one has called me. But I reread the piece and fuck it, it *is* good. It is there on the page in black and white and no one can take that from me. It exists and therefore I exist. It will be the first of a collection of dozens of stories. Of hundreds.

Haim opened a cheap bottle of champagne in congratulations. Dagmara brought a cake home and we had a small celebration. I guess they're the only family I've got now. Later when Haim, high from the booze, started making his usual embarrassing erotic overtures to Dagmara, I lied and told them I had to go see my boss about something.

I called Zim. He sounded depressed. Insisted I come over. But I knew that I couldn't talk about the story with him. All we'd do is drink and snort drugs and complain about life. Instead, I grabbed a train to Brooklyn.

I was surprised to find John and 'Gitte home alone, *reading*, as sober as Ozzie and Harriet. I felt like I was intruding. It never occurred to me that they would have a private home life. John's loft is like a public place, like the library or a bar.

Finally, John rolled a joint and for the second time that night I felt like I was part of a family. What's that about? I decided not to tell John about my story being published. John doesn't care about the real world, doesn't care about ambition. Also he would never admit he was jealous.

'Gitte disappeared into the kitchen to make lemonade and John told me stories about bullfighting. I relaxed while he described Mexico and the stadiums and how the matadors aim their stabs so that they cut into the bull's shoulder muscles and force the bull to lower his head. They do this because then the matador can thrust straight down between the shoulder and the neck so perfectly that the blade of the sword cuts into the aorta and the bull dies instantly!

After the bullfight, if the matador has been skillful, he is given the bull's ear, if he has been very skillful, he is given both ears, and if he's been superb, he is given the ears and the tail. Then the bull's carcass gets hacked up and the meat is sold right then and there in the stadium as people are walking out. Fresh bull meat. Thousands of bulls are slaughtered this way every year. Tens of thousands.

John said that El Cid, the famous Spanish medieval military leader, is reputed to be the first person to lance a bull from horseback. I don't know how he knows this, but he says it like he knows. He added that the greatest bullfighter of all time was some guy named Mano-something who died in the ring when he was fatally gored. He had actually retired but another bullfighter dared him to come out to fight because he wanted to impress Ava Gardner.

Ava Gardner was the actress who ruined Frank Sinatra's marriage. She was also married to Mickey Rooney (!), but that had to be a long time ago. Sounds like she had a good time wherever she went. Anyway, Franco (who was the fascist dictator of Spain at the time) declared three days of mourning when this Mano guy got gored by the bull. Sex and death and fate. That's all there is, I guess.

July 27, 1977

I shouldn't be drinking. I wake up every day with a pain in my side. Two nights ago I got a call from that Tim guy from the bookstore. He was hanging out in the Village at the Cookery listening to Marian Mc-Partland, the jazz pianist. Wanted me to join him because he was with a friend who's a big deal editor. It was pretty clear when I got there that both of these guys were very drunk. The editor guy kept smiling at me and laughing and telling me how beautiful I was. What great eyes I have, blah-blah-blah. Asking me all about myself, when did I arrive in New York blah-blah-blah. I'm thinking, "Go with the flow."

So I was trying to be interesting and cosmopolitan, blabbing on about bullfighting and they're both ooh-ing and aahhh-ing like I'm the most fascinating person they've ever met. I told them about my short story and the editor guy said he wanted to read it. Then at one point, Tim the bookstore guy left to go to the bathroom and this editor guy, who reminded me of my Uncle Norman, started stroking my knee under the table. I shifted away and he smiled this creepy grin. When Tim came back, he proceeded to drink three more gin and tonics, then staggered out of the place by himself. I think he was in a blackout drunk.

So I was stuck with this editor guy and after a while we had run out of things to talk about. He said he had a car and would happily give me a lift to the Upper East Side. Which was okay with me because it's a long journey from the Village late at night. Turned out he had a Mercedes sports car and it was pretty fun zipping through the city. We were laughing and joking, he was running red lights and acting like he owned the world.

He stopped in front of my apartment building. As I undid my seatbelt, he reached over and tugged me toward him.

I said, "I don't go that way."

He stroked my leg again and purred, "Doesn't this feel good?"

I said "No!" and flipped his hand back into his lap.

He said, "Come on, don't be like that. You're very very attractive." Gave me this big toothy smile and then he brought his arm up and around my shoulders. He was a big guy. He was trying to hug me.

I said, really clearly, "If you don't take your hands off me, I'm going to break your jaw so bad, you're gonna be sucking cock through a straw." His eyes went all hard and he let go of me. I got out of the car. I was really wound up.

So now I guess I've totally fucked up my big "connection" to the publishing world. I told Zim what happened and he said I should have let the guy do what he wanted. Said I have to be willing to sacrifice everything for my work. I couldn't tell if he was serious or not.

June 11, 2006

Isn't anger the basis for all great art? Why bother trying to make an argument (which is all that a book, or any work of art is: a point of view) if one doesn't have the motivation? And what purer motivation is there than anger? Anger is the emotion that is born when a wrong has transpired. Wrongs must be righted! Knut Hamsun versus Henrik Ibsen! Joseph Conrad versus Henry James. Allen Ginsberg versus T. S. Eliot, Ni

Tsan versus the Sung Dynasty masters! Bob Dylan against the folkies. Bukowski against the world! There has to be some motivation. Contentment doesn't possess enough fuel to feed and stoke the furnace of art.

These assholes cutting into me, each taking their little piece of flesh. Bleeding me. Wearing me down. Trying to smother me. Next time I see Leon I will tell him he can't have my next book. That's all. No one can. I will write it for myself. I don't need this crap in my life.

All the same, the books are my progeny. And my children must be read in order to live. Someone out there needs them, wants them. If I don't fight for them, who will? I need to promote them even if I have to act like a whore. Otherwise my children will die. And if they die, I die.

Others can have their biological children, nagging spouses and spiteful parents. I don't need any of that. I need to define my relationship to the world and I can only do that through words. Even if no one understands me today, they will someday. I am certain of this.

This is the invisible war, the war each author has to fight on his own behalf. They all did it—Hemingway, Capote, Faulkner, Carver, Roth— all. Otherwise the writing is forgotten. A writer's job is to promote himself. And to do that we must take the abuse. Fellini said "I drop my pants and everyone either laughs or applauds." Perhaps my battle is futile, because I am no Hemingway, Capote, Faulkner, Carver or Roth. I'm nothing. Maybe my books deserve to die and I will die with them. For the time being, I'm postponing lunch with Leon.

June 13, 2006

The New York Review of Books (five months too late), with no advance warning or fanfare, has vindicated *A Gentle Death*. In a masterful and definitive analysis, the critique explores the themes in relation to my previously published body of work. The reviewer actually lists my last five books at the head of the article. Has read each and every one. Carefully. Understands my points. Recalls characters who reappear under different nomenclatures. Understands the subtle nature of the love affair as it resonates with the CIA story line. Happily explores the whole tapestry I have woven in which truth plays against fiction, etc.

Someone actually gets it. The review won't put me on any bestseller lists but at least *one* person sees what I was doing. I am reborn.

I need a break. I need to remove myself from these grinding gears of commerce. How can anything constructive be accomplished with so much money at stake? How can I write? Of course it's my own fault because twenty years ago I let them produce a movie based on a story of mine. That started all this, didn't it? I danced with the devil and that's how I ended up in the crosshairs. But how is it possible to be known as a great American writer without the movies? The playwrights all had movies. Arthur Miller's *Death of a Salesman* was filmed seven times! No wonder he got to fuck Marilyn. And the novelists too. Capote, Harper Lee, Steinbeck, Updike, Roth, Dick, Mann. Everything Hemingway wrote. It comes down to this, a movie is the fast path to a reputation. No movie, soon forgotten.

August 1, 1977

The gay editor called me. He was very sober-sounding on the phone. He didn't mention putting his hand on my knee. Talked as if it never happened. Maybe he wants to give it another try. Or maybe . . . he actually likes my work. Said he read "My Lucky Day" and thinks it's terrific. Wants to see more. He also said he's called someone over at *The New Yorker* and sent them "My Lucky Day." I guess I should start reading *The New Yorker.* Now I feel guilty I threatened him. On the other hand, maybe he read the story because I *refused* to blow him.

August 3, 1977

Essentially, John is a pot dealer and people are always there to buy pot. But some, like me, stay a little longer. Or a lot longer. Also John and 'Gitte let people passing through town crash at their place. 'Gitte will cook a huge bean soup (she's vegetarian) and bake bread and feed everyone for days. Sometimes there are people sleeping on the floor (on foam mats) while we hang out and smoke weed and talk. The visitors are usually hippies: ex–Ivy Leaguers (always very WASP-y) with matted hair who have migrated down from some Vermont commune or Amsterdam. They have big-chested, crazy girlfriends, the kind who roll their eyes when they laugh and wear patchouli oil.

A young couple from Copenhagen was crashing at John's last night. Very blond, almost white-haired, very earnest people until the guy got way too stoned and couldn't stop laughing. The girl was outrageously beautiful, but in a way that usually doesn't turn me on, like a female David Bowie. I could see her nipples under the sheer material of her peasant blouse.

Eventually the Danish pastry dragged her imbecilic boyfriend off to bed (and this skinny, pimply guy who came by to buy hash oil also split) so that John and I were left alone. I like it best when we're alone. Then I can really listen to him. With a twinkle in his eye, he pulled out a Baggie filled with these crumpled-up brown things inside. Peyote buttons. We ate a bunch.

John became unusually quiet. Instead of talking, he dug up some old Dylan bootleg stuff he has on cassette tapes. We listened to that for a while. I'm not really into Dylan, and on these tapes he sounded like a cat in a burlap bag. Then John put on "The Night They Drove Old Dixie Down." On the fifth or sixth playing I was hallucinating trails. The last time John and I did psychedelics, I was speeding, so the stuff didn't hit me so hard. Now I was tripping for real. The room shifted into another zone of reality. I kept swallowing back the bitter vomit that lay in the back of my throat, but after a while I forgot about that.

I was staring at the floor when the music stopped. John seemed to be staring at the same spot I was staring at. John stuttered: "Ever see dogs fucking?"

I said, "Yeah" and my voice sounded like a tiny person was living in the back of my throat speaking on my behalf.

John said, "Female dogs are 'bitches' but male dogs are just 'males.' There is no equivalent term for 'bitch.'"

I said, "Why is that?" thinking that was the appropriate response.

John said, "Who knows? But another little known fact is that koala bears have a double-ended penis." Pause. We stared at the floor for another minute. Then John said: "Now you take millions of humans and add gut-wrenching hunger. Throw in a few machine guns, a police state and you know what you got? A perfect formula for any possibility. No matter how far out beyond the imagination. Auschwitz. But even worse. Can you imagine worse?"

I peeped "No." The walls were flowing like lava.

"So now, dial it back a bit. Some starving farm girl from the Ukraine is propositioned by a gentleman in a nice suit who happens to be passing through. He has money. He seems to wield a certain authority. And all he wants her to do is fuck a German shepherd. For more money than she can make in a year growing turnips. She sucks off Augie Doggie while Doggie Daddy plays hide-the-kielbasa. And why not? I mean who's the victim here? The chick or the freak who gets off on this shit?

"So don't sweat it, because that's life in all it's ironic and varied splendor. Right? The agony and the ecstasy. Life happens. Just 'cause you don't *want* it to happen doesn't mean it doesn't. All over the world, right now, while we sit here as wasted as roadkill, people are having sex with dogs, sheep, chickens. Maybe even voles. Murdering each other. Raping each other. Even eating each other."

I said, "I think kielbasa is Polish not Ukrainian. What's a vole?"

John said, "A vole is like a gerbil. Smaller. Easier to insert."

I said, "Insert where?"

John said, "Into the lower colon. Use a tube. Put the gerbil in a rubber glove. Insert into anus. Allow small mammal to go exploring. Stimulates the prostate."

I said, "Whose prostate?"

John said, "Some candy-assed movie star. Candy-assed movie stars will do anything. Because they're rich and stupid. Especially if it has to do with sex. Hey, we could start a rumor! Some movie star has been seen in the emergency room having a gerbil removed from his ass!"

"No one would believe it."

It was around this time that I realized that some new folks had dropped by and they were sitting on the floor a few feet away passing a joint. Every time I glanced over in their direction, there seemed to be more of them. I whispered to John, "What's going on?"

John gave me this Cheshire Cat smile and said, "You can't lie to me."

I said, "I'm not lying. About what?"

And then he said, "I know who you are even if you won't admit it to yourself." As if I had been hiding something from him. More people arrived and 'Gitte emerged from the back and I finally understood that they were throwing a party. People kept piling in the front door. The place started to get crowded and so I wasn't really hanging out with John anymore because John had wandered off to socialize with the new arrivals. Plus I was tripping my ass off. A wave of anxiety tickled my gut, like "Can I handle this?" And as soon as that happened, 'Gitte materialized and said, "John told me to give you this." And she passed me a small pipe. I took a hit. It wasn't weed. It was a bitter white smoke. Opium? Whatever it was, I suddenly went all calm and my fingers tingled.

'Gitte disappeared and I found it impossible to see more than a few feet in front of where I was standing. I completely lost sight of Big John. People were forced to follow the current of the crowd, me included. We were all moving in this flowing stream of partygoers, from one part of the loft to the other. I didn't like it, I wanted to get out from the thick of the crowd so I aimed myself toward the walls. The enormous loft windows had been yanked wide open and people clustered along the sills. The summer air blew in in gusts. I could actually see the breeze. Then some sort of music layered and wove into the babble, and became an indistinguishable part of it. Or was it the pipe that got passed around? Someone said, "dusted," and my ass felt like it had been welded to the floor. I was sitting, but I didn't remember sitting down. A girl with long hair and a headband plopped down alongside me, looked deeply into my eyes and said "Hi," and then stood up and walked away. A long thick python with glittering scales slithered past my hand. I couldn't remember if John had a snake. Unsteady, I rose to my feet.

As soon as I stood up a primal fear of wetting my pants shot through me. I struggled through the throng toward what I thought was the direction of the bathroom. But I had forgotten where the bathroom was. Also there was something very important I had to tell John, but I couldn't remember what it was.

Another pipe was passed to me and I toked on this too. It tasted like the color blue and then tasted of chocolate. A black guy in beaded dreadlocks was laughing at me. "Hold it in, dude, you gotta hold it in!" 'Gitte hopped by, pretending she was the White Rabbit. And I saw myself off to one side watching myself watching her. Then wham, everyone in the room disappeared but her and me.

I thought, once. To have her just once. Why isn't that possible? I hated the fact that there was something impossible in my life. I felt my dick get hard. Blood hard or piss hard? I entered an open door and the couple from Denmark were on the floor screwing. The girl was completely naked and on her back. She turned her head and her eyes locked on to mine. She kept her eyes on me while the cheerful Dane slid in and out. He had incredible stringy muscles all over his body, even in places where muscles don't usually exist. I thought, this guy must do kung fu. The girl stared at me as she was jostled with every thump, as if she wanted me to join in. With great effort I backed out of the room and closed the door.

I found another doorway along the wall and figured it had to lead back to the big room, a shortcut. I wedged myself through the door, making sure none of the partygoers followed. I didn't want anyone to see me piss my pants. This new hallway was lit by wall sconces every ten feet separated by small framed photographs hanging between them. I tried to get a good look at the photographs, but whenever I focused on one, it would become unfocused. Like I could see it, until I stared right at it, then I saw nothing but shadow. I pushed on in the direction of the bathroom.

After passing several locked doors, I found one that swung open. As I entered the room, someone shouted out, "Shut the door, man!" and I could make out in the candlelight one of the foreign guys from two months before. He was barefoot and naked from the waist up, probing his arm with a little plastic hypodermic needle, like the kind diabetics use. His black tattoos were luminescent in the dim light, crosses and black panthers and a heart crowned with thorns.

Blood seeped from the wounds on his arms. Blood dripped from the syringe. Drops of blood stained the old flooring all around him. His bare feet were smudged with blood.

I said, "Oh, you don't want to be doing that." Bookcases lined the walls. I could smell the mold growing on the old paper. Centipedes crawled over the bindings, slithered down onto the floor and ran over the floorboards. I figured they were attracted by the blood. I could see them lapping up the blood with their tiny centipede tongues.

The foreign guy said, "Man, you just don't get it do you?" He stood up. His body was covered with thick scars that lay along the crook of both arms, on the veins of his lower abdomen, on his jugular, his inner thigh. The scars looked like bits of earthworm. He left the needle dangling in his arm, picked his shirt off the floor and daintily slipped the sleeve up over it. "Gotta be coordinated to do that," he said proudly. The worms on his skin began to wriggle.

Then I was walking in an unfamiliar wing of the loft marveling at the immense size of the place. John had told me that the loft had been a mousetrap factory before the Civil War. After that it had become a kind of leather-cutting warehouse, and then a storage house for exotic brassware from Asia. Also, John had told me the place was haunted.

I mumbled to no one, "I'm ripped. How did I get so ripped?" and continued along the hallway, making three right turns figuring that this would have to get me back to the party. I could hear it, I just couldn't see it. Obviously John and 'Gitte only occupied a portion of the massive loft and now I was lost again in a maze of large airless rooms stacked with ancient office furniture, wood pallets and fearsome grease-slathered machines that crouched in the dark like monsters. I could no longer hear the party, but logic told me that I would have to come to the building's outer wall or be redirected back to the main room.

I made my way toward muffled voices. An open doorway spilled yellow light onto the stained oaken floors. With relief I entered, eager to find people. This group was seated on either side of long tables, apparently having a meal, probably 'Gitte's soup. But no one looked up. When I got closer, I could see that they weren't eating at all, but fiddling with small bits of wood and wire.

Everyone was intently constructing mousetraps. Someone glanced up at me. He wore a leather vest over his boldly striped shirt. His sleeves were rolled up under elastic bands and he sported a long scraggly mustache and a hat. He seemed to gaze right through my chest and then returned to cocking the spring on his contraption. I'm not afraid of ghosts, but I didn't think it was healthy to hang around them, so I left.

I smelled 'Gitte's perfume a moment before finding her in the hallway. She said nothing, simply took my hand and led me back to the party. This was the first time we had ever touched one another. A universe of love streamed through her warm hand into mine. I was about to speak, but she let go of my hand and the crowd closed in around me. I was back where I started, in the thick of it. Music, laughter, perfume and weed smoke crowded my senses.

Then the gathering roared in unison, and the horde split open like the Red Sea. In the clearing stood Big John, wielding an axe, tall and broad and fearsome. All I could think was, "He's taller than I thought."

"You have no fuckin' choice!" He bellowed. "Satan wants you! He wants your life! Go for it!" John lifted the axe high over his head, then drove it down onto something. A spray of splinters flew up in response and the crowd gave a collective "Ahhhh!," leaned away, then flowed back into the void they had created only moments before.

John spun playfully, swinging the axe in a large circle. Then he seemed to wilt, I couldn't see him anymore and the twisting bodies closed in and he was swallowed up amidst the froth of the crowd. Someone stuck a beer into my hand and I brought it to my lips, which reminded me that my bladder had become a time bomb. I made for the door. I was suffocating on the exhausted stench of dozens of fucked-up partygoers.

As I grabbed the handle of the heavy door, it swung inward and a tall, thin girl with perfect eyes entered laughing. I stared at her. It was too depressing. Did God make beautiful women only to torture me? And yet, at the last moment, she did meet my eyes as she slipped past. A moment. How painful are those moments? Everything slowed down, I don't know why, so I asked her her name and she said, "Vera," then slipped away into the crowd.

A tremendous yearning shot through my heart. This woman was my soul mate and if I missed this opportunity to grab her and pour myself into her, I would die. This moment would never come again. And if I left now, I would never be able to find her. But she was gone. "Vera." Lost forever.

My mind cleared enough for me to finally escape the loft and negotiate the worn, endless staircase. I lost my balance, flipped forward, completely out of control. I thought I was a goner but staved off disaster by grabbing the ancient railing at the last moment. I could have broken my neck. My heart was pounding. I sat down on the stairs, the muffled roar of the party seeping through the iron door. Time to go home. Go home, go to bed. Give it up. Give it up.

On the street, I found an ancient mossy wall and peed with tremendous relief. As I drenched the cracked foundation stone, I thought, isn't it amazing what can make you feel good? Urination. Then I remembered all the infested nooks and crannies. What if a rat saw my flaccid dick and thought, "Meat!" Rats can jump. A rat could jump up and tear my dick off. This made me think of a life without a dick. Which made me think of returning to John's place to try to find Vera. Or 'Gitte. Or any woman who could save me.

I was defeated by inertia. The smothering August humidity closed in on me, hugged me hard and licked me. It was as if the breath of every soul in the city had been trapped under the sky, building with pressure minute by minute. I had to get back to my apartment as soon as possible. The air would be cooler there. Things would be calmer. This all made sense to me.

Finding one mysterious, magical brass token in my pocket, I rode the hurtling, roaring vibration through the wild subterranean light homeward and did not get singled out and mugged on the way. The 'shroom trip had faded slightly. I regained the ability to think two thoughts in succession.

I woke in my bed, dreaming of knights and kings. Somewhere an early bird was singing. I vomited and blacked out.

June 14, 2006

Received an invitation to visit Israel. All expenses paid. Simply for an in-person interview in Tel Aviv and some kind of "conference" in Jerusalem ("Postwar Jewish Literature and the Modern Sentiment"). The guy who got in touch with me, Lev, was "blown away" by *A Gentle Death*. Knew it better than I do. Cited chapter and verse. Had made all kinds of connections between themes and characters that I'd never intended. Of course, he insisted that this book could only have been written by a Jew. The suffering, the insight, the tradition of wisdom, etc. etc.

The conversation on the phone was embarrassingly cordial. How could I not accept? Of course, Lev was an author himself. If I accepted the offer, I would have to be careful not to be caught alone with this guy too often. But let's face it, I could use a refreshing vacation of praise. Get away from Leon and the blogs. And Elizabeth and the lawsuit. In addition, I would receive an honorarium of five thousand dollars. I called my father, thinking the news might ignite a spark of Jewish pride. He said, "You're gonna get yourself blown up."

June 15, 2006

The sales of my novel are accelerating. Word of mouth? I allow myself a moment or two of serenity.

When a book begins to sell, everyone wants to know you. It's as if you give off some kind of pheromone of attraction. Women, men, show biz types . . .

Met with the famous actor C.G. today to discuss an adaptation of my short story "The Wounded." When I first shook his hand, I was smitten by his tremendous projection of *substance*. A man of depth and wisdom and . . . beauty. His hazel eyes, his thick animated eyebrows, his lips as he formed words. Even his eyelashes were perfect. The man is beautiful, no wonder he is a star. And he's used his power as a star to make movies that "say something" and get nominated for Oscars. Here was a man, a true man, I thought. I had an instant sense of familiarity with him. We could become close.

All such notions evaporated as we tucked into our meal. After discussing my story, the sum of his discourse was a) his girlfriend and how she wants to get married and have a baby with him and b) his other girlfriends who have amazing bodies, breasts, asses, legs, vaginas, anuses, toes, lips, tongues, etc. and c) what a headache it is to sell his fifteen-million-dollar estate so that he can buy the new twenty-two-million-dollar estate. When the waitress visited us, agog and flirty, C.G. flirted back, and when she floated off with our order, he launched into a discussion of *her* breasts, *her* ass, *her* navel, *her* lips, *her* hair, *her* ears and *her* barely hidden thong.

He did this because by doing so, he reminded me that all these were his for the taking. He can have any woman he wants, whenever he wants her. He makes millions of dollars. Lives in a magical gated estate. I can't and I don't and I don't. He wanted me to understand, that, yes, he was coming to me as a supplicant because he "wanted" my story, that I am a "genius," but I should be ever mindful of the fact that he was still boss.

Once we had eaten, perhaps because the food had satiated something deep within his second chakra, he finished unveiling his plans for my short story. As the obsequious waiter scraped crumbs from the tablecloth, C.G. said that not only did he want to star in the film, he wanted to *direct* it. Dramatic pause. He gazed into me with all the charisma at his command.

I wouldn't mind receiving a small pile of cash for the option, so I said, "Great! Let's do this! I'm excited!" and we shook hands. He grinned brilliantly. We amiably stood and said our adieus. And then he added, "Oh, one last thing. When I told Elizabeth that we'd be having lunch today, she said to say hi." A twinkle in his eye let me know he'd fucked my girl. Or could if he wished.

I returned his smirk ("Just us guys!") and said, "Tell Elizabeth hi back from me." But his cell phone was already out and he was talking to someone else about something very important as the door of the Mercedes was slapped shut by the chauffeur. I walked to the Village and grabbed the A train on 4th Street. On my way there, I decided I didn't need a new car so badly. "C. G." would not be getting my story.

As I entered my place, the phone was ringing. Leon wanted to know how the lunch had gone. I said it had gone well. He said he would sniff around, call C.G.'s agent. I said, "Keep me posted." Which is my way of saying, "Whatever." Maybe Leon knew about Elizabeth and this guy. Did he get a kick out of my discomfort? The whole deal was sick. The only revenge is to take the money. Take the money, take the money, take the money. Without pain, how would we ever know we were alive?

June 20, 2006

On the El Al flight to Tel Aviv, the cabin attendant was a tall, sturdy, unsmiling, dark-haired Jewess. About an hour in, she began to warm up to me. I assumed it was because of the charm I'd been projecting every time she brought me a drink. I fantasized a liaison under a Mediterranean moon.

Alas, it was not my charisma she'd been responding to. As it turned out, another flight attendant had let her know that I've been interviewed on TV by Charlie Rose. My dour stewardess began to pump me for inside info on Charlie. Was he fascinating? Was he sexy? Was he as good-looking in person? I told her Charlie played a mean game of squash implying that a) I played squash and b) I played squash with Charlie Rose. Neither of which was true. Perhaps I should have told her that my appearances on Charlie Rose were brokered by a publicist? That Charlie has never said more than two words to me backstage? That I'm not even sure he's ever read one of my books? That every question he threw at me was written by one of his producers, culled from a "pre-interview" on the phone? No. I would not tell her any of that. But when she found out that I'd never been to Israel before, she gave me her phone number in Tel Aviv. Mission accomplished even though I won't call her.

August 15, 1977

They caught the "Son of Sam" a few days ago. Serial killers interest me. I wonder if I could become one. It must require a great deal of discipline.

I'm trying to figure out if I'm a good lover or not. Not really sure. I think I have a good body and I have a lot of energy. I think I'm a good fuck, but I'm not sure if I can tell when a woman has an orgasm.

I hid a small tape recorder in my pocket and made a recording of John while we hung out two nights ago. I've been transcribing it. He was revisiting the world of castration:

Farinelli! Farinelli! Farinelli! The most famous of the illustrious castrati. The power of adult lungs forced through the vocal chords of a boy. The castrati, from the Latin word castrare *meaning to prune (how great is that), were the most popular performers of their time* and Farinelli was the greatest of the castrati. He was world-famous. Then Farinelli gave up public appearances and sang only for the k-k-k-king. Isn't it interesting that royalty love eunuchs? Eunuch-dom is so special. The hole in the doughnut, when you think about it! Did you know that the Ethiopians castrated seven thousand Italian soldiers during a campaign in 1896? They went home minus their balls and believe you me, it was fucking hard recruiting a second team to go back there! Although despite what people think, a man doesn't need the jewels to get an erection. No sir. You are surprised, young scholar, but it is true! Little known fact. Many of the castrati were the greatest lovers of their time!

Emasculation, now there's a horse of another color. Definitely can't get an erection if you don't have a dick. Peter Abelard, did I ever tell you about this guy? Loved Heloise. One of the great love affairs of history. Unfortunately, she was the daughter of a church father back when shit like that really counted. So Heloise's pop had old Peter's peter snipped off. One of those middle-of-the-night operations. The thugs probably crawled through the window. Held the randy monk down. I bet he was conscious when they did it. Knives were very sharp in those days. Carbon steel, a formula perfected by the Chinese. No, stainless steel wouldn't be invented for a couple of centuries. But carbon steel was always much sharper than stainless. Definitely could do the job.

But Abelard didn't let de-penalation get him down. Guy was a major brain. See that's the thing, in the old days, people just kept on moving, no matter what happened to 'em. Till they croaked. They took it for granted that their bodies were going to get scarred and wear out. All the more reason to do what you can, while you can.

Abelard was a relativist, which pissed off the church. But he was always looking for truth. Questioned shit constantly. So they labeled him a heretic. Condemned his ass. Maybe he was focused on the truth because he had no dick to distract him. Like that German artist Schwarzkogler who chopped his own dick off as part of a performance art thing. You know "performance art" young scholar? Now that's what I call making art. Because by doing that, this Kraut really did something special. Know what I mean? He made a real name for himself.

Because who ever does anything really different? Not many of us. Not many. Once in b-b-b-b-blue moon you run into a bigamist. Or a cannibal. Cannibalism, now there's a statement. Serial killing and eating human flesh, that's existentialism. That's performance art.

Kill someone else's body and you're really living. Because the body is all there is. Lose your body, lose your self. Chop off a finger, you're still there. Ch-ch-ch-ch-chop off a hand, an arm. You're still there. But kill the body, destroy the body, and the "you" doesn't stand a chance. Take the body, stick it in a furnace, burn it to ashes, and there's no more "you." Eat it. The old you is inside the new you.

Right? So here we are, hanging out in these bodies. The body is a vehicle, a spaceship. Need the body. No body, you're out of the game. In the old days, there were ghosts. But no one believes that anymore. And so it's not true. Truth is belief. Belief is truth.

Herophilus of Chalcedon, this guy from the old late Roman Empire days, used to dissect corpses. He thought the soul was hanging out in the fourth ventricle of the brain. He would actually get hold of criminals while they were still alive and cut 'em up, trying to root out the soul. Trying to find it, you know?

Now you take Wilder Penfield, there was an MD who would crack open your skull and stick electrodes in there just to see the results. He'd mess around while a patient was still awake. Claimed that mucking with the gray matter cured epilepsy. And it did, even if you ended up a cauliflower for the rest of your life. Wilder was a *brilliant guy. And no one said "no" to him because he was a scientist. A man of learning.*

Then you've got your Dr. Cotton. He'd pull out your teeth, tear out your tonsils, chop out your stomach, spleen, extract a couple of yards of intestine. Considered it a kind of self-improvement program. Figured if he took out enough stuff, he'd get to the bottom of things. Most of his patients died, but he was venerable in his day.

And then those wild and crazy guys, Drs. Freeman and Watts. The lobotomy men. Drill a hole in your head, stick a swizzle stick right down in there, swish around the buttery brain. Did you know that the human brain has the consistency of warm butter? Swish, swish, swish. All the bad stuff is swished away. Ask Rosemary Kennedy. She's still drooling on a porch somewhere. While they were hacking into her cerebrum, they had her sing "God Bless America"—but after a while, she stopped singing. Like HAL 9000. Veggie-time. For-ever.

Mengele, Sievers, Krebsbach, Kiesewetter—Nazis, each one worse than the other. Loved messing with the living body. What makes it tick? How does it work? Of course it's only human nature to be curious. Like a six-year-old kid with the watch he got for his birthday. Takes it out to the backyard, smashes it with a rock just to see what's inside. How it works. Oh, gee, it doesn't work anymore! But now I can see inside! So it was worth it. Right? It's just human nature to want to see inside. That's what no one wants to admit.

Those patriotic eugenics guys sterilized tens of thousands down South. Legally. Poor people. White trash. Niggers. Jews. No one really knows how many. No one cares. Because in those days scientists thought you inherited poverty through your genes. "Planned Fuckin' Parenthood" Margaret Sanger wanted to make sure those poor girls didn't have too many babies. That's what all that birth control was

about. Bad genes. This guy Davenport, big deal at Harvard, said if
you crossbreed a black with a white you'd get inferior genetics. That's
Harvard my friend and not even fifty years ago.

Everyone wants to know! So they eat the apple. Adam! Faust!
They want to know as much as God. More! But listen to me, young
scholar, you cannot know more than God! Still, everyone wants that.
Because we're curious. Because we need to know.

I ran out of tape. I have to write a story about John.

June 21, 2006

I am in Tel Aviv. Jet lag. The place is chock-a-block with Jews in identical
polyester short-sleeve shirts, no suits or ties. These aren't lox-chomping,
New York Times–reading, twenty-thousand-dollar-a-pop Bar Mitzvah
Jews, but Israelis. Mostly of Eastern European descent, some Russians.
But they've been hanging out here in the desert for a long time. Not like
us. Not like us at all.

These Israeli Jews are beetle-browed, hunched over and fuming,
permanently defensive, simmering. Middle Eastern in every way.
The whole place is in a never-ending state of war—physical, mental.
Everything is on the verge of total chaos. Anything could happen at
any moment. Everyone on red alert, not only to the potential harm
to themselves but to everyone they love, to the buildings that house
them, to the buses, the coffee shops, discos, to the existence of the race
itself.

I am completely unprepared for the weather. The sunshine is reso-
lute. I thought the Mediterranean would cool things down, but instead
the steel gray sea throws off heat like a gigantic boiling cauldron, cooking even the air above us. They've lodged me at a miniature hotel with

feeble air-conditioning that doesn't cool the room. If I try to crank it, an aroma of mildew permeates. I'm two blocks from the beach, such as it is—not a beach for swimming but for noshing and sunbathing.

I went out for a stroll along the shoreline. This is where the young folk hang out. They cluster at the food stalls drinking freshly squeezed orange juice, munching fried fish, their backs turned against the flat, scentless sea. Nearby the U.S. embassy bristles like a massive citadel, looming over the lounging Israelis, not as a protector but as an unwelcome visitor. More a bunker than an embassy. What is in there? Torture cells? Electronic equipment? Filing cabinets filled with the state secrets? No one knows.

I ambled southward along the shore and ended up in Jaffa, the Arab quarter of the metropolis. In the market merchants sat listless and depressed. There was nothing interesting for sale. It was all dust-covered, worn, tarnished. I followed the ancient sea walls and fortifications northward. Very beautiful but it was hard to believe that in those limp unimpressive waves Jonah got swallowed by the whale. I guess I'll get the historical vibrations when I get to Jerusalem.

In an alley, I found a falafel place filled with dark men sitting at laminated café tables. I ordered a small salad, hummus, pita bread and a Coke. No one seemed to give a shit about the stranger in their midst. Olives and Coke. This is Israel. As I left, I bought a box of baklava that turned out to be sodden and stale. I crammed it into an overflowing trash receptacle. I considered buying a pack of cigarettes. Probably not good for the heart.

Back at the hotel, I recalled that I had Haim's number in my wallet. This fact had been in the back of my mind for weeks, but up to this point, I'd been too busy to consider it directly. I've done many unforgivable things in my life, but to avoid Haim while I was here seemed particulary heinous. I made the call on the gray industrial-strength (wartime!) phone.

Haim didn't seem surprised to learn I was in Israel. It was as if we had last spoken only a few days before, not thirty years ago. Said he'd "heard" about my books. I asked how he was doing. In a hoarse voice, he said he was tired. We agreed to meet and have coffee in a small café near the hotel tomorrow.

June 22, 2006

Began the day with a newspaper interview at the café where I would be meeting Haim later. Ridiculous. First of all, guy's name was Avi, I had heard, "Amy." I had hoped Amy would be one of those red-haired freckly Israeli chicks, veteran of the army, iron-thighed and pruriently curious about aging Jewish American writers. No such luck.

Second, the hairy-chested Avi had read nothing but the first two collections of short stories. Didn't know the new book at all. Asked two perfunctory questions about the old stories ("Where do you get your material?" "Is it true, you tape-record your subjects, then transcribe what they say?"). He warmed up while grilling me on my position regarding the Palestinians! Wanted me to declaim on Bush and the war! The war! What can anyone say about the war? It hit me that while I'm in Israel I represent the United States of America. God!

After I offered only the blandest, most noncommittal responses he gave up with the political stuff. Grinning, he shook my hand with nasty vigor. I was finally left alone with my espresso and a tattered, day-old *Herald Tribune* while the mustachioed waiter fussed nearby. The service personnel of this country are dedicated to making guests feel uneasy at every opportunity. I have not had a conversation with one cabbie, waiter, stewardess, tour guide, museum guard, nor one immigration or customs officer, who did not possess the chilliest poker face. It's my assumption that no one is really happy here. This unhappiness transmutes into a deep resentment when they are faced with an American. They hate Americans for being able to go home to a safe place.

When Haim entered, I didn't recognize him. What was left of his fringe of furry hair had turned white. He was clean-shaven. His buoyant vigor had been replaced by a tentative creep. I embraced him in the classic bear hug of long-lost friends only to find that he'd lost his bulk and shrunken into a little old man. The meekness of our embrace undermined the very notion that we were ever friends. What were we exactly?

In the ugly/modern café the stiff chairs reinforced the formal relationship between Haim and me. This is something we never had when we were living together. We were no longer the roommates who once shared the common denominator of struggling in New York City. We were only two strangers having a coffee.

A view of the morose sea filled the walls of tinted glass. On the horizon line, freighters passed like distant Silk Road caravans. Athens to Cairo? Albania to Somalia? I wondered what filled their holds. Crude oil? Machine guns? Loaves of plastique? Every action and surface here has a sinister vibe. The buildings, the streets, the people are all either girding for war or recovering from the last "conflict."

I broke the ice by handing Haim an autographed copy of *A Gentle Death*. He riffled the pages as if he'd never touched a hardbound book before. He scanned the inscription. His expression revealed nothing. I had written, "To My Good Friend and Plum Eater, Haim, Yours—Richard." He smiled and gently put the book down beside his coffee.

Haim filled me in on how he had returned home to Tel Aviv to recover from his New York adventure. His father owned a small offset shop and Haim had relented and joined him. He spends his days printing menus and wedding invitations while his old father lives in a back bedroom of Haim's apartment. Haim effectively manages the company. I asked him how business was and he said "Bad, somedays. Worse other days."

I mentioned Dagmara and Haim dreamily said that she might still be in New York, he wasn't sure, they hadn't been in touch. Did she ever get married? He didn't know that either.

I described running into Tony the hot dog guy in the park and Haim smiled for the first time since our bear hug. I suggested that Haim take a vacation and visit New York. He gazed out upon the flat Mediterranean, left my offer hanging in the air. I described my heart surgery but he wasn't impressed. He had drifted into some sort of reverie. Had I crossed a line, inviting Haim to New York?

I abandoned the present and reminisced about the night of the blackout. I managed to coax another smile out of him when I mentioned all the pot we used to smoke. I accused him of contracting infectious hepatitis and passing it on to me. And then . . . the well ran dry.

I paid the bill and we stepped out into the brittle sunshine. The dazzling light illuminated Haim's face and now I could see how thoroughly unhappy this man was. He told me he was glad I had come to visit because lately he had been thinking about Dagmara incessantly. He turned his large sad eyes on me and said, "You took her away from me. But it was just as well."

In sum, he confessed that he had never loved a woman so deeply as Dag, that he had worshipped her, but that she and he had not meant to be together and that he could never have made her happy and he was grateful to me for killing the romance. He said that seeing me again was God's way of telling him that she would never return to him.

A thread of pain stitched my chest but the feeling passed in a moment. I didn't have the clarity of mind to think of my heart. Instead I was filled with wonder. Was this man talking about me? Was he talking about something that had happened between us thirty years ago? But it hadn't happened that way. He wanted it to be a revelation, and it was. A revelation of massive delusion.

As Haim said goodbye I anticipated an offer of a tour of the city. But he made no such proposal, so I didn't have to turn it down.

August 20, 1977

From William Burroughs, *Naked Lunch*:

> *Masturbating end-over-end, three thousand feet down, his sperm float-*
> *ing beside him, he screams all the way against the shattering blue of sky,*
> *the rising sun burning over his body like gasoline, down past great oaks*
> *and persimmons, swamp cypress and mahogany, to shatter in liquid*
> *relief in a ruined square paved with limestone.*

Crazy huh? Been writing like a demon. Four stories in the last two weeks. I am boiling and churning with ideas. I am a juggernaut, sparks fly from my wheels. I can't write fast enough. And the guy from the first magazine wants more. Also the guy from *The New Yorker* called and was all enthusiastic and chatty. Said he wants to see what else I've got. Can't promise anything. I don't care. I don't even read *The New Yorker*.

I'm off work from now until mid-September. My parents called inviting me to some kind of suburban barbecue. The whole family will be there, everyone wants to see me. Blah-blah-blah. And so I'm heading up there to take a break. These breaks are important. Without rest, I can't keep going at this pace.

Me and Zim and Katie went out drinking two nights ago. Ended up at Zim's at around four in the morning. Chugging Hennessy and snorting coke. Out of the blue, Katie came on to Zim, and they started French-kissing, rolling around on the floor right in front of me. I decided it was time to go. I said, "Okay, guys, later." Zim reached out, took hold of my wrist and pulled me toward them. Then Katie turned and smiled up at me and started kissing me. I could feel Zim's breath over her shoulder. Katie undid my belt while Zim pulled her clothes off her slim body, I guess we ended up in a ménage à trois. The whole time we're doing this, I'm thinking: I'm in a ménage à trois! It was like I was floating over our bodies watching us do it.

So Zim fucked Katie while she sucked me off. It wasn't totally satisfying because I was distracted by Zim pumping away at my girlfriend (Is she my girlfriend? Not really.) which made her teeth scratch my dick. It was more strange than satisfying. She wanted me to fuck her next but I was so distracted I figured I was never going to come so I tried to concentrate on one of her nipples and then I came in two seconds. Plus I kept worrying about catching some kind of disease from Zim, who messes with hookers and junkies. Also seeing Zim's dick was a strange experience. I don't think male friends should see each other naked.

Got home around dawn. Jerked off fantasizing about what we had done. Way more satisfying than actually doing it. I think I've had sex with Katie three times now (once with Zim. Does that count?).

My train to Boston leaves in three hours. My dick is itchy. I hope I don't have herpes.

August 22, 1977

I'm back in Stoneham, staying in my old suburban bedroom where I used to smoke dope and listen to Hendrix. I would get completely hypnotized by the wallpaper. That's when I wrote my first stories. There's still an old John Coltrane poster up over my bed. And all kinds of shit stored away in the closets. All my high school stuff. Old sneakers. Yarmulkes from my buddies' Bar Mitzvahs and Grampa's funeral. A guitar with a warped neck. My writings, my journals. A dried carnation from a prom. I guess I should keep all this stuff. Never know when someone may want to write my biography.

Yesterday the whole family came by. I have so many aunts and uncles I can't remember their names. They behave like they haven't seen me in twenty years. Plus the cousins. And the cousins of cousins. Some of them are married and have bought homes already. Our great-grandmother lived in New York City, worked in a sweatshop on the Lower East Side. Once the family escaped, New York was always seen as an evil place. I can tell from the way they look at me what they are thinking: Richard's living in the corrupt big city answering phones.

Dad tells everyone that I'm not going to be in New York much longer. He explains that I'm going to law school "once he gets this *mishigas* out of his system." I don't remember discussing law school with him at any time. Of course he's clueless regarding my writing career.

I hung with this old aunt of my Dad's, Sadie. Everyone treats her like a boring spinster, but she tells great stories. I think she was a WAC during the war. She worked on soup lines during the Depression. I should write something about *her*. She has absolutely no life in the present. A big event for her is visiting her nephew down the block. She always brings pound cake in a little white box tied with peppermint-striped string.

I smoked a cigarette with my "uncle" Dave (not really my uncle, not sure exactly who he is). Dave used to be a butcher and so he tells butcher stories. Nowadays he sells life insurance. Has a hearty laugh, wears gold jewelry and heavy diamond-studded rings. Sadie dotes on him. I guess that's where she gets pleasure out of life.

Almost everyone in my family smokes. There's one guy whose name I can't remember who just sat and drank whiskey. I think he's a bookie in Boston's "Combat Zone." Most of them were fat and out of shape. But the barbecue was good. Dad cooked steaks. He's a good barbecuer. I guess it's a tradition, men and charcoal.

I can't figure out what's up between Dad and Mom. They seem to be getting along at the moment. Maybe they've just given up on fighting. Decided to bury the hatchet in preparation for their golden years. Or maybe it's because Ma's been sick. Not sure exactly what's wrong, but she's been different. She barely did any cooking today. She's going in for some kind of "exploratory" tomorrow.

I snuck away around eight. Went over to Rick and Judy's. They just had a baby. We pretend that I don't think they are condemned to this hell on earth forever. All the dreams we had in high school! "The Revolution, man!" Their baby's cute. If you like babies. I mean, it sleeps. It shits. It cries.

Rick's older brother showed up with a case of beer around ten. He sees me and the first thing out of his mouth is "How's New York City? Gotten knifed yet?" Nice. We work our way through a whole case of beer, about six joints and some schnapps. On my way home to my parents, I miss a curve in the road and hit a tree.

August 23, 1977

Heading back to the city. Things kind of helter-skelter in the old homestead because Mom's going to the hospital today. Everyone's all worried and freaked out. I took her aside and tried to calm her down. I said, "People go to the hospital all the time." Right? "Doctors know how to deal with whatever the problem is." Which I don't specifically know.

Bought a copy of *The New Yorker* at the train station and found a Raymond Carver short story in it. He's kind of inspirational. Also this guy Bellow who I'm getting into more. On the train I ate hot dogs, drank black coffee and wrote a story about the barbecue. Wrote a million notes.

June 23, 2006

Lev picked me up as the sun was rising and we spent the morning crossing the interurban desert on the way to the holy city of Jerusalem. One leaves civilization behind in Tel Aviv and skims over a world of home-less bedouins camped out under cardboard and plastic tarping, endless sand, Orthodox settlements. More sand. Rusted-out tanks squat aban-doned by the road. They have been left there as memorials to the 1948 war. You can't go two feet in this country without being reminded that Arabs are evil and want all Jews dead. We passed through checkpoints. And of course, The Wall. The ever present wall, a typical nonsolution solution, creating more confrontation (although it does keep the suicide bombers out). The days of dialogue, if they ever existed, are over. The soldiers are stern, but much too young, hiding their fear behind offi-cious grouchiness. Because I was traveling with an Israeli, our passports were scanned quickly, then handed back with a snap. Nothing more was said. We moved on.

Lev wanted to talk about writing. My writing, his writing, the writ-ing of Kafka and Heller and Mailer and Roth! He wanted to discuss method and theme and Judaism and "the problem of the Palestinians" and honestly, I didn't. I pretended to fall asleep.

I checked in at the King David. Much nicer room. But the whole town was so tense my stomach ached. I knew the Holy Land was physi-cally dangerous before I arrived, but in Jerusalem it's clear that this place is potentially dangerous to *me*. No matter who's aiming at whom, a piece of stray shrapnel or a bullet could easily find its way into my body and kill *me*.

The old city is entered by gates, each specifically named (Herod's Gate, Lion's Gate, *Sha'ar HaGai*, which in Arabic is *Bab el Wad*), supposedly going back two thousand years. But these actual walls and parapets weren't here two thousand years ago. They were built by the Ottoman Suleiman the Great. At Jaffa Gate Lev pointed out yet another example of Muslim brutality, the grave of the architect who designed the walls. Once he was finished with his work, Suleiman kindly had him beheaded.

Made it past the checkpoints to the Wailing Wall where the davening Orthodox clustered like fat black crows. Individually, they are just bearded men wearing hats. Together, they might just deliver the apocalypse in their attempt to regain the Temple Mount.

In contrast to the two-tone Jews, Christian pilgrims sporting brightly colored baseball hats and pastel sweatshirts followed flag-waving leaders from one Station of the Cross to the next. We ran into them visiting the cave where Jesus was supposedly entombed, memorialized by the Church of the Holy Sepulchre. Illogically the church was constructed hundreds of years after the death of Christ by Constantine the Great for his mother, who located the holy spot through a visionary dream. It was subsequently destroyed and rebuilt by alternating generations of Persians, Christians, Ottomans and Crusaders. (The Jews were long gone.) These pious modern-day Christians had no use for the enormous mosques on the Temple Mount, only a stone's throw away (recently rebuilt by the bin Laden construction company). Is it sacrilegious to say the whole enterprise feels like Auschwitz meets Disneyland?

Lev left me on my own when I insisted on visiting the major mosques atop the Temple Mount. I negotiated the cool, shadowed alleys of the old city, finding the bright open area of crumbling tan stone and checkpoints that is the base of the Temple Mount. I ascended up over the Jews bowing to the wall and up to the plateau. The Arab security detail that loitered by the entrances to two of the most holy Islamic shrines in the world probably detected my Jewishness, but also my Americanness. I removed my shoes and they let me pass. Breathtaking beauty within. The Arabs/Turks sure knew how to throw an architectural party.

Footnote to the afternoon: I found an Internet café and checked the sales of A Gentle Death on Amazon. The number, for whatever reason, had leapt upward again! The book is now sitting above two thousand! The sunshine seemed even brighter as I left the café.

Later I made my way down through a much more satisfying bazaar in the Armenian quarter. I bought some ceramic stuff from an old Armenian potter. All very authentic and old world-y until I met his twenty-five-year-old son who couldn't wait to return to California where he could have his fill of cars and babes. The truth is, no one wants to be in the Holy Land but the crackpots. All the normal people want out. Who can blame them?

Under an archway, someone had stuck up a leaflet protesting the Turkish avoidance of culpability. It was an old photograph of a stack of severed human heads. Armenian I presumed. What did Hitler say, "Who remembers the Armenians?" These Armenians are interesting. I should write something about them. What really happened ninety years ago?

August 30, 1977

Really late. Drunk. Six hours ago Katie and I were headed over to her place. We started kissing under a streetlamp. Then she told me that she'd just had surgery and couldn't have sex. Refused to explain what *kind* of surgery. (We had had a nice night together two nights ago. Just when it gets good, she runs away from me.)

We had been drinking and I was very horny and not happy about this state of affairs. I got angry. She jumped in a cab and left me there on the street. I was pretty high, so I decided it was very important to get more alcohol into my system. I ended up in front of Tier 3, a nightclub down in what we call "TriBeCa" (triangle below Canal Street). I went in for a nightcap. I paid for my drink and since I didn't know anybody there, I started hanging out by the door, welcoming people in as they entered. A crew of young guys showed up. From the way they were laughing and whisking their hands about I figured they were gay.

One thin guy with big brown eyes was the center of attention. He was so beautiful he could have been a girl. He was wearing a leopardskin headband. I gave him the once-over and he did the same to me and then, for some reason, I stepped up to him and kissed him on the mouth and he kissed me back. Then I fell in with his group and followed them to a booth in the back of the club. He seemed amused by me and then I realized that I was drunk off my ass and didn't have any idea who these people were. So I demanded that this beautiful guy give me his phone number.

Now I'm back home and I'm staring at this phone number trying to figure out if I'm a homosexual or what. I'm still really horny. Can't think. Drunk. I'm drinking now. Everyone's alseep.

August 31, 1977

Woke up at eight with a throbbing hangover and the phone ringing. I think I called that guy. Did he come over? Did we have gay sex? Am I gay? I can't remember. I was very drunk and very horny and this isn't something I want to do again. I think.

I'm at the airport. The reason I'm at the airport is that Mom's in the hospital. It's definite, she has lymph node cancer. Dad kept repeating himself on the phone. I think he's afraid. Now that Mom's at the hospital, he's got to deal with everything all at once: cleaning the house, cooking his own dinner, checking in on her. I called Mom and we spoke for two minutes on the phone. She sounded far away and weak and I'm not even sure she knew who she was talking to. She's on morphine.

So I'm headed up there and my head feels like a bag of angry cats. It's hard to think about Mom because I don't really know what this cancer thing means.

Is cancer a death sentence? If it is, and if she dies, Dad will totally spin out of control. He may even kill himself. Then I would have to take care of the funeral.

I want to feel bad or sad about this whole thing, but deep down all I feel is a strange fascination. Something in my gut likes disaster. Sis is completely freaking out. She's angry at everybody for not telling her sooner how serious Mom's illness was. Her hysteria is going to make all of this very difficult. But one way or another, something big is going to happen.

June 24, 2006

The Jerusalem Conference!

Meaning, a short statement, followed by questions from the audience.

During my statement, I decided to commit and criticize the war in Iraq. Probably not the right move. I assumed these were intelligent people, who also happen to be my fans. I had an obligation to be honest with them. Two mistakes right there. First question: "You are a famous author in the United States, what do Americans think of your anti-patriotic attitudes?" I replied, "First, I am not anti-patriotic, I love my country. Second, most Americans have never given a thought to my work or what I have to say about anything." My interrogator furrowed his brow, unhappy with this answer. He thought I was being evasive, when for once I was telling the truth.

I was then asked why the United States does not support Israel. I assumed the question was in jest, so I glibly said we should raise the annual support to Israel from four billion a year to a hundred billion, maybe two hundred billion. The questioner seemed puzzled by my reply. Although the questions were in English, everything I said was being translated into Hebrew seconds after the words left my mouth.

Now someone returned to the main fault of my work, my "negativity," my "embrace of the dark side of human nature." I replied that in case the audience was not familiar with it, most of the Western canon is devoted to the "dark side," from Sophocles to Voltaire to Dostoyevsky, etc. etc. I didn't mention any German writers. I added that I was surprised that Jews, who more than most people have been intimately involved with the dark side of human nature, would shun such honesty.

The questioner shouted something in Hebrew and stormed out of the room! Many heads were bowed over notepads. My interpreter made a statement to the assembly without translating. A reply (in Hebrew). A counter-reply! Scribble. Scribble. I shouted into the fray, "How 'bout that Primo Levi! Now there was a lighthearted soul!" A camera crew recorded my feeble sarcasm. Something was lost in the translation. The tension in the room grew. My interpreter attempted to refine my answer and now someone else was shouting from another corner of the room that I was "anti-Israel"! I shouted back that I was against any and all nationalism whether it be fostered by settlers or Nazis.

At that point I lost interest in the fracas. I noticed that the translator had a lovely mouth. I wondered if she'd be interested in seeing my very impressive suite at the King David. But she seemed upset also. Everyone was upset.

Later, at the reception, a man sidled up to me and asked: "Where did you find that interpreter? She was awful! Everything you said she misstated. Many of the people here are very angry with you because they think you have no respect for Israel! They think you insulted Primo Levi!"

I wanted to know more, but I was steered away by Lev, who led me to a tall man in wire rim glasses, the director of the institute where the reading was being held. The director smiled politely, but didn't engage me. After a few minutes, he drifted away. I found Lev and asked him if I had said something wrong and he said "No, of course not! These people are very difficult." But for the remainder of the evening Lev also kept his distance.

September 1, 1977

So I'm here at Dad's, which is très weird because Mom's not here and the neighbors arrive every fifteen minutes delivering covered casserole dishes. They sit with Dad in the living room. I can hear the murmur of their conversation all low and depressed and then I hear the front door opening and closing and they're gone again and the house gets very still. Sis showed up this morning before we all drove over to the hospital. Dad looked like he'd aged twenty years.

Mom looked like she's aged a *hundred* years. She lay motionless in her bed, her face the color of sand. There was this little plastic bag hanging off the side, half-full of her yellow pee. There was another plastic contraption that dripped the morphine into her arm. She was asleep most of the time we were there. I didn't realize she was so fucked up. I guess it will be a miracle if she lives.

While we were in the room, my grandmother arrived with Aunt Sadie. They stood at the end of the neat bed, smiling at Ma, holding back their tears. Sadie brought a plate of homemade hammentaschen. Then my sister had a total meltdown and had to leave the room. I stayed in a corner trying to make myself invisible. Sadie was curious about New York. I don't think she wanted me to fill her in on the after-hours club scene, so I kept quiet.

I felt like if I didn't move, didn't talk, then I'd be okay. I think Dad felt that way too and I think we had this understanding that neither of us was going to talk about anything of substance. That would make two fewer people emoting.

So now I'm back here at his house with him. I don't know what I'm supposed to do. He wanders around downstairs, sneaking peeks between the curtains. The phone rings every ten minutes. Sometimes the phone rings at the same time as someone is visiting. I want to go back to New York and write a story about Big John.

June 25, 2006

Lev escorted me to Yad Vashem today. He was very somber because an Israeli soldier has been kidnapped and the country is wired for action. Lev needed to make some final travel arrangements so he left me to wander about on my own.

There was an old black and white photograph, blown up to cover half a wall. In it an anonymous woman stood before a railroad cattle car, her arms outstretched toward a child who was being dragged away from her. Was this taken outside the camps? Is she leaving? Is he leaving? The image was horrific. As horrific as it was, I thought to myself, this is going on somewhere right now. Today. Right now. As I stood there. Nauseating.

I thought of Primo Levi's memoirs. All memory is a form of fiction. But all fiction is a form of reality.

How did the Holocaust happen? Why didn't someone stop it? Everyone knew about it, didn't they? Was there an alternate explanation? Or did they just not "see"? Not acknowledge what they were seeing? Isn't that always the way it is? Isn't that what's happening right now? "If we had known the truth, we would have done something." A lie.

The Nazis were the essence of the modern. Stalin and Mao were inspired by them. Now Cheney. In Hitler's vision lay the germ seed of the modern admixture of desire and violence. Technology allows distance. Distance denies accountability. We can see it, but we are not responsible.

Same now as then. We all deny responsibility. That's not *me* burning that village.

And what do I do about it? Nothing. I write.

The act of making art is obscene because it is built on the premise that there's a safe place and from this safe place, we keep an eye on the "other" place. We pretend that this safe place, this castle high on a hill, isn't mortared brick by brick with bone dust and blood. We honestly believe that we live in a place that is *not* a product of tragedy. That *we* are civilized. That *we* are good. But how could that be? It's never the case. Ever. Where there is affluence, there must have been horrific violence. All wealth is born of violence, there is *no* other kind of wealth, and to protect that wealth, violence must continue. Ask the Indians. Ask the blacks.

Something happened to me: I flew to Israel. I entered a building that is a memorial to the victims of a grinding engine of bloodlust and hatred and horror. It is very probable that not ten miles from where I stood, someone was packing ball bearings around a wad of explosive, rigging a vest, blessing a bomber.

Who am I to condemn that act? The coldness, the impersonality, this is *my* way too. I have no empathy for anyone in my own life. Haim's indifference to me is evidence. What else could I expect? We once lived like family, I hurt him, or he *thinks* that I hurt him, and I forgot about him as soon as he was out of sight.

Has anyone ever had any significance for me beyond what I could get from them?

But, but! I have a saving grace! I possess insight and *I tell the fucking truth!* I admit my faults. I admit that I am selfish, that I am indifferent.

At least I'm not lying to myself. Or am I? Because despite my objectivity, I subscribe to the biggest lie of all, that I am enlightened. I tell myself I've finally "got it." That I've learned the great Augustinian lesson, that I am evolving toward a better life with my eyes open. Progress! I will tell you that I *know* I'm a sinner. And so in my heart, I'm certain that I'm a good man because I feel guilty. I confuse *guilt* with *humanity*.

September 20, 1977

Mom is in a coma. I have to go up there again because she will die soon and we're supposed to be there by the bed when that happens. I feel nothing. I have been hanging out at John's every night. I tape him and he doesn't know it. I am going to write a story and make him the centerpiece.

I've managed to get an apartment for myself. It's actually a storefront down in Little Italy. Two hundred a month. Nothing in it yet. Just a piece of foam rubber on the floor for the past two nights. I've been moving my stuff down there. Haim and Dagmara are all upset. But what can I do? I have no privacy. I can't get laid when they're hanging around. Plus they're both nuts. Dagmara got really angry at me, said "that wasn't the deal." Jesus!

Bought a used black leather jacket. And I've cut my hair short. Since the mugging, I don't want to look so innocent when I'm walking down the street.

From Kenneth Patchen, *The Journal of Albion Moonlight*:

I am an idealist in a quagmire . . . I am on fire . . . farewell Death . . . what burdens are mine! . . . I come with my guns blazing . . . I am going to beat in your heads and kick out your teeth . . . I'll make you listen to me!

I "christened" my new place with Katie. She came by and we had pizza and red wine and snorted some coke. I don't have any electricity yet, so I lit candles and I think she dug that. We fucked, which wasn't particularly exciting. I mean, I love her, I think, but she just kind of lay there like a dead fish. Later when I asked her to stay the night she said "Do you have any more coke? I have to get up early for this job at Barnes & Noble and I can only stay if you have more coke." Logical.

It's okay. That's life right? I scratch your back, you scratch mine. I love her and she loves drugs. So we made a deal. I don't think she loves me the way I love her but I don't care anymore.

September 30, 1977

My mother has died. I've been up here for a week. I don't know what I feel. I'm forcing myself to write about it. Copped some coke from Zim before I left New York and have been completely wired through the whole thing. Even sat shiva fucked up. It's so sad. But we all die, right? Everyone is hysterical because Mom's death reminds them that they're going to die some day too. They're nostalgic for their own memories and past which will never return. It can't be that they loved her that much. If they did, why wasn't everyone happier when she was alive? I'm sad too.

I called Katie long-distance and cried on the phone. She sounded like she was actually concerned. I stopped thinking about Mom and starting thinking maybe Katie'll fall in love with me now. Deep down I want her to love me.

I am a hypocrite. I am Satanic. My mother is dead and I don't know what I feel about that.

Sitting shiva, I ran into this second cousin of mine I haven't seen since we were both little kids playing in my grandmother's backyard in Newton. Very pretty in a JAP kind of way. Usually I don't go for Jewesses. I imagine them old, turning into Zsa Zsa Gabor strolling the Miami Beach boardwalk. But she's so young and fresh. Or maybe I wasn't that attracted to her, I just chased after her because it was such a perverse thing to do. Anyway, I offered her some of my coke and we hid out in my dad's attic and sniffed drugs and smoked grass and smooched. While we were kissing, I undid her blouse and kissed her breasts, she began to give me a hand job. Then suddenly she got all upset, like we had committed some major sin. I don't understand people. Honestly I don't. I mean, I know it was "wrong" but so what? We weren't planning to raise a family, we were just fucking around. I mean, isn't the taboo part of the fun?

At the funeral service, I looked up to see old Aunt Sadie staring at me. Like we shared a secret or something. Creeped me out.

I think about Mom's body cold and alone in the casket underground. She's not really there. She's inside me. I will write about her too.

I take the train back to New York tonight. I've got all my stuff moved down into my new place. I called Dagmara and said she should come see my new apartment. I think she's afraid I'm going to rape her or something. (It isn't like the thought didn't cross my mind.) Getting her alone, having real sex with her for once.

Maybe I'm a sex fiend? Or a drug fiend? But I *should* do these things. It's essential to *live* life if you're going to *understand* life. I have to push things to the edge.

June 28, 2006

Finally back in Connecticut. The departure from Tel Aviv was extremely stressful. They still hadn't found the kidnapped soldier and a premonition of imminent war was wearing on everyone. The airport security personnel were on red alert for any move that might betray sinister intentions. (Lev informed me that not only were we all being scrutinized very carefully, but the people watching us were being watched by others.

And even those observers were being observed from behind one-way mirrors.) I am paranoid by nature so there was something appealing about these structures of fear and suspicion. Especially when I could walk away from it all.

As I drove up to the property I had this crazy expectation of finding Elizabeth on the porch, arms crossed over her chest, suppressing a grateful smile. As I emerged from the car, she would run up and hug me, admit that she'd been wrong to judge me. She would tell me she loved me too much to see me in pain and so she'd come back to me. We would sit by the fire and drink wine and I would tell her about the Wailing Wall and the press conference.

None of that happened of course. It was all a pure fantasy. Because the other way never existed. No one has ever been happy to see me return.

Fourth of July 2006

Sarah called me after a lapse of a few days. I guess things didn't work out with her new love. (Of course it didn't work out. We penis bearers are all the same. Except that in this case, he's a liar and I'm a truth teller. It was all so predictable. After he got what he wanted, he stopped lying. Suddenly over morning coffee they're looking into each other's eyes and there's nothing to talk about. So now she reaches out to *me*.)

She said she wanted me to be her "friend." Oddly and momentarily, I was at a loss for words. She had this idea that something had gone wrong that could be made right again. "Richard?" There was a desperate tone to her voice.

I invited her up to the house but she realized that I expected more than a platonic visit. Not an uninsightful premonition. Why shouldn't I have expected that? When did we *not* sleep with each other? Mind you, I made a point to avoid saying anything explicit about fucking. No. She probed for this information. Sensitive to it. Testing. In effect she asked: Are you going to be a "good friend" or do you "expect something" from me? Do you expect to get laid?

"Yes," I wanted to shout, "I expect something. I expect things to be what they should be."

But she didn't want that. Had Sarah ever wanted that? She had been insatiable. But had she been faking it? Was that just something she had done to keep me around? Is every human relationship founded on a lie? Can we only get along with one another by hiding the truth? Are all projections of desire promises made, never to be kept?

She: "I'll be your fuck-bunny."

He: "I'll be there for you. I'll be gentle and sensitive to all your needs."

These are competing fantasies. What we project on the situation, not what is. And then she discovers the hidden stash of porn in the underwear drawer. Or he discovers that she wants to organize every minute of the rest of his life. And have kids.

Her endless neediness forces him out the door and that's it. Game over. Women stop wearing high heels once they've had children. They trim their hair short. Their insistence on attention is just one of endless demands. Men turn surly, impatient. Men become drunks. Couch potatoes. Because it's all pretense. All a dance. No one will say out loud what they want. "Be there for the children we will have." "Swallow my cum then go away."

Or do we even know what we want? Even our desires are stand-ins for other desires. Don't leave me alone. Don't let me get hurt.

Sarah's sixth sense triggered her fear of me, so she's not going to visit. She came up with a shabby excuse at the last minute and never showed up.

The town fireworks boom a few miles away. But I can't see them from the house, all I can see is a glow silhouetting the wooded ridgeline. I could drive over to the Little League field and watch the colors, watch the crowd, but who can enjoy fireworks alone?

October 3, 1977

I have quit my job. Mom's passing has made me think about what I'm doing, how little time there is to do it. I have to write full-time. If I can sell three stories a month, that money plus unemployment insurance should be enough to pay the rent. I can always drive a cab if I really need cash. My new apartment is only two twenty-five a month.

And I'll be saving money on subway fare because it looks like I'm not going out to John and 'Gitte's for a while. He caught me audiotaping, which pissed him off.

This is a transcription of the tape of my last night at John's. We were talking about my writing. John:

> Used to enjoy a cocktail every now and then at a place called Musso & Frank's. One day this old dude sits next to me at the bar, orders boilermakers and starts knocking them back. One. Two. Three. This caught my attention because the cat was old and old guys usually avoid that kind of hard-core drinking. Anyway, he started complaining about how Hollywood stole his stuff and never paid him right. Blew my socks off when I figured out this guy was Jim Thompson. You know, The Getaway? With McQueen? He wrote that. Fucking great writer.
>
> You know what Jim Thompson told me, young scholar? He said the writer is the same as an addict—there's no way for either one to be an upright citizen. Just can't happen, it's against the laws of na-

ture. They can pretend they are good, responsible people—even fool themselves that they are, but that can never be—because the artist and the addict has only one responsibility: himself. Will sell his own children to get his fix. Just the way it is.

See young scholar, what's gonna happen is, you're gonna write and then you're gonna hope someone buys your shit so you don't feel like a total jerk for wasting your time and ending up broke— but, even if, and I'm just saying if, you succeed in doing all that, the world's just gonna wait for your next story or the story after that and sooner or later you will fall on your face and then they'll call you a worse failure. And that's how the addiction starts.

Because it ain't about money. It's not even about fame. Why does a serial killer kill? Something deep inside he can't control. It's a tapeworm in your gut. It's a sociopathological drive. The artist must be a lunatic.

When you fail, and you will fail, they'll all be laughing while you lie facedown in the mud. Remember, Big John warned you. Because you have to be able to take it. It's not about winning no game, it's about taking the punches, getting knocked down and getting back up.

(John didn't speak for one full minute here. We passed the pipe. I knew he didn't want me to speak either. Abruptly, he resumed.)

You can't fool me. You are the most ambitious little fucker I've ever met. You'd sell your soul to make a name for yourself. I hope you've read your Faust. Makes no diff. What will happen will happen. So, okay. That's you. That's your fate. You got no fuckin' choice. Just remember this, if you're gonna do it, do it. Don't compromise yourself by thinking about money or fame or any of that shit. Picasso was the richest artist in the world. And he fucked everything that moved. But before any of that, he was the best. Life is too fuck-ing short to write one word you wouldn't want to read yourself.

(Pause)

Don't think. Every time someone has the world all figured out, the world turns around and tosses their ass sideways. Like all those Popes who never saw those Albigensians coming. Freaked 'em out. They even had a Crusade trying to stomp out the "wrong" way of thinking. Didn't work. Inquisition of the heretics? Only made things worse. Next thing you know, old Martin Luther is nailing shit to church doors and the rest is history.

And every time it all shifts, it shifts again. Don't forget that, young scholar. There is no absolute truth. No one knows what's good writ-ing or bad writing. Even Shakespeare was forgotten for a hundred years or so. Fuckin' Bach! Guy spun gold, and he was treated like one more chump.

No one knows. Only you know. The hoi polloi make rules about what's good and what's bad. But only you know. Just when it's all going one way, it will turn around and go the other way.

I mean, what kind of literature do you think ants would make if they could read? Not F. Scott Fuckin' Fitzgerald, not Joyce or D-D—D-Dostoyevsky, not even friggin' Steinbeck. Wouldn't make any sense to 'em. You ever read Nabokov's Lolita? Best book of the twentieth century, but old-fashioned my friend, old fuckin' fash-ioned. Same old story over and over again, one more guy mesmer-ized by his own dick, wandering around the wreckage of his life. Who the fuck cares about that? Give me the Knights of the Round Table! Give me Merlin! Or better, the "wine dark sea"! Much more interesting.

(John took a massive hit and held it in. Blew out a long blue stream of smoke.)

All you got is your memories. If you can't remember who you are, you're nobody. So your personality is all in your head. Anvil clunks you on the head, or your skull gets crushed under a d-d-d-dump truck tire, that's it, it's over: reality, time, self, the whole universe.

So talk, talk, talk. Write. Write. Write. "Truth." No truth. No such thing. Ask an aboriginal. They think dreams are truth. A geologist will tell you that a chunk of rock is two hundred million years old. But if there's no geologist standing there, telling you about the layers in the rock, then there is no time.

And if you remove time *from the equation, then you remove "fate." You remove ambition. You remove "luck." You remove "success." Animals don't know time. Don't know ambition. Don't know who the fuck they are.*

So think about that the next time you sit down to scribble, young scholar. "Ah, but you say, how will I know what to do?" You won't. You can't. Best thing to do is lie on a couch like Bukowski did. Get drunk and pop the pimples on your ass. Because there's nothing you can do. *You will* do *only what you will* do. *That's God. That's what's called the . . .*

(Click of the tape recorder running out of tape.)

John stopped.

"You hear something?"

"Uh, a . . . my tape recorder."

"Tape recorder?"

"I was taping you. Talking."

"You're taping me? Why would you do that?"

"I was going to listen to it again when I got home. So I could think about what you were saying."

"You done this before?"

"Some nights."

"Why would you do something like that?"

"I told you."

"Yeah but you're lying to me, young scholar." John doesn't stutter when he's pissed off.

"I thought—"

"You were going to write something weren't you? Write something about your pal John."

"Maybe."

"This is my home."

"Sure, I know."

"This is where I eat. Where I shit. Where I ball my old lady."

"I know."

"You are spying in my *home*."

"No."

"Big Brother. In my home. Lemme have that tape."

"No, John."

"Give it. Now."

I took the tape out and gave it John. "John, I didn't mean to—"

"But you did. You did." John examined the tape. "Changes things."

"No."

"It's an attitude. Difference between being inside and outside."

"I'll never do it again."

"True. You won't."

We sat. John said nothing for a full minute. It was strange to be in that room and John being silent. John held the tape in his hand, then without looking at me again, gently placed the cassette on the coffee table pile in front of me, stood and left the room.

I saw 'Gitte out of the corner of my eye. She was wearing a funny sad smile. Then she followed John. I picked up the tape and split.

On my way to the subway, through the old dark streets of Brooklyn, I tried to distract myself from the emotional situation that had just happened. I thought about what John had said and what it had to do with ambition. But ambition is not about seeking fame, but using fame is a tool. It's something you have to have to protect the work. It's all about the work. So it's up to me to protect my work by any means necessary.

I realized I have to force people to think of me as an exciting person. Then people will notice me, notice my work. I should have controversial girlfriends. Develop a reputation for being undependable, but in the end be brilliant. Show up late everywhere, talk about how hard I work, how I work through the night, get in fistfights, drink more booze than everybody else, do drugs in public, even narcotics, hang out with criminals, etc. This is important. It's as important as making the work. I need to get as much publicity as possible. Celebrity earns respect.

July 15, 2006

There is one percent of human experience that has nothing to do with relationships and this honest experience exists in maintaining solitude. In solitude there is truth. In solitude, instead of planning the next lie (which is necessary in order to preserve the "relationship"), one concentrates on living, pure and simple.

There are writers who embrace solitude with their eyes open. Who have the courage to do this. Roth. Coetzee. Naipaul. Truth tellers. Courageous men who only want the truth and understand that it is their mandate to seek it, that it is their obligation to report the truth, unobscured by sentiment. They don't romanticize friendship and love and family. They are beyond that. Memento mori!

She gazes into my eyes and wants my truth. She wants my courage and my intellect. But if I give it to her, she weeps. So I have a choice, be honest and be alone, or lie and enjoy some kind of companionship.

This is the ageless struggle between the male and the female, positivism and romanticism, science and superstition. In our time, Venus is ascendant. She is so beautiful, we forget who we are, what we are capable of, and we dreamily follow her as we stroll off the cliff and fall to our deaths.

I'm too old to change. I can't do this.

Oh, today's news: Joe Versa, Leon's wunderkind, was awarded a MacArthur "genius" fellowship. I have nothing to say, I'm too busy gnashing my teeth.

July 17, 2006

Woke at four A.M. and could not get back to sleep. Couldn't get Leon out of my mind. How he's never really respected me or my work. I was actually talking out loud to myself, lying in bed having conversations with Leon. When I realized I was moving my lips, forming words, I forced myself up. Brewed coffee as the sun came up over the maples. Showered, dressed, drove to the minimart. Ended up sitting outside waiting for Don to unlock the place at six. He said something like "You're up early." I bought my *New York Times*, a corn muffin, more coffee. These are the solid elements of reality that reassure me every morning, let me begin my day.

I got home and settled down with the paper and my muffin. Pulled out the magazine. Got about five pages into the accursed thing and who was being interviewed? Elizabeth! I pressed on and read the article. Why should I deny her her life? What she does is not something I could do, be in the public eye continuously, talking to reporters, photo sessions, and on and on.

Of course, in the interview she dithered on about her involvement with "the animals rights movement," the benefit she did for PETA at the Hollywood Bowl and the wonderful relationship she has with her English springer spaniel, Joey. (Named after Joey Ramone.) Discussion of her "activism" ignited a flurry of snide remarks about George W., global warming, etc. There was a brief mention of her stint in the rehab for cocaine abuse. (She had once tried to get me to go. I wasn't the one with the problem. She quit when she wanted to get pregnant.)

I don't mind that she never mentions my name, not even in the past tense. I know that she does this to protect herself. I understand that. But about halfway through this particular interview she commenced to expound on her love of literature. Now I scanned the pages for my name. *We were together for fifteen years!* But no, it wasn't *my* work she was reading. No, she was reading Brett Easton Ellis. "Can't get enough of him." Claimed to have read *Glamorama* twice. Twice! How is that possible? She has erased me.

It's not fair. I'm not bothering anybody. I'm just living quietly by myself in the tranquil Connecticut woods. I never asked that this information be laid at my doorstep. When I read the *Times* in the morning, I want sustenance for my life, not disruption of it. I want to learn about chaos far away from my country estate. I want to read about poverty in Rio or the lastest clash between the Israeli army and the Palestinian troublemakers. Along with all that, I don't mind a little seasoning, the odd dumb review of Updike's latest effort or the sports page.

I felt woozy, untethered. An anger bordering on madness tightened like a wire around my skull. I shivered. My teeth chattered. I had to do something. Killing myself was an option, but not a very good one, since I knew that I would never carry through.

I left the house and stepped into the great New England out-of-doors. The air pulsed fresh and clean. No sounds, nothing but balm. A brand-new sun warmed the dew-stained grasses. I was drugged by the gravitational pull of beauty.

In an amnesiatic state, I tripped down to the barn, unhooked the latch and let myself into the dark. The air hung chilly and damp, scented with the aroma of pinewood and ancient straw. I ascended the ladder to the loft. There I found the old army cot Elizabeth and I hauled up there almost twenty years ago when we would loll around and smoke grass and fuck. Twenty years ago!

In the hayloft, it was dry and warm. Small cracking sounds peppered the roof as the sun heated the slate shingles. I could hear wasps orbiting a nest outside. I slipped down onto the cot, exhausted and fell asleep. Ninety minutes later, I awoke minus my bearings. Cautiously I made my way back down the ladder. Still dizzy, I almost broke my neck. Safely in the house, I brewed yet more fresh coffee, polished off the muffin, sat down to write. What else could I do? Nothing.

I wrote all morning and into the afternoon. I broke out of my trance to discover it was already five P.M. I knocked back a middling tumbler of whiskey and drove into town for a steak. Though I was happy to be alone, the proprietor, Ed, a pink-faced guy with a massive potbelly, stopped by my table and we made small talk about the Red Sox, my Yankees, the local mayor. Ed filled me in on his daughter's wedding. And that was that.

I headed home. The tousled newspaper was where I had left it, splayed on the oak table. I was afraid to touch it but because I knew I would see it in the morning, I scooped it up and took it out to the recycling bin in the barn. No sign of raccoons.

So that was that. Another crisis, another day. Good night.

October 11, 1977

The editor invited me over to have dinner to discuss publishing my
new story. What he really wanted was to fuck me. My writing's good. I
don't need to do that to get it published. Again he was saying things like
"Doesn't this feel good?" And I was so drunk, I didn't even realize he
was down there. I didn't have the energy to threaten him. Also he frightened me in a way. He's not a small guy. I let him do what he wanted but
I couldn't cum. He asked me to take all my clothes off. He said, "I just
want to look at you." I said I wasn't feeling good and left.

I ended up over at Zim's. We snorted some cocaine, but he also had
some heroin. I guess he's been buying it since I showed him the cop
spot.

This time the H lingered in my bloodstream after I left. I was weirdly
energized. I wanted to come home and write but instead I wandered all
through the Lower East Side, rode the trains for a while and ended up in
Times Square. I perused the porn for an hour, smoked some cigarettes,
ended up back at my tiny storefront apartment.

I drank half a beer and woke up on my own linoleum floor around
four A.M. I thought my heart had stopped beating. I got up, made coffee,
tried to write. Nothing came. Still angry at that fucking editor. Writing
this. Agitated. Need more. Something. What? Gonna get as drunk as I
can.

October 12, 1977

Woke up with a monster hangover. I had been drinking vodka. Only
had about a third of a bottle. Remembered going out the front door.
Don't remember anything else. This morning my head feels like someone stuck a knife into my eye and left it in there. My teeth hurt.

Also something else, there's blood on my pillow and there's a huge bruise on my right arm just above the elbow. The knuckles of my right hand are red and scraped. My eyes are swollen. Did I get in a fight? I can't remember. I don't remember coming home. No, wait, I do. The sun was coming up. I was eating a slice of pepperoni pizza. Where do you get pizza at dawn? And I remember dropping my keys about ten times trying to get in the front door. I smoked a cigarette. I'm lucky I didn't burn the place down.

I have to slow down.

October 13, 1977

Woke up in the middle of the night. Katie lying next to me asleep. All I could think was, who is this woman? She feels nothing for me. I think I love her, but it's because she rejects me that I want her even more. What is that? I want someone in my life I can feel real affection for.

July 21, 2006

I was outside sitting under the shade of my vast boxwood tree when I heard the phone ringing. Something told me I shouldn't bother answering. I ran in nonetheless. I had been calling Leon for two days to discuss the book sales.

It was not Leon on the phone. It was Russell. Just wanted to give me a heads-up that he would be appearing in court in Manhattan on Monday to seek an injunction to stop distribution of *A Gentle Death*. I told Russell to go fuck himself, then called my new guy, Jessie, who told me not to worry about it, said he would call Russell. If necessary, he would appear in court on my behalf Monday. For six hundred bucks an hour. And so it begins.

I called Elizabeth and got her answering machine. I wasn't thinking about her not five minutes before. Now she's all I can think about.

October 14, 1977

It sucks not being able to go to John's. I'm polishing the story about him and 'Gitte and it makes me nostalgic for them.

I've been drinking.

My editor-buddy called and was all apologetic about our sex adventure. To make it up to me he said he got me an invitation to this artsy loft party in SoHo. I figured I better go. Good for the work. It was a catered party packed with women with hennaed hair and black fingernails and ponytail guys wearing handcrafted silver bracelets. Ironic people. People who like to drink hard liquor. The host, Stephen, was this tall, beaming, square-jawed guy who is without question an alcoholic. I guess he's a big deal critic, also a big name dropper. He's pals with Rauschenberg and John Cage and Lady Astor. When he tells stories they begin with "We were sailing off the rocky coast of Delos . . ." or "Polo season had just ended in the Hamptons." This guy also hangs at CBGB and Max's, so I guess he is a modern "Renaissance man." How many people can say that they know Sid Vicious but have also gone deep-sea fishing with Fidel Castro? How many people give a shit?

Zim was there, so we spent the night in a corner, smoking cigarettes and arguing aesthetics.

We were doing blow in the bathroom when Zim pulled some folded pages out of his stained suit jacket. I scanned the creased sheets while he cut lines. My heart rang with jealousy. Somehow this fucker has a book coming out. I'm not sure when he has the time to write a book. Maybe it's because all he does is write and drink, drink and write. He has no relationships. For Zim sex is a bodily function like having a bowel movement or blowing his nose. That's what I should do. Write and drink. Not even bother eating. We got very drunk. Now I'm trying to write my John story but I'm too wasted so I'm going to get all this down, maybe throw up, then hit the sack.

July 23, 2006

Been hard at work all week, cranking out five pages a day. Drove into the city twice since my last entry. Couldn't resist dropping into the St. Mark's Bookshop. They had nothing of mine other than the second short story collection. Grabbed a cab and met up with Leon at Nobu. For Leon, *A Gentle Death* is already no more than a faint memory. Ditto my heart surgery. Leon lives in the "now" with no interest in yesterday. His only concern is the upcoming Sunday *New York Times* bestseller list.

He gives me the respect due to someone who once made a mark. No more than that. What more should I expect? Is the world of Sonny Mehta any different from the world of Roger Ebert or the world of Jay Leno? Literature, movies, variety shows—it's all entertainment isn't it? I am only one of many projects of Leon's. It is a conceptual problem. That there are other artists as committed to their work as I am to mine is as impossible to imagine as my own death. Leon has other writers in his stable who excite him as much as I do, if not more. Writers like Joe Versa who win the MacArthur. Of course, it must be that way, but I can't accept it.

Leon boasted that he had cajoled Kurt Vonnegut into squeezing out one more short book. So that was a big deal. He also mentioned the "lost" Nixon papers, co-edited by Norman Mailer, which is going to be huge. I guess there's a passage in which Nixon describes meeting the young George W. Bush at a Washington party and gives his opinion of the future President. That chapter, having already been placed in *Vanity Fair*, guarantees the book at least one month on the bestseller lists.

Why do I care? What does any of this have to do with me? All the same, I am jealous of Leon. His ongoing engagement with the greater world is something I miss. In that way, Leon is still alive and I am dying. Or dead. Despite the fact that I have no appetite for it anymore, if I ever did. Fuck it. I don't believe in unrequited love. The world isn't interested in me and I don't have the energy to bang the drum hard enough to revive the interest. So that's that.

There is no safe emotional cave in which to hide. I am perpetually agitated. I reread my old journals again and again. The young cocksure dynamo who wrote them, I don't recognize him. He left town. He's not here anymore.

My back hurts. I need a massage. I need to find someone, hold them close and have them tell me that I mean something to them. I dialed Sarah's number nine times today, hanging up before the first ring. I can't tell her what she wants to hear.

I have a recurring fantasy of kidnapping Elizabeth and imprisoning her in an underground bunker, shackled to a damp wall. Deliver her meals on battered aluminum dishes. Stockholm syndrome would set in and she would have no choice but to love me. It's not so far-fetched. In fact it's an option. I would go to prison, but my reputation would be guaranteed. Everyone would read my books.

I went online and found my old roommate Dagmara. She is living and breathing in Warsaw as I write this.

July 25, 2006

Thunderstorms rolled through in the early evening, followed by a stupefying humid heat that has lingered all night. Mosquitoes and crickets thrummed in an immense concert of mindless orthopteran communication. Sleep came on so suddenly, I woke up immediately, quaking. A deeper morbid mood was seeping into my consciousness. Spending time alone in the house has never bothered me before. Now I lie in bed calculating how long it would take me to retrieve the shotgun wrapped in a towel on the closet shelf. To do what? Shoot an intruder? Shoot myself?

I roused myself at six-thirty and again motored to the minimart. The city newspapers were stacked beside the bundled firewood. Don had just finished brewing fresh coffee. The corn muffins were warm from the oven. The guy who looks after my place, Nat, wasn't there and I didn't really know any of the local guys by name. On my way back to my car, I felt them appraising me.

At home, drinking sour coffee from a Styrofoam cup, I scanned the obituaries. I do this every day now with an eye out for the sixties generation of wildmen who burned the candle at both ends and so paid the price of "early retirement." The ones who did not have the sense to jump the Good Ship Lollipop when they had the chance. The reckless fools who lived without thought or care, now dying like flies. The aging rock stars and photojournalists and forgotten novelists. My mentors and peers, going one by one, out the door. And this trend will only accelerate until the obit editor gets replaced by a younger obit editor and the new guy doesn't remember the quasi-famous well enough to bother memorializing them at all. Only the old movie stars will be remembered. "After a long illness . . ." or "In recent years, Mabel lived at the Sunset Nursing Home in West Levittown."

I almost missed the name. Katherine Makous Walters. A designer.

Makous was Katie's last name. Was this my Katie? Fifty-five years old. It must have been her. Would I have even noticed her name if I hadn't been reading my journals?

Her obit filled in the time since I'd last seen her. Katie had become a success. Not as an artist, but as a designer. Designed lighting fixtures for important architectural projects. Her work was seen around the world, including the new Sony pavilion in Osaka. It will be a major element in the new Goldman Sachs building downtown. She had won awards. She was respected and admired by her peers.

We had been lovers. Or had we? We had sex. But not that much. Is that important? How well had we known each other, really? I barely remembered what we would talk about. I did remember that her skin was very warm to the touch. She was soft and slim and very pretty. I remembered her eyes and her fluffy hair and her small breasts.

Was she a good artist? I couldn't remember. Her success must have come later after we lost track of each other. And never saw one another again. I guess we didn't mean that much to one another. Where was that perfect peach skin now? Six feet underground, boxed in bronze or pine? Probably not. She was cremated certainly. So now she doesn't exist at all. Better that way.

Did we discuss her art? We must have. I couldn't remember. She must have been intelligent, she made a big success of herself in a very competitive scene. I wondered if she ever thought about me? She must have. I should go visit the Sony pavilion. See what she created. But I won't.

Why hadn't we ever seen each other again? Maybe I called her and she didn't return my calls? No voice mails in those days. No e-mails. The answering machine had just been invented. Her voice is probably on a tape somewhere, stored away.

According to the obit she had had breast cancer. My old girlfriend was survived by her husband and two children. Certainly her family had surrounded her during her last moments. As we had with my mother.

They were all there with her in the end. It had been worth it. She had died, but she had made her art and she had had her children. And long ago, when she was first trying to become an artist, she had slept with me a dozen times.

What if she had slept with me fifty times? A hundred times? We could have been together for years, but if, in the end, it came to nothing, then that's all it was. Nothing. How it ends is what it is.

Ten o'clock in the morning and I was sitting at my kitchen table weeping for someone I hadn't seen in thirty years. I'd fallen in love with her all over again. She had been an artist. We could have supported one another's work. I would have been at her bedside when she passed. I would be a widower now, crying with good reason.

One by one, each will die. And whatever we had will die with us. Outside my window a catbird bobbed her tail. Dagmara is living in Warsaw. I could get on a plane tonight and find her and talk to her face-to-face. I could do that.

October 15, 1977

Went out on my own tonight because Katie was busy with her upcoming show. Saw something I have to write about, not sure if I know how to do that. It was early. The club was like a empty barn. Populated more by the staff than by anyone interesting.

I went upstairs and found a spot at the balcony rail and kept an eye on the meager crowd clustered beneath me. The music thudded, the blue-white auto-spots rotating in an attempt to liven up this vast black hole. Congregating at the bar were the usual drips and assholes.

In the middle of the floor a girl danced alone. She wore sneakers and a short cheerleader's skirt, her hair was long and she flipped it with her movements. Her moves were lithe and sexy. She was exhibiting herself.

Not one person tried to talk or dance with her. Instead, a circle of emptiness moved with her as she drifted across the floor. The longer I watched, the more curious I became, because the girl was so sensual, so lost in her own freedom. Clearly she had been a professional dancer at some point, maybe still was. What kind of movement was this? Ballet? Jazz?

I headed downstairs to get a better look. In the center of the dance floor, under the swirling lights, she never stopped moving. The bemused crowd stood and nursed their drinks, all oriented toward the girl, appraising her with cool detachment. She pumped her legs in a way that invoked athletics. Her short schoolgirl skirt flew up so that her pale legs were exposed up to the pantyline. She let her arms swing around her body, her breasts high and full. Her head hung slightly, as if she were dancing not to the house music but her own soundtrack.

The tempo slowed as the DJ searched for something that would tempt the onlookers onto the dance floor. The night was building, soon the dam would break and the room would flood with bodies. The girl stepped up and down in place, the way joggers do when they come to a busy intersection. Her perimeter of influence had become vague and ragged, the crowd inched forward, tightening what space she had cleared for herself.

She turned and faced me. Her hair cast deep shadows that covered her expression. Her body was perfect, her rhythm perfect. And then, suddenly, with a roar, the music swelled and the girl lifted her face to the ceiling as a swath of limelight washed over her.

I got a good look. She had a small mouth, like a hole in the middle of moonlike surface. Her eyes, what was left of them, were sightless. She had almost no nose. No real brow or cheeks or even a chin framed a "face." If this was a face, it was the face of a snowman or a Mr. Potato Head. She was a living, breathing, dancing . . . cartoon.

An old guy nudged me. He shouted into my ear, "Survived a fire." He wasn't smiling. "They say she has no tear ducts."

I almost ran home to write this down. She will make a great story.

July 30, 2006

Things have happened in my life I can barely remember. Things I've done that have hurt people. Does that make these actions bad? Not if I had no choice. And isn't every artist selfish? How could he not be? But I have to keep things in perspective, I'm not a Stalin. I'm no Mao.

Most people have nothing to brag about but an unexceptional and mundane life marred by the most insipid indiscretions. I'm one of those people. I have secrets. Every man does. My saving grace is my capacity to forget my secrets. It's the saving grace of all great men.

October 18, 1977

Just finished my delicious lunch of Yung Chow fried rice. Two bucks a pint. Packed with vitamins and minerals and cooking oil. Now I'm knocking back a couple of pots of espresso and I'm burning to work. Wrote about fifteen pages yesterday. It's all going well. When I begin it's still light out and the next time I look up from the typewriter the streetlamps are on.

The Big John short story is working out. It will be one of a series of short pieces, a portrait gallery of men I've met here in the city. Each piece is not a short story, rather it's an *impression*. These individual portraits will combine to make a larger statement. The whole thing hangs together like a Calder mobile, each piece interacting with the next. I won't have them published separately. The reader will have to dive into the whole thing all at once or not at all.

Last night I worked until midnight, then went out with Zim. New clubs are opening up. Not like the discos, these places are gloomier and no one's dancing. The bands onstage are more aggressive, it's not about music it's more about anarchic theater. It's about attitude. The bathrooms are packed with people filling syringes in the sinks and shooting up in the stalls.

Zim and I stay out until dawn every other night. There's always something to do. Two nights ago we crashed an opening reception at Andy Warhol's Factory near Union Square. This isn't the original Factory, this is the new one. Lots of people trying to look cool. Zim has a simple philosophy: Drink the free booze until there is no more. Then leave. Which is what we did.

Zim said, "I know a place." Under a dilapidated hotel near the meat market was a small stairway descending from the sidewalk. At the bottom sat a nude man with a guitar in his lap who collected the five-dollar cover. Inside people milled around. We found a table in a corner.

We were drinking Budweisers, discussing *Gravity's Rainbow*, when about ten feet from us, someone looped a length of clothesline through a metal staple driven into a ceiling beam. Two guys in leather masks led in a manacled, blindfolded, naked masochist and proceeded to yank on the rope so that his arms were wrenched up behind him. While we sat conversing nearby, the two masked guys whipped the blindfolded guy with a cat-o'-nine, followed this with melting hot wax onto his bare skin, then started to shove ice cubes up his ass. Finally, they began ass fucking him right there in the middle of the room.

Zim ignored all of this. They could have been dancing to Donna Summers for all he cared.

I said, "That's pretty weird, huh?" Zim picked up his beer and took a sip. He said, "Look at it this way, the guy's gonna sleep real well tonight."

Zim's a genius.

August 1, 2006

At the airport. Leaving for Poland in about an hour. I have accepted an invitation to visit the Film Institute in Lodz. They will pay for the flight and a stipend. I guess they're big fans of the film adaptations of my stories, especially "Philosophy of Paradise." (Of course.) Normally I wouldn't have time for something like this, but I have a reason.

On the Internet, I'd found her address and phone number. Unbelievably Dag answered after one ring and suddenly the same warm, amorous voice of my roommate and lover was whispering in my ear.

I said, "Dagmara? It's Richard."

There was a pause. "Richard? Where are you! You're not in Warsaw?" I gave her the details and detected a gradual cooling, nonetheless she invited me to visit her while I was in Poland. She lived only a two-hour ride from Lodz. Once I had heard her voice, I understood the danger of being in her presence again. She had been safely tucked away in my journals, put to bed as it were. A different Dag than this one. Dag of thirty years ago.

Nonetheless, I will see her. We will talk about old times. I will leave. Perhaps I will write about the visit some other time.

August 2, 2006

I'm in Lodz. My deluxe accommodations consist of a spacious suite of rooms dating to the mid-nineteenth century. The floors gleam with a thousand polishings. Amidst the fluted and ornamented cabinets, framed mirrors and faux Empire-style furniture sits an incongruous Soviet-style television set. Is someone watching me? Possible.

Along one wall, floor-to-ceiling windows overlook the town's main drag, a museum of empty storefronts and modest shops, all garnished with the most elaborate architecture. There is no color in this world. No flowers or vivid posters. Only gray sky, gray buildings, and gray, barely ambulatory people, smoking, hauling along carts piled with root vegetables or walking bicycles.

Was this country ever in any way affluent? Perhaps centuries ago. Since then, nothing but desperation. The Poles are a proud, hearty people. They survived the Nazis, the Russians. They are survivors. They rebuilt a country that was smashed to smithereens. The only price they had to pay was killing all the Jews. No more Jews. All taken away, the children, the old folks, everyone. But no one talks about that.

In the early evening, I attended a public reading of my novel. An impressive actor with tremendous gravitas recited my work in translation. When he concluded, he bowed ceremoniously and received ovation after ovation. I felt the love. I was led up onstage. Someone handed me a bouquet of roses. I wasn't sure what to do with the roses.

More irony: After the reading my hosts took me out to dinner at a "Jewish" restaurant off the main drag in Lodz. As we munched on kasha and pickled beets, a smallish woman played a violin while perched upon a makeshift chunk of thatched roof built over the bar above our heads. She was playing Jewish folk tunes. My host's eye twinkled as he pointed at her with his fork. "The Fiddler on the Roof!" he laughed as he munched his cabbage roll. Then he knocked back his fourth shot of the house speciality, an intensely evil vodka/turpentine concoction.

Stoned on booze, I am now in my cold room auditing Slavic soft porn on the retro TV. A faint smell of lavender oil pervades. If someone is watching me, I hope I don't disappoint.

October 20, 1979

I can't do this. I have no work, no money. I am seriously thinking of moving back to Stoneham to live with Dad. I mean, what's the point? And as far as writing goes, why do I have to be in New York City to write? Why is it so important to make money writing? I can go back to Stoneham, work as a landscaper and write at night. Why do I need to be in the thick of things? Anonymity was good enough for Dickinson, good enough for Kafka. I need to write like a madman, then when I have achieved my goals, I will burn everything.

Zim says the objective of the writer is to persist, to survive, like a cockroach. Katie says I have no choice. I will have to stay until I get run out of town.

Katie has convinced me to give myself another six months. The only way I can think about it is "If not me, who?" I know my writing is better than the others. But there's no proof of this "fact."

Katie is getting ready for her first gallery show. I've never seen anyone work so hard. She never shows any sign of doubt. It's like she's going to war, she's so determined. She won't let me visit, won't let me see her work.

August 3, 2006

My driver waited in his idling Honda as I rang the doorbell of Dagmara's flat. A buzzer sounded, the electronic latch released. I shouldered the tall heavy street door inward and waved the driver off. Everything in Warsaw is styled à la nineteenth century or earlier. Except, as I was to learn later, virtually everything has been reconstructed. My eyes adjusted to the dark corridor within. A stairwell. Clean, dark, cool, and sterile.

I climbed the scrubbed cement steps to the third floor, confused momentarily because floors are counted differently in Europe. The third floor landing was actually what I would count as the fourth. I heard Dag's voice one story above me, calling from her opened door. "Richard?" I rounded the final flight to discover her silhouette. Why was I here? Why couldn't I leave her in the petrified forest of my memory? I brought her back to life. Here she was. All of her.

As I moved closer, she cross-faded from an outline into something with a face. Her hair was darker. But her eyes were the same, large, innocent, searching. Dag had not gone to fat. She was herself, only older. The perfect slope of her nose was still there, her cheekbones. She had matured from ingenue to fading beauty.

She said: "Look at you!" I kissed her cheek, because it seemed to be the thing to do. She presented the other and I kissed her again, inhaling her scent. It felt as if we were the last two people in the world. I wanted to hug her tightly to me and not let go. Instead I handed her a gift-wrapped copy of *A Gentle Death*. She accepted it the way a turnpike clerk might take a toll. In singsong, she said, "Come in, come in!"

Dagmara's place was surprisingly sunny and roomy. I stood in the middle of her small kitchen as she brewed a pot of tea. I told her I saw Haim in Tel Aviv. Dag smiled weakly, and asked, "Is he well?" Something happened between them after I had left, that was clear. I abandoned the topic and described my heart surgery for the umpteenth time, my story polished and supple. Dag half-listened while she poured out the tea.

In her living room I sank into the old-fashioned couch. I asked how her life was in Poland. She replied that it was quiet. Since the dissolution of the Soviet Union and the subsequent reforms, she had returned to real estate. Without any prodding, she let me know that she has been married for ten years but that the husband was no longer around. They had had one child, a girl, who was working in Kraków. She smiled gently and added, "You look prosperous, Richard."

"I am." What could I tell her about my life for the last twenty-five, thirty years without sounding boastful? My pursuit of success, my achieving it, my struggle to maintain some sort of dignity with my work, my slow but sure transformation into a wealthy hermit. Describing any of this was pointless because it had no meaning in this context of post-Soviet drudgery. What it would be like to sleep with her now?

I asked Dag what she did for fun. She said that she worked long hours and that she spent her nights alone at home. She enjoyed American television shows, especially *Law & Order*. She was enamored of Sam Waterston. I told her that I often see the film crews working in the streets of the city. She replied, "Really?" with faint interest.

I couldn't help myself. "Don't you miss it?"

"What?"

"The city."

"I still live in the city."

"But Warsaw is so quiet." A faint clatter in the cobblestoned square below filled our silences. When I drove up, workers were erecting stalls. I rose from the armchair and found a window. Below, I saw a man serving ices to children. A mime was pestering people. Groups strolled through the historic center, checking out the makeshift market. It couldn't have looked more dreary.

Dagmara said softly, "I like the peace. In the end, New York frightened me."

"Certainly not when you were with me. You liked to party. You and your blond friends."

"Did I?" An offended tone crept into her voice.

"Of course! You were a hot ticket. You had a hundred boyfriends. You and I had fun."

"Yes, fun. You made me do things I wouldn't normally do."

"I *made* you? In what way did I 'make' you do anything? Are you saying, I forced you to do something against your will?"

"Yes. Of course. You know that." Her clear and virtuous eyes searched mine.

This seemed to be a ruse, to what end I had no idea. "What could you be referring to, Dag? We had a great time when we were roommates."

"You perhaps. *You* had a great time." She was examining her teacup, as if she could see us in the bottom, thirty years ago, in the apartment.

"Wait a sec. Not me. *Both* of us. Both of us had a great time in New York."

"Some memories are enjoyable from one perspective and not another." Her accent had become much stronger over here. It gave her speech a formal quality. She drained the dregs.

"Wait a minute, what on earth are you talking about? We lived together as friends."

"As 'friends.' Like the TV show, eh?"

"We were young. And it didn't work out as a stable relationship, but I have no regrets. Do you?"

"*D'accord. C'est ça.*"

"So tell me."

"Richard, you haven't changed in, what is it, thirty years? You intentionally forget."

"Dagmara, I didn't come all the way here to play twenty questions."

"Okay. Okay. I don't want your trip to Warsaw to be a waste of time. I don't want to play games." She collected my cup and headed for the kitchen. "Do you remember the night we got very drunk on port wine? My family had sent me a bottle of very old wine. Someone coming to the States had brought it to me from Warsaw. Do you remember that night?"

Water was running in the kitchen. If I could make an inventory of every single second Dag and I had spent together, I probably would not remember the night "of the port wine." In fact, I didn't recall specifically any of the nights we had spent together. I only recollected her white skin, her mouth. Her endless fussing over her hair and clothes. I recalled her perfume. I remembered her tending to me when I was ill. But not much else. From the journals I had the idea we didn't fuck much. Certainly I never penetrated her. But now I remembered, we had, I did. I called out to her: "The port wine? We drank the whole bottle, right?"

"Oh yes. Very like you. It was special, that wine. I wanted to save it, but you insisted that we continue drinking. We became quite drunk." She returned to the living room, drying her hands on an embroidered dish towel.

"I'll take your word for it."

"You don't remember anything else from that night?"

She wandered out again, forcing me to raise my voice. "I think we were kissing on the couch. We did that often. Haim never knew. He still doesn't."

She called out from the kitchen: "You told me you enjoyed keeping secrets from Haim. It gave you power over him. And me!"

"Well, it didn't make sense to give him the sordid details. He worshipped you. You know that don't you? I'm sure he told you. It was obvious."

Dag reentered and sat down next to me. I could smell her perfume. "Let's not discuss Haim." She sought my eyes. "The night of the port wine. You don't remember anything else?"

"You got sick?" A vague memory asserted itself. But parts were missing.

"I got very drunk. And you wanted to have sex. Do you remember that?"

"I always wanted to have sex."

"We had actually begun to break it off. It was getting too tense in the apartment and you were seeing other women. You had sex with my best friend."

"Right." When had Dagmara become a nun?

"But that night. We got drunk. And then, well, if you don't remember ..."

"What?"

"No, it's okay, Richard."

"What? Obviously you've remembered. It's something important to you. Tell me. I want to know, because it's important. To you."

"Use your high-powered imagination."

"I wanted to have sex. You didn't want to have sex."

Dagmara lit a cigarette. "Your eyes. What's that Eagles song? 'Lyin' Eyes'?"

"Lemme guess, we had sex!"

"Yes. We had sex."

Okay, time to fold. "And you didn't want to."

She kept her gaze steady, as if bequeathing a great truth. "There's really no other way to describe it: You raped me, Richard."

Why was she doing this to me? "We were seeing each other. It isn't rape if you're sleeping with someone."

"I was sore for a week. I got an infection. Don't you remember, I couldn't get out of bed the next day? You crept around the house, looking guilty."

"Are you saying I had sex with you in a blackout?"

"Okay, okay, you don't remember. Very flattering. But there's more. Do you want to hear this or what?"

"Of course."

"I became pregnant. From that night. I couldn't bear to tell you then. I knew you'd just make a cynical remark and pack me off to the abortion doctor. Besides, you were just a boy, what could you do about it? We weren't about to get married!" Dagmara laughed out loud, as if genuinely amused. "Still, it made me crazy knowing I was carrying your child inside me. Because I could have loved you and I was certain you didn't love me. Oh! Don't jump to any conclusions. There was a, how do you say it, miscarried before this good Catholic girl had to face the music. But not before I passed through a very struggling time in my life."

Dag's command of English was decaying. This had always happened when she was upset. No point in correcting her. "I don't remember any of this, Dag. How could I, since I didn't know?"

"In those days, you were spending more and more time away at night. With your friends in Brooklyn, I think. That woman 'Gitte, who you worshipped. And her husband."

"I'm sorry . . ."

"Fortunately I didn't do anything dramatic like jump myself in front of a subway train. What made it more depressing was that you didn't notice my sadness. I reached a time when just seeing you in the apartment upset me. I told you I was taking a night course and had to study, so I had an excuse for staying in my room. Then one day you announced you were moving out and suddenly you were gone. And I did not see you again until right now, today. We both, Haim and I, missed you for different reasons, although by that point, I was happy that you left. There was a sense of relief."

"I shouldn't have come here."

"No. I'm *glad* to see you. You're not the only one who becomes curious with old age. I had read about you in the American magazines. And besides, what happened was a long time ago. Deep down, I still care for you. Love you, in my way. How can I not have those feelings? And I'm happy for your success. There's a lovely sense of accomplishment when someone you know has done well. I feel like I share it in a way."

"You're making me feel very guilty."

Dagmara smiled warmly. "I had made a—how do you say it?—deal with myself not to mention any of this today."

"You left New York because of me?"

Dagmara slapped her thigh. "Now, wouldn't that be a souvenir you could take back to New York? An idea you could *cherish*! Unfortunately, no! Well, not because of you, specifically you. It was the whole thing. You were a part of New York for me and my New York experience had many unpleasant aspects. It was all too rough for me. Too heartless. And so I left, yes."

My book lay on the coffee table. I wondered if she would ever open it. "You're telling me that no man in Poland acts selfishly?"

"No, I'm telling you that in Poland there is some sense of another person. What's the word? Empathy? There is some sense of *love*. My husband is an alcoholic and so we had to separate. But we are married to this day. And as selfish as he was, he admits it. He is remorseful. He goes to church and confesses. You did what you did as a young man, and then you just kept going, same as before. What you did is a part of you, your modus operandi. It's what makes Richard Richard. It's what attracted me to you. You know? All those adages about leopards and spots and scorpions and frogs. Your destiny was clear."

"You have a few spots of your own, Dagmara."

"Maybe. But different, eh? Not as black."

I had hoped for a quiet afternoon, maybe some sightseeing. The driver would not be returning to pick me up for another two hours. I didn't want to spend another minute with this narrow-minded woman who had once been so lively and sensuous and was now sitting here trying to wound me with a thirty-year-old resentment. Her husband had left her angry and bitter. Who needed it?

She said, "It's in the past, Richard. You should eat. " And again, she disappeared into the kitchen. My anger vied with my pity. This is what Dagmara's life had come to. She was trapped in a vapid day-to-day existence in a struggling country. She hadn't had the guts to stick it out in New York. And so now, here she was. Confined to the prison cell of her own nonhistory. Why should I be angry with her? She had the worst of it.

We consumed a boring lunch of sliced cucumber, cheese and bread. Later we visited perhaps the most tedious museum in which I have ever set foot. Gallery after gallery of oil portraits of royalty long turned to dust in their graves. Men who ruled an empire no one now remembers.

The driver was waiting for us when we returned, so we said our goodbyes quickly and without emotion. Exhausted, I slipped into the car and dozed all the way back to Lodz. At the hotel dining room another overwhelming dinner of fish and veal and potatoes and cabbage. Tomorrow the flight leaves at eight A.M.

August 10, 2006

After days of jet lag, I decided to make the trip to the city to a backyard barbecue at Leon's brownstone in Brooklyn. I have so few friends in the world, I must cherish the remaining few I do have. This is without seriously looking at whether Leon is in fact my friend. We've been through a lot, so I suppose he is. We amuse one another. We laugh out loud when we're together. That's friendship, right?

Once it was so much easier to motivate myself. All I had to do was follow my desire: money, fame, women. I had goals that flowed from my gut unbidden, seized my heart and set me in motion. I had no choice, I had to pursue what I wanted. I never questioned the imperative. I no longer have that drive. So I set goals to force some direction to my day. Ergo my attendance at Leon's barbecue. Having made the commitment, I forced myself up at a reasonable hour, showered, shaved. I drove into the city, daydreaming as I plied the traffic.

The Polish trip had left me feeling rancid and irritated. I knew it was just fatigue and some viral bug I had caught, probably in the restaurant. All the same, I was not myself. Thirty years ago I was a rapist. Live and learn.

It's funny how Leon has kept up with the times. Me, I'm content to have an apartment on the Upper West Side and a country house in

Connecticut. But Leon is much hipper than me. Long before it became fashionable, Leon lived in a loft down in TriBeCa and then ten years ago, with perfect timing, he sold the place for two million bucks, and moved his young family across the river to a brownstone in Brooklyn. At first it seemed like a crackpot move. Why would anyone want to live in Brooklyn? He appropriated a massive brownstone for a sum in the low five figures. Repointed and reroofed the whole damn thing, installed a new furnace, landscaped the backyard and in the process became two million dollars richer.

And so there we were, the literati of New York, circa 2006, decked out in linen and starched cotton, packed like sardines onto the grounds of Leon's miniature estate, a patch of carefully manicured lawn, replete with a tiny pear tree and a brick wall covered with climbing tea roses. The whole thing maybe forty feet by twenty feet. In the corner stood an antique lawn mower. Leon loves irony.

Leon himself was playfully adorned in a chef's cap and apron, doling out burgers and hot dogs and skewers of sushi-quality tuna from behind his brand-new five-thousand-dollar gas grill. When I arrived, he made a cynical remark about "the recluse" deigning to make an appearance and then promptly turned his back on me to huddle with his current bestselling discovery, a colorless WASP who writes unreadably dense semifiction inspired by maritime law.

An attractive young woman found me and it took ten minutes for me to figure out that this babe was Leon's grown-up daughter. I'd last seen Nina fifteen years ago in her Halloween costume. She was a novelist now, of course, and approached me as a fan before confessing that she hadn't yet read *A Gentle Death*. It hurt, but I pretended an avuncular amusement. Why should I care if the novelist daughter of my editor is so incurious about my work that she can't be bothered to pick up a major effort of mine? I can only imagine the dinner table conversations, Leon and Nina, dissecting my career while passing the steamed asparagus. "Whatever happened to Richard? He used to be so *good*!" "He's lost his edge. It happens." I ducked away from Nina and searched out more drink. Over my shoulder I saw her moving in on the maritime guy.

Because Leon thinks of himself as an old anarchist in the Bob Dylan mold, he had invited not only the moneymaking luminaries but the anonymous old dogs who were the young rebels of their day. Most of these characters have secured cushy jobs at well-endowed universities and have a safe manger from which to bark. A few have left the profession altogether. I guess I fall somewhere in between. Neither here nor there.

Juggling my plate, I managed to consume half a tuna shish kebab and two mouthfuls of wild rice while listening to a discussion regarding the legal transgressions of the Bush regime pinging between Doris Kearns Goodwin and Jane Mayer. Jane confided that Dick Cheney had been a bed wetter until he was ten years old and with that knowledge, I moved on to my third plastic cupful of a very tasty red.

As the bartender handed me my wine, I scanned the crowd for a smoker from whom I might cadge a cigarette. Suddenly before me stood Zim, like Marley's ghost.

As if picking up on an ongoing conversation, Zim launched into a critique of the crowd. As usual, he was hilarious. In a sea of luminaries Zim is an alchemist who can transmute every atom of their sacred being into pure caricature. And like a dummy, I stood next to him, grinning into my wine, chuckling along at his rancorous fusillade. I knew I looked stupid and I didn't care.

Then Zim lobbed a grenade in the direction of Sharon Woodward, an old girlfriend of mine. Sharon writes small novels about isolation and probity and suicide. A kind of mini-Woolf. We slept together off and on for about a year after Elizabeth and I broke up. In those days, Sharon was still pretty and buxom. Now she was menopausal and sagging. Zim dug in: "I fucked her once. She saves her passion for her crappy writing. I gave her a couple of helpful hints, but she was too dumb to take them."

I hadn't read Sharon's last two books because I didn't feel I needed to. Nonetheless I've always been her cheerleader, enthusiastically composing letters of reference for MacDowell and Yaddo and the Guggenheim. I'd done so with absolute candor. Her work *should* be supported. I was grateful it was out there. Writers like Sharon are the bread and butter of . . . something.

So here was Zim, demolishing her cottage stick by stick, lighting up her straw roof with his Zippo of sarcasm. He was right, of course, about everything he was saying. Her work is dreary and prim and self-pitying. But fuck him. And so I defended her. "Sharon is an innocent, but she is an authentic innocent."

Zim nursed a brimming glassful of iceless iced tea. When he grumbled, "What the fuck do you know?" I could smell the tang of whiskey on his breath.

"I know." There was danger in this conversation.

"Richard, you wouldn't know authentic if it fucked you up the ass."

I tried to stare into Zim's flat, rheumy eyes. Having made his move, he assumed a poker face, as if he hadn't just stabbed me to the spiritual core.

Did I mention Zim is a full-blown alcoholic now? If he isn't juiced round-the-clock, he gets the DTs. A few years ago, his esophagus detached from his stomach and he almost died vomiting his own blood. Thus his own unimpeachable "authenticity." He is an authentic drunk and so his work is "grounded" in a way that every college sophomore loves. And editors embrace him because his writing is always nasty and easy to read. That is, when he manages to write at all.

I took the bait. "Hey, asshole, in what way is anything you do more authentic than what I do?"

"Richard, you've never had defeat or disappointment. All you know is pussy and money. You are soft and you are decadent and you are addicted to fame and what it can bring you. So you write what the academy *wants* you to write. They tell you you're a genius and you believe it. But believe *this*, my friend, you're nothing more than court jester. You can't tell the truth. It's not in you. Your job is to *distract* from the truth."

"Are you accusing me of being commercial? Because I'm not."

"No, you fucking idiot, I'm talking about your total lack of spine. The *academy* only recognizes ass-licking, nonauthentic, pseudo-intellectual, grade-A bullshit like yours. The frightening thing is that you believe in your bullshit. It's actually your worldview."

A nauseating fatigue set in. Why had I come to Leon's? To please him? To network? To remind people I have just published a new book? Zim needed an answer. "This is a rhetorical point, one I can't dispute because it's based on vagaries and syllogisms. You are jealous of me, so your entire argument is poisoned. "

"How could I be jealous of a man who doesn't even know what he is? A man who writes and writes and writes only the most empty and soulless self-reflexive prose. You haven't written one honest word in twenty years. In your coward's heart, you know that. When did you last take a risk? When?" His lips were screwed into a sneer.

I smiled to cover my anger and said, "It's moot. I'm not writing anymore. I have heart problems."

But Zim wouldn't quit. "No, my friend, what you're saying is, 'You and me, Zim, deep down, we're the same.' But that's not true. We live different lives, Richard. It's wonderful to be rich and famous. It's intoxicating. And the intoxication has ruined you."

"Intoxication? Speak for yourself."

"I will, my friend, my good old friend. For myself and for you. Because when I leave here today, you won't give me another thought. You will return to your favorite topic, yourself. But nobodies like me, we must keep you in mind always. We have no choice."

How much fun were *we* having? Two old bums struggling to land a good square punch, staggering, falling down, finally forced to retreat to separate corners or worse, shake hands. Obviously, that's what I should have done. Walked away. But I'd been drinking too. Leon kept an eye on us from across the yard.

"You're drunk, Zim. You're not making sense."

Zim faced the milling crowd and shot me a sideways glance of pure red-eyed disdain. "Sure. That's right. Fuckin' wimp." Then he poured what remained of his drink onto my shoes.

Jane Mayer stood only a few feet apart from us. After the briefest of pauses, she and her companion resumed their conversation.

I saw Leon look away. Something in my chest swelled and puttered. Was I going to have a cardiac event right here in front of everyone, on Leon's perfect little estate? Over my dead body!

Without saying goodbye, I entered the house, walked straight through it, down the front steps and out to my parked car. Fifteen minutes later I was on the BQE, driving drunk, aimed for Connecticut.

November 1, 1977

So this tall, red-haired guy wearing a London Fog raincoat came to my reading down at Franklin Furnace. I heard about him when someone "backstage" said there was an FBI agent in the audience. Typical downtown paranoia. Why would a government agent give a shit about what we had to say? This isn't tsarist Russia and there were no Dostoyevskys here.

The red-haired guy approached me after the reading, told me he liked my story very much. Handed me his card. "The William Morris Agency— Blake Lansford, literary agent." Okay. We strolled up to SoHo and I conned him into buying me a triple espresso cappuccino in the Cupping Room. We sat. He was very nervous. Like we were breaking the law by sitting in a coffee shop talking. I began to think he might really be an FBI agent.

Blake asked me where I thought all this was going, my writing. I wondered why he asked this, but when I told him I was writing a book of short stories that would be very different from the usual collection out there, he got interested and wanted to know more.

I'm not sure if Blake followed what I was saying. But he said my work should be in magazines. That if I could get three more pieces published, he could swing a deal for the book I wanted to put together. He said he could get me an advance of *five thousand dollars*! So we shook on it. And now I guess I have an agent.

Blake said he would hook me up with this editor at *Esquire*, Leon Koppler. Guy's supposed to be "hip," probably means he sniffs cocaine and dates models. I haven't read *Esquire* since I was in high school but Blake says it's a good place to sell material. If I do do this, it will just be for the money. I figure, make the money writing for *Esquire*, then write what I *really* want. I told this agent guy I could write a short essay about a Talking Heads concert gig at CBGB. He said "Leon would love that."

So, who knows? Maybe I can make money doing this. And more. Get a book published. I wish Mom could be here for this. I miss Mom. Where is she?

November 2, 1977

What does an artist think he's doing when he attempts to make art "successfully"? What is "success" in art making? An artist is successful when he's BLASTING THE WORLD! There is no other kind of success. Money and power mean nothing. There is no power but the power to write. To create. To attempt immortality.

Katie's show opened. Hundreds of people crowded into the gallery. She was surrounded all evening and we barely got to talk. Every time I got near her I could see she had a wild look in her eyes. Excitement. Fear. Madness.

Everyone was telling her the work was terrific. But I also heard people whispering in the corners. They were *laughing* at her. Myself, I don't know. I didn't get it. It had something to do with the alphabet and poorly executed paintings of naked women. It was a lot of effort but in the end it was very art school. No, worse than that. It was mediocre. I don't care what anyone says or if she gets a good review in *Artforum*, the show sucked. Sorry. But if I can't be honest, what's the point?

I didn't know what to say to her. This is a problem now. How can we have a relationship if I can't tell her what I think of her work? Who is she if the things she makes are awful?

I saw Zim at the opening. He was standing in front of a huge letter V composed of spread legs. When I asked him what he thought, he said, "You've got to be kidding me."

Being an artist isn't just a matter of *wanting* to be an artist. It isn't just about *wanting* to share a point of view. It's about the logic of being and that logic must be aggressive, undeniable. Katie wants to share her insecurities and anger with the world. It's not enough.

What *is* enough?

August 12, 2006

I've been asleep in bed or catnapping on the couch for two days straight. Waiting for Leon to call. One would think he'd be curious as to where

I'd disappeared. But no one has called. I could die here in this decaying house and unless Nat happened by to mow the lawn, that would be the end of that. This is an untenable situation. I don't have a solution. I am alone. That's it. Why?

My barbecue hangover has forced things to a head. Woke yesterday completely wrecked. Despairing. Sick. Burning with fever, my chest hurt, I vomited. I was afraid that I was having another heart "episode," but I didn't call anyone. No one *to* call. Nothing to do. Took it easy all day, made myself some Lipton's chicken noodle soup, read, drank tea. Dragged the quilt from room to room, filled in the crossword. Slept as much as I could.

I'm too sick to drink. Fruit juice, tea, rest. I'm not trying to figure anything out. Not yet. I don't give a shit if Leon calls. I'm going to gather up my strength and head for Cape Cod. I need to watch the waves.

August 20, 2006

Drove for two days. Stopped overnight in West Dennis at a tourist hotel, an overpriced, industrial-strength human warehouse packed with chubby sunburned kids and eyeless (sunglassed) smokers. Avoiding the drab breakfast, I took a walk and discovered a charming pancake house down the lane. A simple bungalow painted yellow and white, surrounded with gnarled pines and sea sand. I walked in. The place smelled great, fresh-roasted coffee and baked goods. The sun-drenched walls were festooned with shark jawbones, plaqued trophy fish, and hand-painted signs boasting "the BEST coffee this side of Cape Cod Canal" and "No IOUs accepted."

Crisp bacon and maple syrup is good for the soul. As I watched the sunny, lithe waitress (probably a college student up for the summer) glide from table to table with a grace and serenity only innocent women have, I wanted to reach out and touch her. This wasn't horniness. This was devotion.

After breakfast, I paid my hotel bill, and headed north on the two-lane that leads to P-Town. The ride relaxed me. Dunes, clapboard-sided liquor stores, a length of black asphalt and the steady, streaming traffic served as a kind of narcotic elixir. Every now and then, through the pitch pines and scrub oak, I caught a glimpse of the indigo sea. The only radio station featured oldies but goodies. In this peaceful state of mind, all other emotions were checked. I could do this forever. But following a highway on a peninsula is a doomed agenda. Sooner or later one must arrive at the sea.

In Provincetown I found a B&B twenty paces off the main drag. The proprietess, possibly a lesbian, handed me a steel skeleton key and I shuffled up the wainscotted stairwell to a dry, pleasant room, freshly painted in a cheery pastel. It lacked a phone, had no air-conditioning, and shared a bathroom with the neighboring room. Good, I thought. Simplicity. All I needed was here. Entering a rented room is about a new beginning. An empty slate. No need to be anywhere else, and so, peace. The calm of the room settled me.

I lay down on the firm spring bed and immediately fell into a dreamless nap, waking an hour later to the sound of water running in the bathroom. Of course my bladder ached but I lay still and waited until I heard the slamming of the opposite door, then rose up off the bed, snuck in, peed and rinsed my face.

I strolled the main drag. To what end? None. I could have marched into the sea and no one would have known or cared. I visited a men's shop on the pier and bought a light pullover. As I stood before the dressing room mirror I wondered what Elizabeth would say about me in lavender cashmere.

Across the street I bought a cup of coffee, and took a position on the pier. The gulls circled the lobster trawlers. The sea breeze swept over me.

I considered the deep water and all that the ocean implied: infinity, rot, adventure.

At first I didn't hear my cell phone when it beeped, only sensed the almost imperceptible vibration in my pocket. The world beckoned.

Leon's number on the screen. Finally! I hesitated. I didn't want to seem to be waiting for him to call me. But fuck him. I needed to speak to someone, anyone, and that took precedence.

"Yeah?"

"Richard?" He sounded like he was standing behind me, whispering into my ear.

"Leon?" The gulls circled.

"Are you in Connecticut?"

"No." I refused to be generous. It was his turn.

A pause. Leon didn't seem to want this call either. He murmured, as if afraid of being overheard by someone, "Listen, uh, Zim is dead."

"I wish."

"No, man, he died. Last night. I guess it was his liver. Did you know he had Hep C?"

"Zim died." The gulls became more than gulls. They turned into portents, signs, metaphors. But I couldn't decipher their meaning. The gulls were Zim? What kind of idea is that? The fishing boats bobbed in the rising tide, not the same boats of minutes ago.

Leon's voice formed buttery shapes. This was his area of expertise, human communication. "That's what I'm saying." Pause. "Ironic, isn't it?"

"Why?" I felt as if Leon killed Zim as a way to indict me. And why should I feel guilty about Zim?

"I don't see him for a year. He dies the next day? I almost didn't invite him. He was such a mess. When was the last time you'd seen him?"

"Didn't Zim have some kind of book deal with you?" The gulls, the trawlers. For one moment, I had been in the center of everything. Now I was on the outside looking in.

"What deal? Years ago, Richard. Years ago."

"So, what happens now?" Keep it to the practical. Get off the phone. Gulls. Waves. The air in Provincetown is imbued with a soft light. That's why the painters came here. Was it the humidity that thickened the air?

"The funeral. Tomorrow morning. Downtown, Old St. Patrick's. Apropos of nothing, where the fuck are you, Richard? What's that sound?"

A hundred feet away a swordfish trawler reeled cable onto a massive pulley system. Puffs of soot from its smokestack melted into the pale sky. The gulls screeched. "I'm away. I'll come down." I hung up.

November 20, 1977

It's time to work. I've quit drinking. Quit smoking weed. No more distractions. I must finish my book. Writing a book is like preparing for a prizefight. I'm so focused, I'm not even masturbating. How else can I make the work that will pierce the world?

My schedule: Get up early, seven or eight. Read the newspaper. Thirty-five push-ups, a hundred sit-ups, stretch. Make a huge pot of espresso coffee and write until I can't write anymore. Usually until four or five. Then go out for a long walk. Breathe. Try to gather up more ideas. Then I eat something. Usually, I go by and visit Zim, talk philosophy and watch him sniff heroin.

Using this system I've cranked out sixty pages in the last week. And the stuff is good. I'm halfway through the second week of this. I'm going to dedicate this book to my mother.

Blake, my new agent, checks in every couple of days. He has sent samples of my writing to magazine editors. Then he asks me how the book's going. Sometimes he dishes about his star clients. He knows Raymond Carver personally. Represents a guy named Richard Price, who is very interesting. I guess I'm in the big time now. But I have to get the writing done.

I visit Katie. We have bad sex and talk. She's depressed about her show. There haven't been any reviews. I don't know what to say. I can't tell her what I really think. I tell her her work is good while I rub her back so I don't have to meet her eyes when I speak. How can I be with this woman if her work sucks? The whole time I'm reassuring her, I'm thinking about my own work. I know this book is going to work. I can feel it. Blake has confidence in me. I look at the writing of the establishment and I know I can kick their ass.

Deep down, I don't care about Katie or her work. There's only one thing I care about.

August 22, 2006

I arrived late to the two-hundred-year-old Little Italy church packed with Zim's mourners. I squeezed in, nudging and wriggling my way toward the front. How is it that a guy who was a pain in the ass to almost everyone he ever met has become, the minute he croaked, beloved and celebrated by all of those people and more?

Of course, the little magazine publishers/editors, the ones who saw Zim as the second coming of Bukowski, were all there. His "publisher," Joel Flowers, always believed in him and for Joel, it worked, because the cash flow kept his little press afloat. College kids couldn't get enough of this stuff. Probably read all of three pages and stuck their copy of Zim on the shelf, never to be looked at again. But books are artifacts. They don't have to be read to sell. Ask William Gaddis. Ask Stephen Hawking.

The pseudo-wise R.C. priest intoned the standard lines from Corinthians: "For as in Adam all die, even so in Christ shall they be made alive." "The last enemy that shall be destroyed is death." I fantasized Zim leaping out of his casket to pick a fight with the good Father. But Zim was dead and he wasn't debating anyone.

I have never been comfortable in a church. When I was a kid I discovered that Catholic churches were particularly eerie. The melancholy Christ bleeding on the cross, tortured to death, malnourished, miserable. And not just Christ, but a clubhouseful of plaster saints. Hung upside down, beheaded, burnt to a crisp. Ronald Taft, who sat across from me in Mrs. Graham's fourth grade class, once slipped me a color picture of Saint Sebastian, bristling with dozens of arrows. I said, "This is a joke, right?"

Ronald replied, "No, Richie, this is their *religion*! They love this stuff."

A burnt-out Rod Stewart wannabe crooned while someone strummed a blues progression. He bowed when he was done. Were we supposed to applaud? No. Now three hefty black chicks belted out a gospel number. Zim had always liked the sisters. Part of his mystique. He dated them too. Zim must have known that this gave everyone the impression that there was more to him than met the eye. Gotta be a real man to bang a black chick, right? The entertainment portion of the afternoon came to an end when a bad poet strode up to the altar and recited a poem about a train leaving the station. Gawd! The guy was obviously auditioning for Joel. Sad.

Leon read his prepared pages and opined that Zim was the "purest" writer he'd ever known. Whatever the fuck "purest" meant. A saint? If there was a Saint Zim, he did not preside within the Satanic church that Leon attends every Monday through Friday. Death is the great transmuter in the arts. What was no good yesterday is what we all love today.

When it was my turn, I launched myself at the altar with a jocular stroll but as I struggled through the crowd, I tripped and almost fell on my face. I had wanted to tell the story about the night Zim and I drank beer at the Hell Fire Club and watched the guy getting whipped, but after my awkward landing I lost my nerve. So I recounted a cute anecdote about the first time Zim and I ate sushi stoned on a half-gram of red Lebanese hash. Warm laughter. Sniffles. Okay. I looked up and saw appreciation on the faces of the mourners. Enough. He was pure, he was courageous. We mere mortals would have to soldier on without him.

Zim's young nephews, possessed with the violent mien of Serbian soccer players, easily hoisted the coffin onto their broad shoulders. I imagined them beating someone to death with baseball bats. They were part of the extended family members who had arranged and paid for Zim's funeral, paid for the flowers and the cemetery plot.

Zim's two sisters and two brothers followed. The brothers had a comic resemblance to Zim. Zim without style. Zim without intelligence. One was actually handsome in the same way as Zim, but endowed with a slightly dazed expression. The sisters were middle-aged, heavyset and grim. Their expressions said, "We saw this coming." The fact that Zim had predeceased them only served to reinforce their collective opinion that they were right and he had made a big mistake moving to New York City to be a writer and now justice had been served.

Zim's dad, stoic, slab-faced, brought up the rear. Retired, preparing for the last stages of his own life: bouts with diabetes, emphesema, maybe a touch of cancer. Probably counting the minutes till his next cigarette. And angry. Very angry.

The crowd filed out behind the family. We understood that most of us would not be driving out to the cemetery. A cold luncheon buffet would be served later, but since the family was paying, none of us were invited.

The mourners milled around by the worn brick walls of the churchyard as the cortege loaded up to leave. A few ventured onto the street only to be warned back by the honks of passing cars. I corraled Leon and shook his hand. He absentmindedly took mine as if he wasn't sure who I was. He was riding with the family to the cemetery. For a moment I wondered if I should join them, but no, it would be an empty gesture. If Leon wanted to play this farce out, that was his choice. He felt guilty about Zim. I didn't.

The remains of the crowd broke up. I drifted off in an uptown direction, toward the bookstores.

"Rich! Richard!"

A wino approached me. Somehow he had harvested my name and was attempting to snag a couple of bucks. I assumed a stony expression. But then the years fell away like a computer-generated aging program run in reverse. The guy became more and more comprehensible. First the smile, then the eyes, the gait. It was Jack. Good ol' Jack!

"Jack?"

Grinning. Limping? "Richie!"

"Jesus." How does one show up at a funeral and not run into someone who makes you uncomfortable? Jack had always been a nice guy, but I didn't want this. Not today.

He brimmed with pathos and empathy. "Can you believe it? Poor fucking Zim, huh?"

"Yeah, poor fucking Zim. I didn't know you knew him."

"We worked together on a series of videos. In the eighties." Jack's voice was hoarse, and he cupped a cigarette in his hand. He carried himself with a slight limp and wore a Carhartt jacket, a style that had come and gone ten years ago.

I played along with Jack's good cheer. Tried to make it as painless as possible. "Right, videos, I heard something about that. The thing at the Guggenheim? I didn't know you worked on that."

"Zim always talked about you, man. Especially when you started to hit it big."

"I can only imagine."

"He loved you, man. Guy had a huge heart. Generous."

I didn't want to talk about Zim anymore. "And where have you been, Jack? All these fucking years." I'm good at this, making a bad situation worse.

"You know man. Doing my thing." We're moving northward now, Jack dipping ever so slightly with each step. The limp, was it from the motorcycle accident?

"The bartenders don't miss us, huh?"

"No more barhoppin', Richie, no more barhoppin'. And you, you're a busy man. Must be so cool. I saw a picture of you in the paper hanging out with Alec Baldwin. Proud of you, man."

"Thanks. The funny thing is, I don't really know Mr. Baldwin. We just happened to be at the same place at the same time. You live in the city still?"

"Same place I always had. Richie, you remember! Right up the street here. Bleecker. Come on up for a drink!"

Could I have said, "No, Jack, I don't want to come up and have a drink because something about you frightens me"? No. So I said, "I only have an hour." He had called me "Richie."

"Sure man, sure. I understand. No problems." Big grin. He was missing a tooth. "Just great to see you, man."

Was his enthusiasm genuine? Even though I saw him as a failure, Jack didn't see himself that way. He was still dreaming his dreams, scheming his schemes. And now, who showed up in his life again, but the big writer, the star, "Richie." I girded myself.

At Bleecker Street, instead of the dilapidated neighborhood I remembered, we were met by three active construction sites that were once trash-strewn, rat-infested lots. A warehouse next door to Jack's place had been gutted and renovated. It featured a slick foyer complete with the ubiquitous doorman, minimalist art and potted fig.

With a flourish Jack unlocked the building door (clean and freshly painted, no longer stuccoed with peeling flyers and stickers) and we mounted the two flights. As we passed baby strollers standing outside his neighbors' doors, I wanted to ask him how much his place was now worth. A mil? Two mil?

The loft was almost exactly as I had last seen it. Lots of stuff: a bicycle, a tire pump, stacks of record albums and CDs and videocassettes, books, milk crates, half-disassembled electronic equipment, tripods, skis, balled-up clothing, cowboy boots. The light was muted and pleasant, tinted the color of late summer afternoon. A faint breeze freshened the room. The rear windows, veiled by a security gate, faced the back side of another building, one still clearly in use as housing for welfare recipients. Jack's yard had been manicured, but on the other side of the razor-topped chain-linked fence, a bare-branched tree dominated a muddy yard. That tree had been leafy when I had last seen it.

Jack dug up two pint cans of Newcastle Ale and a fifth of Talisker single malt scotch. Once we were committed to getting fucked up, it was a swift ride back to the seventies. Back to all the good times I barely remembered. With alcohol in me, the tense morning evaporated and I was no longer the "busy guy" who "has to get going." And Jack was no longer a scruffy and annoying street person, but the great guy he always was. I became "Richie" and he became "Jack."

My cardiac condition made no impression on my old friend (He is an overgrown kid. Age, illness mean nothing to him.) until I showed him my scar, whereupon he showed me his mangled leg. It must have been very serious. Why hadn't I seen this before? I couldn't remember.

We began to talk about women. I gave Jack an abbreviated history of Elizabeth and Sarah. He then filled me in on *his* women, a remarkable parade of choreographers and poets and journalists and filmmakers. The standout was one well-known *New York Times* columnist who wrote on photography. They had lived together for a number of years. No children because, as it turned out, Jack was sterile. The couple discussed adoption or finding a donor but in the end, they had broken up. "Better that way. I'm not a family guy," Jack confided with jocular manliness. But as he said it, his eyes conveyed the opposite.

I tried to help him out. "A lot of horny women out there. Someone's got to take care of 'em. If you and me don't do it, who will?" We laughed, enjoying the lie. In the old days, when we had been two guys out there carousing, on our own, unfettered, we thought we'd wanted that. But we'd never had a choice. We were lone wolves, condemned to be lone wolves forever. Old lone wolves. Older and grayer and slower.

I was high on the scotch and ale when Jack suggested we go out. I knew this wasn't a good idea. I was more than happy to waste another hour with Jack, but only within the safety of Jack's four-walled "pad." Hidden away from the eyes of others, Jack and I could stroll memory lane with easy abandon. In public we would be nothing more than two pitiful, drunken, middle-aged men.

We reminisced about one drunken night that began in the East Village, moved onto the Staten Island Ferry for six round-trips and finally landed at the Brooklyn loft at three in the morning. After making respective toasts to John's superior weed and 'Gitte's delicate, overwhelming beauty, Jack paused, dropped his smile and said, "Something happened between you two guys."

"Yes." I tried to stand, but the whiskey had cooked my legs into limp pasta. I stayed put.

"I mentioned you one night and John's face turned red. He didn't want to talk about you. All he would say was—excuse my French—'Fuckin' rat.' What did you do to him? I thought you guys loved each other."

"I'm not sure. I just stopped going over there."

"Yeah. He seemed pretty pissed off."

Why not tell Jack the truth? "I taped him."

"Taped?"

"I audiotaped John talking."

"Why'd you do that?"

"I was inspired by his persona, his style. I wanted him to be the basis for a character in my first collection of stories. Not really stories, more a set of profiles. Not really fiction or factual."

"Yeah, I remember that book. I think I have a copy here somewhere."

"It's still in print."

"That was a funny story. He was pissed off at you for that?"

"That and the taping in the first place. He saw it as a kind of transgression. And then, John's 'portrait' got a lot of attention. But by the time the book came out, I hadn't been to John's for a year. Then one night he called and started ranting about how he wanted compensation. Said he was going to have my legs broken. Scared the shit out of me. I had to change my phone number and everything. Listen, John knew I was a writer."

Jack lit a joint and passed it to me. "You ever write about me?"

I took a drag of the weed, exhaled, passed it back. "Nah," I said. There's a limit to the usefulness of truth. What Jack didn't know wouldn't hurt him. Using all my concentration, I rose from the low futon couch and lurched into the bathroom. Everything was adrift, the hair-streaked bar of soap, the cat box under the sink, a roll of toilet paper next to it, the *Men's Health* magazines strewn around the toilet bowl. Under the vanity mirror stood trendy perfumes and hair dressings. I was nauseous, the room swung like a pendulum. I held on long enough to piss.

Stiff-backed but shaky, I made it back to Jack and announced my departure. I fumbled with my cell phone as if it were the reason for my exit. I thanked Jack for his hospitality.

After that, I have no memory. Whether I passed out on his floor or cabbed home, I don't know. All I recall is trying to fit my car keys into my apartment door, then, morning.

December 15, 1977

I've sent my raw manuscript to Blake. I figure he can read it over the holidays and then we can make a plan. I told him he should send it to Random House and Viking first. Been hanging out with that *Esquire* guy, Leon. He's got a great sense of humor. And great coke.

December 16, 1977

There's been a new development between me and my girlfriend Katie. We had just had sex and I was falling asleep when a sniffling sound woke me.

She was crying. Just lying next to me crying. And then she made this big confession about how she's always been so fearful and intimidated by me and Zim and the whole scene and now her show's been a failure and she feels like killing herself.

I held her close and tried to soothe her. I didn't really know what to say, so I said that no matter what happened, I loved her and she could always depend on that. She hugged me hard and sobbed and told me that she loved me but had been afraid that if she ever admitted that, I would leave her!!!

My heart flooded. I wanted to cry! What an incredible breakthrough between us! We started to kiss and then I got hard again and then we had the most amazing sex we've ever had!

This morning she was like a different person. Very quiet and shy with me. She kept smiling at me. I'm not used to this. But it's good.

August 23, 2006

Jack called today, checking to make sure that I made it home safely. I don't remember giving him my phone number. No suggestion of "getting together for a cup of coffee," none of that. He had been satisfied with our short bonding session. Trying to cut the call short, I lied and said I was going out. He repeated that it was great seeing me again. I said the same. He asked me if I wanted John's number.

"John's number?" For a moment, I wasn't sure who he meant.

"Big John. He moved to western Massachusetts years ago. Him and 'Gitte. Thought you might like to have it."

"John doesn't want to hear from me."

"When I saw them, 'Gitte asked about you. I couldn't tell her anything 'cause I didn't know."

"'Gitte asked about me?"

"Yeah, man. And as far as John goes, 'time heals all wounds,' right? You should call him. I bet he'd be happy to hear from you. What's the worst that can happen?" I took down the number, then Jack said he had to run, as if he had completed his obligation and didn't want this call to be misinterpreted for friendship.

September 30, 2006

It's been a wicked, as we say in New England, couple of weeks. I had planned to take a day to gather my wits, buy books, find Leon, perhaps have a good meal somewhere. Instead I got a hysterical call from my sister. Dad was in the hospital with pneumonia. I promised to drive up.

I found Dad tucked away in an anonymous hospital room, dwarfed by his massive mechanical bed. He lay there with all the animation of a large deflated balloon. His eyes signaled resignation, blurry and moist, like a blind man's. Dripping bags of sugar water, oxygen tubes stuck in his nose, other cables leading to monitors and beeping machines, the whole shebang encircled by a flimsy curtain symbolizing privacy. Even the smell was a cliché: baby powder and urine and shit.

Two days later, Dad graduated to the "rehab." This place offered a more active set of indignities, the daily ritual of inconvenience and humiliation spiced up with round-the-clock harassment. Maybe the idea was that the patient would be badgered into leaving the facility. Or if that didn't work, die.

I've been sleeping in his house. Not because I wanted to but because the place is a ruined mess and Sis thought it would be efficient if I organized the clutter Dad has been accumulating. I had no idea know where to begin, so I resigned myself to wandering from room to room, picking up stacks of old magazines, hauling them a few steps, then placing them back down on a different dust-covered spot. I hadn't cleaned a bathroom in twenty-five years but I scrubbed his to the best of my ability. I emptied and swabbed out the fridge. I swept the cellar stairs. I washed his car and raked his leaves. At the local Kmart, I picked up a portable vacuum and trimmed back as much of the dust as I could. I found clothing I had bought him decades ago. I inventoried his neckties, some with price tags still on them. I selected a couple and tossed them into my bag.

Dad had spent years collecting a houseful of garbage. It took a special talent. Pulp novels, each one bookmarked twenty or so pages in, then forgotten, lay on every horizontal service. Alarm clocks and egg timers stood ready in each room, often one clock displaying one time sitting upon another in contradiction. The stacks of magazines and newspapers already mentioned. Little bags of candy, opened, reclosed and carefully wrapped with rubber bands. Dried-out, half-eaten bologna sandwiches, mahogany-colored bananas, wadded Kleenex. Calendars were tacked up in each room, one to a wall. Compact plastic transistor radios, the kind you never see anymore, aimed their antennae toward the cobwebbed ceiling corners. Vast collections of empty plastic take-out containers.

Frayed terry cloth towels tanned with grime lay on the arms and backs of his couches and armchairs. Cloudlike balls of dust gathered beneath the furniture, a mixed affair dating back to *his* mother's old place. Here and there were a few bizarre items he'd picked up at yard sales since Mom died (e.g.: a planter/table lamp constructed from a bronze replica of a 1939 Cord automobile, minus plant). Many framed photos of Mom. And of me.

I discovered a steel file box, unlocked. Inside were ancient insurance policies, rings of keys, defunct savings passbooks, black and white snapshots of the family at the beach. In one I'm standing alongside my father. We're both wearing bathing suits, showing off our naked skinny chests. I'm six or seven.

Also in the box was a diary, one my father kept when he was a schoolboy during the Great Depression. I find an entry marked with a paper clip, "Today is my birthday. I am 13. All I got was fifty cents. Nothing else." The date was June 29, 1935. I tried to imagine myself in his place, impoverished, frightened. I tried to hear his boy's voice. I couldn't do it. I placed everything into the box and stuck it back in the closet where I found it.

I found a bottle of twelve-year-old bourbon I had given him for his birthday a few years back. I plopped down on a dusty couch and commenced to drink.

While musing upon my own ineptitude, the phone rang. The doctor was looking for me. My good old friend! He informed me in his usual unctuous tone that the rehab was releasing Dad the next day. Also that they'd updated their diagnosis. They were now fairly certain Dad was suffering from Alzheimer's. I hung up and refilled my glass. What else is new? Oprah was discussing it just that morning.

December 18, 1977

Blake read the book in two days. Said I should do more work on it before he sent it out. He made some suggestions, cuts, rewrites. I got off the phone, went to Zim's and got wasted on Ballantine Ale and bad marijuana. Fuck Blake. What does he know?

When I got home, Katie was waiting by my front door. She said she was worried about me. I was too wasted to fuck, but she said she didn't care and came in and we ended up talking for two hours. She listened and held me and in the end I kind of woke up and we fucked and it was amazing. She is so much on my side, believes in my work. I'm lucky.

December 20, 1977

I've begun the rewrites. I'm not going to do everything Blake says, but in a way, he is right. But only partially. Ultimately he doesn't understand what I'm doing. I'm not on my schedule anymore. Instead I sleep until eleven or noon, then I write until about nine, go to Zim's, we get fucked up, then we go out nightclubbing. We usually end up at Max's Kansas City and when it closes, the after-hours clubs. It's important to live, otherwise there's nothing to write about. I told Zim what Blake said about my work. Zim said, "Fuck him, what does he know? What did he ever write?" But I know that when Zim says that, he's not thinking about me and what's good for my work. Zim doesn't care about what happens to me. Artists are like jackals. We travel in packs, but in the end, each is only looking out for himself.

December 22, 1977

Had a monstrous, painful fight with Blake today. I went to his office and demanded to know when he was going to get off his ass and find me a writing job. He got all silent and pretended to be offended, which pissed me off even more. I ripped his phone out and threw it at the wall. When I blew past his assistant standing in the doorway, I could see that all the nearby offices had gone dead silent, no agents or assistants visible. Fuck them. I need money to keep going and Blake had said he was going to get me some work writing screenplays or magazine articles and that's not happening. Later I apologized to him on the phone. Then I hung up on him. Now I'm not sure if he's still my agent. It's probably not a bad thing. Have to make my reputation somehow.

October 5, 2006

As awful as Dad's house was without him, it was even worse when he came home. I'm amazed by the power of a patronizing, contemptuous old man. He's gripped in the jaws of something he can't control and so he takes it out on me.

When they delivered him back to me I made a decision to smother him with love and kindness. I couldn't change the guy, so what else was there to do? Sis was on a tough work schedule so I was left there alone with him. I broiled a couple of tuna melts, his favorite. He sat at the table, brimming with mistrust, eyeing the food as if I had laced it with cyanide. I commanded him to eat and he began to take small, hostile mouthfuls.

I mentioned "home care," i.e., bringing in someone who could come by and tidy up, cook a meal, be an object of his derision. His jaw stopped moving and his eyes narrowed. He placed his food back onto his plate. He wiped his mouth and launched into a tirade, listing my shortcomings as a son, as a caregiver, as a human being. Flecks of tuna spittle fired from his lips and the creases on his forehead etched black against his flushed skin.

Fortunately, I'd had a drink before the Ambu-care van delivered him to me, so I greeted this outburst with a placidity that only served to enrage him further. He swept the sandwiches onto the floor. I told him that the food could stay where he threw it, that I wasn't his mother.

He rose from his chair and a scent of urine drifted toward me. He leaned on the table as if to catch his breath, staring at me with cold eyes, gathering his strength for another attack. Then he threw up.

I could have walked out the door. But that would be inhuman, right? He may have deserved it, but what if the guy died on the spot? My sister would never forgive me. I took a step toward him. Fortunately he couldn't puke and scream at me at the same time. A string of drool hung from his lips. At his feet, the brightly colored meds freckled his tuna puke. They must have topped him off at the rehab before sending him my way.

I slipped an arm around his thin chest and led him toward the freshly scrubbed bathroom. He barfed in the doorway, on the floor, into the sink, everywhere but into the toilet. I nudged him to his knees and aimed his face toward the bowl. He was limp, defeated. He spasmed as I steadied him, his bony shoulder blades sharp under his yellowing T-shirt. Tears rolled down his gaunt cheeks.

He stank and he shook. All meek and vulnerable. What a con artist. What a selfish prick. He had me right where he wanted me, overwhelmed by *his* needs, *his* wants. Using every molecule of guts I possessed, I resisted the urge to feel sorry for him. No. I would do what I had to do, but I was not going to give him that.

No need to continue this description. There are volumes on the subject. In fact, there's too much on this subject. The point is, I didn't murder him. No. I wiped him down, diapered him, wrangled him into his pajamas, then tucked his lank body into his bed. Nestled in his sheets and pillows, he cursed me softly as his eyelids drooped. His voice grew fainter, and fainter. He began to snore.

I made a phone call to the doctor and reviewed the situation. We discussed the meds. There wasn't much else to say. The doc's patronizing tone had been replaced by a clipped intonation giving me the impression that he couldn't wait to get off the phone. It occurred to me then, that perhaps I should have taken a moment and thanked him for saving *my* life, but fuck him. He assumed that I *wanted* to know all this information about my father, about myself. But I never did.

October 8, 2006

Back in Connecticut I walked in the door of my house to find that Sis had left a long message on my voice mail informing me that Dad couldn't stand the home care worker I'd hired. While the woman collects his laundry, or dusts or washes his dishes, Dad harangues her from his armchair. He'd told my sister that "the Jamaican" (that's what he calls her) vacuums incessantly so that she doesn't have to listen to his carping. I almost laughed out loud. The kicker is that Sis wanted me to go back up to Stoneham. I put that on the bottom of my agenda.

I called the number in Massachusetts Jack had given me for John. A woman answered, her voice mature, hoarse with age. When I said, "It's Richard," 'Gitte knew me immediately, which I hadn't expected. In fact,

I had prepared an introduction for myself. ("I used to come by when you lived in Brooklyn.") She and I had never talked much "in the day," so now the dialogue had an odd lilt to it, as if we were both playing parts and hadn't fully memorized our lines.

I asked after John. 'Gitte said that John had not been well, that he was in the hospital. This news caught me unprepared. I had imagined he had simply shipped his Barcalounger to his new country home and was tilted back, smoking bowls of weed there. I inquired whether his illness was cardiac-related. 'Gitte said no, but didn't elaborate. Did I detect a lack of affection in her voice?

'Gitte invited me up to "the woods" for a visit. A three-hour drive, but why not? If this was the 'Gitte of my dreams and yearnings with whom I was speaking, and if indeed, she *did* remember me, then how could I *not* see her? What else did I have to do with my dilapidated life than to go rummaging around in my own lost fantasies?

December 25, 1977

Staying in the city. Not going home. There's too much work to do here. I can't leave. Katie's Christian, but she's not going home either. We had a wonderful Christmas Day meal at a diner in Chelsea. I don't know how to say this. I think I love her.

December 28, 1977

Cold these days.

Zim called. I told him I was working. He said, "Doing those rewrites for your agent? You're such a pussy." I decided I needed a break. Zim and I went up to the dollar movie at the Playboy movie theater on 57th this afternoon to see *Towering Inferno*. (It was either that or a John Holmes porno on 42nd Street.) Got seats in the balcony, smoked a joint and shared a pint of Old Mr. Boston Peach Brandy. Laughed our asses off. The film is packed with all these amazing stars like Steve McQueen and Paul Newman and Faye Dunaway and Fred Astaire. What would be the literary equivalent to *Towering Inferno*? *That's* the book I want to write.

As we left, Zim laid three hits of white cross (amphetamine) on me. Said he bought it from the Hell's Angels on 3rd Street. (These are the same Hells Angels who threw a hooker off their roof two years ago.) I chugged the speed with a can of Mountain Dew, and headed home. The chemicals hammered my brain stem just as I was unlocking my front door. It's quite a feeling. Like being reborn. I sat down and started writing. Did not stop until about an hour ago when my thoughts got too tangled up. I washed the floor and I sorted my books. Talked to Katie on the phone for two hours. Now it's about three A.M. and I'm crawling the walls. I have to go out.

December 29, 1977

The new year started early. Just woke up and it's dark out already. I think I ended up in Chinatown last night, not sure. Fuck. The pages I wrote yesterday are almost worthless. Yesterday was a waste of time. I have to edit. Have to focus. Drinking coffee. This is painful, but this is good. This is how it's done. Keep going, whatever it takes. And stay away from Zim.

LATER:

Katie came by. She's been nursing me out of this hangover all night. Behind her back, I sniffed some heroin and we fell asleep in each other's arms. She's a good woman.

December 31, 1977

It's snowing. Zim called with a list of parties we can crash but I told him I wasn't feeling well. I copped some H and I'm going to watch the ball drop on TV, sniff drugs and smoke cigarettes. Katie's in a bad mood because of her work and we argued, so I'm alone tonight. This isn't fair. I should finish my book, dedicate it to Katie and kill myself.

January 1, 1978

Completely obsessed with the fact that Katie is angry at me. But I went for a long walk along the ruts of the snowy streets and figured out my situation. There is no such thing as unrequited love. If Katie doesn't understand that she needs me in her life, then I don't give a shit if she abandons me. It makes no difference. This is a woman who has tremendous difficulty with her own emotions. Obviously. But *she* is not the issue. I can't do anything about her art. The only person I need to think about is *me*. I'm free. I have things to do. She'll be sorry.

January 2, 1978

Worked all day today. Made the big mistake of calling Katie. It was a short cool phone call. I said, "I just wanted to wish you a Happy New Year." She said, "Oh, okay" with this tone, like why in the world would you call *me*? I tried not to sound desperate, but her silences were damning. What crap. I'm so full of crap. One minute I'm making her come, the next minute she won't speak to me.

October 13, 2006

I am in the northern Berkshires. The trees are bare. Everything up here is frozen. My footsteps crunch on the scatterings of icy snow. My nose and eyes itch. The skies are high and empty.

I arrived last night, checked in after ten, got settled. The motel bed was too soft but the food wasn't bad. I was lucky to get a room at all because I guess it's "bow season" or "turkey season" or something. A season for hunting and killing. Inside the inn, guys in camo outfits bustled around, anticipating the hunt. Very few women in evidence, the hunters like an invading army, only interested in force and functions thereof. They spend their time in the antler-festooned bar, watching vintage football on ESPN.

I called 'Gitte first thing this morning. She sounded cheery on the phone. They probably don't get many visitors up here. I made small talk, as if I just happened to find myself in her neighborhood. She invited me over to their place for lunch.

Her directions were straightforward: Drive twenty minutes north on a two-lane out of the center of town, then turn right past an abandoned gas station, go six miles and locate a hand-painted sign nailed to a tree. I did all this. Once off the two-lane, I endured twenty minutes bouncing along on a rutted, unpaved passage through the thickening woods hoping not to break an axle. In a clearing stood a brown-shingled affair, probably constructed by local volunteer help (a pound of potent weed for a day's work?). It looked like a typically suburban split-level transported to the bowels of a witch's forest. I was surprised. I guess I'd expected a geodesic dome or a large teepee.

As I popped the car door, two yellow dogs trotted toward me, tails whipping. One sidled up and I patted his neck. He crouched and began to bark viciously. The second dog followed suit. They flanked me. I

was midway between car and house. I'd have thought it was abandoned were it not for a ribbon of gray wood smoke trailing from the
chimney.

One dog nipped at the other's rear as they circled me in an
ever-tightening orbit. The barking became ominous whining. I had no
options. I was surrounded by thick, dark woods, home to wolverines
and possums and other ravenous nocturnal animals that feed on the
rotting deer corpses abandoned by careless hunters. My body would
never be found. Saliva dripped from the dogs' fangs. One was barking so hard, he had begun to go hoarse. John's dogs. Probably bred
to kill.

A form appeared in the front door and the dogs ceased their clamor
instantly and trotted off like two spring lambs. The woman left the
doorway and moved toward me. She took me in her arms and hugged
me. She smelled of roses.

Throwing me a shy smile and taking me by the hand 'Gitte said, "Let
me show you around!" She pulled me toward the back of the house,
like a schoolgirl eager for flirtatious mischief. We turned the corner
to discover cages and fenced-in areas beside a weed-choked subsis-
tence garden. I learned that all of this was housing for a medium-sized
menagerie. 'Gitte introduced me to her pony, her turkey, her rabbits,
her six dogs, each by name. Dozens of cats, unlike the pony, turkey and
rabbits, were semi-free and anonymous. 'Gitte proudly showed me the
reeking manure heap banked up against an abandoned car. I wondered
where the marijuana field was hidden, but did not ask.

We entered the house proper. The place smelled like a pet shop/
health food store combo, incense and dry herbs and wet fur. An oat-
colored macrame weaving hung above a dusty bookshelf upon which
stood a well-thumbed copy of *The Road Less Traveled*. 'Gitte doesn't
drink coffee, but she had picked some up just for my visit, recalling my
fondness for caffeine. She peppered me with questions about my life

and my work and before long I was babbling, providing much too much information. As I spoke, she fixed me with a loving gaze, as if she had been waiting for years to hear every word of it. A dog bounded in and 'Gitte stroked him, while keeping all her attention on me.

Over the organic lunch of bean paste slathered onto thick slices of homemade bread (topped with alfalfa sprouts), I picked up more information regarding John's absence. He had gone in for observation because he had become forgetful and now the stay had been extended. I inquired whether a visit would make sense, trying to get a bead on whether John was still angry at me. 'Gitte said that she was sure John would love a visit from me. Her blue eyes twinkled. I resisted the urge to reach out and stroke her cheek. I wanted simply to take her hand, just hold it for a while.

We ran out of things to talk about. It became clear that the only way to get closer to 'Gitte was to go spend some time with her spouse and then report back. 'Gitte wrote the address on the back of an envelope in a perfect cursive. I appraised this woman one more time. Her hair was now a whitish blond. There was a slight darkness under the eyes and her smile was more weary than bright. But she was in good shape, thin, lively. Her eyes sparkled with life. She was who she was and would ever be.

We hugged goodbye and I harvested her warmth. Beautiful 'Gitte. In the car as I drove off, I realized that I had not mentioned my heart surgery. Then another thought struck me, is 'Gitte the woman I am meant to be with? Crazy.

February 18, 1978

No money. No friends. Haven't heard from Katie for over a month. I try to write, then throw it all away. Drinking too much.

October 15, 2006

I have been to see John. An hour's drive to a town near Williamstown. After receiving directions three times in the small hospital, I entered a room and found a man seated by a window. John had lost weight and his skin was pale, no longer cherubic. When he turned his numinous gaze my way, I saw that despite the changes, it was him. Later when he relaxed, he laughed and his eyes crinkled and he was the old John.

What did I expect? Thirty years. But in actual years, how old could he be? Sixty-something? He appeared much older than that. He immediately launched into a discussion of his situation. As he did, he deftly opened the can of fancy butter cookies I had brought along, then absentmindedly munched them as he talked. By the time I left, he had eaten the entire tin.

John: "I try to remember things and the information is not there. Can't remember the names of my children. Or even whether or not I have kids at all. People come to see me. I don't know who these people are! People. From long ago? Who knows? My kids? Relatives? To me they're just strangers.

"Don't know where I am. Don't know why I'm here. Don't know what year it is. Couldn't tell you many things. Many many things have slipped away.

"For example, I've completely forgotten major historical events. Presidents! Who was the President between Carter and Reagan? Have no fucking idea. I kind of remember some wars, there was a war in Vietnam, right? And I remember some space exploration, the moon. But not Mars. Did we put men on Mars? See I *know* we did, but the details are just outside my reach. Can't tell you the names of the tallest mountains. And you know what? When you can't remember shit, it's scary.

"I know you, buddy, know your face, but I don't know *you*. There's so much about you I've forgotten. Emptiness instead of stuff."

I began with the obvious and said it was nice seeing 'Gitte again. John replied, "Don't know her either. Don't want to know her! Who is she? Some bitch?"

Patiently, I said, "No, not some bitch. Your wife."

"My wife? Right. Tell me another one. Who the fuck are you again? My doctor? Where did you get your degree? And don't tell me Harvard, that's what they all say." I noticed that John's hair had been unevenly sheared to the scalp, allowing tufts to spring up between what appeared to be fresh scars.

I said I was not a doctor, but an old friend. I purposely left out the part about being a writer but reminded him of all the nights we had spent together passing the pipe. His response was: "I hate drugs. Fuck drugs. Don't gimme any more drugs." But when I brought up facts I'd gleaned from his encyclopedic monologues, he brightened up. "Yes, Farinelli! One of the greatest, if not the greatest, stars of his time. Like a Caruso. Everyone knew him. But what was his brother's name? See, I can't remember that. Farinelli's brother's name. I knew it once. Fuckin' Farinelli! Say, did you know that Caruso was in San Franscisco during the earthquake? Walked through the rubble in his bathrobe."

As far as I could tell, John bore me no ill will, whether he recognized me or not. All of his venom was saved for his "imprisoner," the doctor. John said there were details of his former life that he did remember but could not divulge and that because of "my other life" as he called it, there had been an ongoing conspiracy (which involved his doctor), to keep him locked up. I vaguely remembered Jack telling me of rumors that John had had an "other life." Could it be possible that John was being kept here against his will? Maybe he had been a spy?

I stayed for about forty-five minutes. John grew restless, migrated toward the window, as if on the lookout. I left him at the window.

I sought out John's physician and baldly asked, "Why is John locked up like this?"

"And you are . . . ?"

"An old friend. Richard Morris."

"*The* Richard Morris? The writer?"

"Yes."

"Wow! I read your short stories in college. John said you two were friends. But with John you can never be sure."

I didn't have time for this, though it was significant that John had admitted knowing me. "You didn't answer my question."

"Mr. Morris, you saw him. It's pretty obvious." The doctor's mild face matched his voice.

"He's in a very excited state of mind, I'd be too if I were locked up."

"John runs the risk of hurting himself. Or others. Obviously Brigitte took part in the decision to place him here."

"He says he doesn't know 'Gitte. Brigitte."

"He says a lot of things."

"But can't Alzheimer's be treated? Or slowed down or something?"

"Alzheimer's?"

"John has early onset Alzheimer's."

"John doesn't have Alzheimer's any more than you or I."

"Then why is he in an Alzheimer's ward?"

"He isn't in an Alzheimer's ward."

"But he has trouble remembering things."

"Mr. Morris, let's back up a sec. Where do you think you are?"

"A nursing home. Assisted living, whatever they call it these days."

"Mr. Morris, your friend was brought to us five years ago in an agitated state. Under observation it became clear that psychosis had rendered him incapable of handling his own affairs. We tried medication, we tried counseling, even electroshock therapy. Occasionally there would be a slight improvement, but eventually he would return to this delusionary state in which he insisted he had forgotten essential aspects of his own life. Often this was accompanied by a form of catatonia. We eventually made the diagnosis that John suffers from a perpetually mutating form of shizophrenia, shifting from hebephrenic to catatonic to paranoid manifestation. He is totally detached from reality and obsessed with 'remembering' things that don't exist. He does this to a point of distraction. The bottom line is, he can no longer take care of himself."

"Electroshock therapy? They still do that?"

"It can be very effective. For a while we considered his state to be a manifestation of bipolarity, and if that were the case, then EST would be a proper therapy. But we've abandoned that idea. The EST did provide some relief. But it had no effect on the central problem."

"But maybe he really can't remember things and this bothers him."

"We considered that too. We even considered the possibility that the problem lay with Brigitte and not John. Sort of a *Gaslight* situation. But I have thoroughly fact-checked his personal biography. In most cases, the events or people he can't remember either didn't occur or don't exist. The same is true of places. Historical events."

"Places?"

"The most terrible of his delusions. He will fixate on returning to a place he claims to be very familiar with, then is tortured by the fact that he can't remember where this place is. Two of his favorites are an abandoned harness horse track somewhere in the middle of a forest and a tenement on the South Side of Chicago. He's never, as far as I can discover, *ever* lived in Chicago. But the obsession is not frivolous. Once John gets it in his head that he must find a place, if left on his own he will pursue this objective to the point of, well there's no other word for it, psychosis. They've had to call in air marshals to remove him from airplanes five or six times. In a straitjacket."

"He might have visited Chicago once."

"It's possible. But I don't think so. The street names are bogus. Furthermore, on the two occasions when he actually got as far as Chicago, he had no familiarity whatsoever with the layout of the city. He has never been to Chicago, except for these wild, manic goose chases."

"Maybe it *is* Alzheimer's?"

"None of the major indicators of the disease present themselves. He can carry out tasks, he can drive a car, he can complete crossword puzzles. He can watch the evening news and give you a full report the next day. He knows what's going on. His problem is that he is completely obsessed with the idea that he is senile and this in turn paralyzes him."

This was not a hospital. This was a nut house. I repeated the word, "Paralyzes?"

"John becomes so stricken with fear, he can't move a muscle. In that state, he can't do anything but spend the day obsessing about his memory loss. Which as I said, is nonexistent. He drives himself into a fury attempting to remember information that doesn't exist. He honestly believes that a world war took place in 1994. He insists atomic weapons were used. But beyond that, he can't remember the details. When we seek to reassure him that no such war ever happened, he says we are humoring him. He honestly thinks that everything we say or do is part of an elaborate scheme to shield him from the pain of loss. When he enters this frame of mind, he can become completely inert, frozen and catatonic for days at a time. This is an indicator of mental illness on the order of schizophrenia as opposed to an organic illness such as Alzheimer's or vascular dementia."

I said, "He doesn't stutter anymore."

The doctor replied, "When did John stutter?"

I left the hospital. As I drove away, I thought, John is nuts.

October 16, 2006

Well, there is some justice in the world. The nominations for the National Book Award were announced. *A Gentle Death* is on the list. Leon called me and breathlessly confided he'd known the news for a week but hadn't been allowed to leak it to anyone. Right. No matter. It's not that I care about the prize itself. But it will boost sales.

I'm still at the hunting lodge. I feel inspired to use this time to write, to collect my thoughts. Find myself thinking about 'Gitte. How is it that beauty can endure for so long? I haven't seen her in what, thirty years, and yet she has the same hold on me she had when I was just a kid. What makes beauty so powerful? How far from symmetry does beauty have to stray for it to be less than beauty? Isn't that how art is judged? The elements must fit together harmoniously to create the whole. 'Gitte is like that. I can't get her out of my mind. Crazy. If I could only touch her, for just a moment.

March 19, 1978

The unexpected becomes the norm. It's all happening now. I can feel it, like surfing a tidal wave. And it's up to me to take it all. Blake knows a movie producer who wants to buy one of my stories. For *twenty-five thousand dollars*!

I hang out down at Max's every night. Sometimes I have nosebleeds in the morning from all the blow. Makes no difference. The hand of God, the hand of God, nothing can stop the hand of God. My spit is golden, my jism is golden. I'm like some ancient king, even my hair and fingernails are holy.

It's important to get really fucking drunk at least once a week. To clean the slate. Renew the spirit by obliterating the spirit. I am the Phoenix! To catch the pulse of the universe in my alcohol-saturated veins. To scream and laugh and dance like a lunatic. Like a religious experience. Except *my* church is a shithole bar on Spring Street. My holy sacraments are speed runs and drunken fights and quick sex with strangers. Fighting and fucking is what God *made* me for. And writing. And writing.

Got eight stitches in Roosevelt Hospital last night because Zim and I decided to hang out in Times Square. We were walking along 44th Street and this sleazoid emerges from the shadow of a doorway and wanted to know if Zim and I "like girls." The guy said he "has girls." All we had to do is follow him! Zim and I did the sideways glance bit knowing full well that there were *no* "girls." But what the fuck, why not? Nice night for something, whatever came down. We followed this asshole out of Times Square down Eighth Avenue past the darkened post office to an abandoned building. While we were trotting along, the hustler's like, "You guys visiting the city?" Zim's like, "Yeah." And the creep was like, "What do you guys do for a living?" Zim said, "Computer sales." The guy was like, "Yeah? A lot of money in that?" Zim said, "You better believe it."

My face was hurting from trying not to laugh. The character focused on me, "You like girls? I got a great place with girls." Zim said, "Are they virgins?" Guy was like, "Some, yeah." Then out of the blue, the character asked, "You guys don't have any weapons on you, knives or anything?" Zim and I got all blank-faced. So this was what was going down. No girls. Something else.

We entered this apparently empty building, and followed the guy up a short stairway. At the landing, we encountered two thugs waiting in the shadows to pounce. Zim didn't hestitate, he just lowered his head, butted the chest of the first one, grabbed him around and flipped him. Punches flew. I fell backwards down the stairs, which must have been when I cut my forehead. A lot of shouting and cursing, like we were the ones who had done something wrong. Zim grabbed me by the collar and dragged me out the door. Probably saved my life. We tried to flag a police cruiser, but the cops had no interest in two knuckleheads on a dark street. We had to hike all the way up to the Roosevelt ER. Since I was bleeding all over the floor, they took me right in.

We spent the rest of the night hoisting free drinks while recounting the story of our battle and my wound. I woke up at six A.M. on the floor of my bathroom, my house keys in my hand.

Five messages from Katie on the answering machine. I guess we're back together.

October 18, 2006

Found John in the day room parked in his wheelchair. Another six people were scattered around the room, also in wheelchairs, oriented toward a widescreen TV upon which a chattering fat lady baked a batch of Christmas cookies. A pumpkin sat on the windowsill. A festive touch, like a bouquet thrown on a grave.

I wheeled John into a corner. He squinted at me, I said, "John, it's me, Richard."

He said, "Big deal. You wanna medal?" He looked away.

I said, "You know who I am."

John replied, "I know you're someone. Right? You're someone? That I know. And I know that you're someone I don't know. I know that I don't know. I don't think, therefore I am."

"Richard. I'm Richard. From the old days in Brooklyn. You told the doctor you knew me." John smiled benignly. Was this an act? I continued: "The loft. Smoking weed. Talking about life. Knights of the Templar? Flesh-eating bacteria? Pentacostal miracles?"

"Richard. Okay. I get it. Get me the fuck outta this place, 'Richard.'"

"I can't."

"You have any idea what I'm going through? I'm using my mind and then, *boom*, like a pothole in a road, a bump and I'm lost. I used to be a sharp guy."

"I remember."

"You do?"

"Sure. I loved listening to you."

"Those were the days. Exactly when were those days?"

"In Brooklyn."

"Yeah but exactly when were they?"

"The seventies. Thirty years ago. That's when I knew you."

"Thirty years ago? That's a long time. So how old am I now?"

"I don't know. Sixty-five?"

"Old man. See that's the problem. Time won't stop. And if it won't stop, then where the fuck are you? Or *when* the fuck are you? Good as dead. Everything dies. So why not now?"

"Not that old. You remember Jack?"

"Don't remember anyone."

"No one?"

"I remember Nixon. Bob Dylan. Lyndon Johnson."

"The Vietnam War."

"All the wars. I remember all the wars. Except one."

A young attendant entered the room and loitered by the window, as if waiting for me to leave. I said, "You need John?"

The young man replied, "You're Richard Morris, aren't you?"

"Yes." I assumed my poker face. You never know what's coming from people who recognize you.

"I'm Theo. Very happy to meet you." He extended a hand. We shook.

"You know John, of course." With a wave of my hand, I indicated John in his wheelchair.

"Oh sure. But John says he doesn't know me. Right, John?"

John kept his eyes lowered and grumbled, "Never met you in my life."

"Okay, okay, don't get all riled up, big guy. I'm only stopping by for a minute." The attendant glanced at me.

John glowered. "All the guessing games. Okay, I give up. Who are you?"

"You know who I am, John, and if you don't, I'm not going to make it easy for you, you fucking asshole." The young man delivered this statement evenly with no anger, then turned to me. "Can you step out with me for a sec, Mr. Morris?" Theo gave me a confiding glance.

John growled, "No smoking."

Theo said, "I know, I know, John. Relax. I'm not talking to you."

As we left the room I said to John, "I gotta go, man, see you tomorrow."

John smiled at me, a tired, yellow grin. "Thanks for dropping by, young scholar."

In the parking lot, the kid lit a cigarette and said, "Mom said you drove up to visit John. She always talks about you guys hanging out in the bad old days. I thought she was bullshitting me. I love your work, man."

He looked about twenty-seven or -eight. Was this John's son? Was 'Gitte pregnant the last time I saw her in Brooklyn? I said, "John made a big impression on me when I was your age."

"Yeah? Made a big impression on me too. Guy wasn't really a father figure in the traditional sense. When I left home, I didn't have to deal with his crap anymore. We lost touch. Then he got sick. I don't visit that much. But Mom said you'd be here, so I thought, I have to meet my hero."

"Hero?"

"Dude, don't get me started."

"You live up here?"

"Up here? In northern Appalachia? Nah, I live in the city. Brooklyn. Greenpoint. Trying to make my bones, you know? You have an apartment on the Upper West Side, right?"

"What do you do?"

"Write, man. That's what I'm saying. If there's one thing I can thank John for, it's turning me on to your stuff. He had all your books. I started reading them when I was like, ten. I read your shit and I thought, this is what I want to do. Write like this."

"I'm flattered. Thank you." Nothing more to say. "Well, it was a pleasure meeting you, John's son. I'm sorry your father's not well. I'll stop by again tomorrow. Good luck with your work." I moved toward my car.

"Thanks! It was great meeting you, man."

"Same here." I resisted saying, "Feel free to . . ." Didn't matter. Theo was one step ahead of me.

"Maybe we can catch each other in the city? I'll buy you a coffee? I know you like coffee. 'Gitte told me."

This was the child of my own hero. Couldn't blow him off. "'Gitte has my number. Call me anytime." And I left him standing in the parking lot.

I drove back to 'Gitte's. Is there an inevitablity to life we just can't detect? Isn't 'Gitte why I came up here in the first place? Not to see John. Once upon a time, thirty years ago, I met a woman who was everything a woman should be. Was I wrong to want to see her one more time? Talk to her? Maybe touch her hand again for a second or two? Life is short.

The dogs didn't bark this time. When I entered the kitchen, she was rinsing parsley. I pulled a chair up to the table and 'Gitte fetched me a cold beer. As she handed it to me, she paused. However it was communicated, it was communicated. I drew her toward me and I kissed her.

She took me by the hand, led me up the dimly lit stairs and into the bedroom where she undressed me. We kissed again. This time it was a real kiss, unsymbolic, forceful, aggressive. We separated and she undressed, almost shyly, like a girl. Trembling with anticipation, I touched her breasts, every part of her, kissed the nape of her neck, her ribs. She lay back and invited me into her. The word "fucking" doesn't describe what we did. More like an old-fashioned dance. As we swayed in and out of one another, I saw myself, my young self, in bed with young 'Gitte.

All things come to those who wait. Very softly she whispered into my ear, "Richard." And that was it. I came. If this were twenty years ago, that would have been the beginning of a long winding road. Elizabeth would bring that out in me. Could never get enough of her, was surprised by my own appetite. We would fall asleep at dawn, as if we were on a long voyage and the sex act was our vessel.

But this was not that. This was expectation fulfilled, plain and simple.

We lay there for fifteen minutes or so. We didn't speak. Out in the yard, John's dogs snarled and woofed. The oil burner kicked on and the radiators clicked with the expanding heat. She touched my chest but my thoughts were already drifting. The National Book Awards. It is possible I could win. That would be good. It would change things. People would return to me, read me more carefully. I glanced at 'Gitte and she was watching me. She smiled.

I rose and found the window. A gray day, or perhaps the sun was setting. Hard to tell this deep in the woods. The unblinking pony stood by his shed. The dogs circled my car. One peed on a rear tire. 'Gitte and I still hadn't said a word. The lengthening silence generated more silence. The growing chasm between us was pushing me out the door.

'Gitte watched as I dressed. I stepped over to where she lay and kissed her. She was so warm. My last image is that of the lovely 'Gitte lying on the bed, beaming at me, eyes brimming with love. At that moment I finally put it all together. 'Gitte had slept with me because of who I am, not who I once was. The kid I was thirty years ago, she barely remembered that guy. Young Richard was nothing more than a shadow to her. No. It was the guy in the magazines, the guy she told her son about, that was who she was after. Of course.

As I escaped down the rutted road, the woods darkening all around me, I prayed out loud that I didn't bust a spring and have to return to the house. I made it out to the two-lane. Relief eased me into a meditation on what could have been, should have been and was. Such a short distance between fantasy and memory.

In my old journals, I called 'Gitte an angel but the truth is that in the day we'd never said much to one another, John did all the talking. I had always assumed she was brilliant, but quiet. Naive on my part, I guess. And was she genuinely beautiful once? Who knows? I was stoned every time I saw her. Never saw her in daylight. If she was a beauty, that was no longer the case. Not really. Her belly was wrinkled and her legs were thin and varicose. I don't know what I'd been hoping for. She was a middle-aged woman who lived in a house in the middle of nowhere. With dogs.

October 19, 2006

I spoke to 'Gitte on the phone the next morning. Oddly, she had yet to mention Theo, and I was not about to bring him up. I told her I had to get back to New York, giving her a complicated excuse relating to the National Book Award nomination. I implied that I would be up again before Christmas. Not sure why I said that, but I did.

I could have headed home right then and there, but I had to see John one more time. I had the tape of our last night together in Brooklyn. I had thrown it into my luggage at the last minute.

He listened to the old recording with suspicion. When the voices ran out and I clicked it off, he said, "Yeah, so?"

I said, "Do you remember that night?"

I was gazing into the mad eyes of the guy I knew thirty years ago. John knew me, he remembered. "Young scholar" indeed. Anxiety pulsed in my stomach. Obviously John saw right through me. He knew I'd been out to see 'Gitte. Knew that I had come only for that. How hard was it to figure out?

All of this passed in a moment. Then John lowered his head, turned away from me and snarled, "Too many people. No time to rest. However it ends, that's the way it stays."

Without a word, I left his room. He did not watch me leave. I'd fucked his wife while he was locked up. Can't get any lower than that, right?

Regret is only a function of time. You can learn to regret anything. But also, in the moment, in the startling, brazen moment, anything is possible. Was I sorry? Fuck no.

October 20, 2006

It's not over till it's over. I checked out of my hotel only to find young Theo waiting for me in the parking lot. "I hate to bother you, man, but I had to take a bus up here and 'Gitte told me you were leaving today and I was just wondering if I could catch a ride back to the city with you."

What choice did I have? My balls were probably still damp from sex with his mother, so there was an obligation, right? It's only when I had thrown his stuff into the trunk of my car that I remembered that I was not planning to drive back to the city. I had planned to stay at the country house in Connecticut. Too late.

Do I have to describe the ride or the night Theo stayed in my house? Despite my reservations, Theo was a brilliant young man, and it was pleasant to spend time with him. He knew my work and the work of most of my contemporaries. He understood the context. He understood how the writing came together and what my part had been in it all.

The next morning, we picked up coffee and corn muffins at the minimart and drove into the city. By the time we got there, I had given an entire seminar on method. And recounted all the "John" stories I could think of. Theo hung on every word.

Theo confessed that since 'Gitte gave him my books to read, he had always known he would meet me one day. He was almost tearful with gratitude to have had the time together. He asked me if I would read his work. Of course I said yes.

October 25, 2006

I invited Theo to my reading at the St. Mark's Poetry Project at the old stone church on 10th Street. This was a promotional event I could handle, safely in the city. Been a while since I had read my stuff to this crowd. Thirty years ago the place was perpetually milling with young writers. Ginsberg and Corso would come by. And there would always be a couple of characters passing a pint of wine in the back rows. Now, the crowd was scrubbed, eager. Out on Second Avenue a cold rain fell. Inside the room was overheated and the smell of damp cloth filled the air. I read from A Gentle Death and then added a few pages I'd scribbled about the heart surgery. The audience was rapt. Huge ovation at the end. Felt good.

When I found Theo afterward I could see that he was impressed. But there was also a glint of agitation in his eye. We got a bite to eat at Veselka's. He picked at his food while I waited for him to laud my reading. Instead, he asked if I'd read his pages yet. I lied, saying I was halfway through them and didn't want to comment until I'd finished. His expression was that of an eager pup, waiting for the ball to be tossed.

Theo is a beautiful young man with chestnut curls and soulful eyes.

He's brimming with his future, with his *need*. As we sat, I noticed two young women at the next table trying to catch his eye.

It was energizing to spend time with Theo. If I had had a son with 'Gitte, would he have been like Theo? No matter. He has entered my life like a gift. And I need a friend right now. I need someone who will listen respectfully to what I have to say.

November 15, 2006

Leon bought an entire table at the awards dinner at the Marriott Marquis. He seemed genuinely pleased and proud. There was a renewed sense of brotherhood between us, a bond forged by all that we'd been through together. Sarah had decided to bury the hatchet and agreed to be my escort for the evening. She was radiant. She held my hand under the table as the winner was announced.

As you know, I won the award. When my name was announced, every part of me knit itself together and my pulse grew firm. The award, however synthetically, amended and improved the world in every way.

After my (brief but brilliant) acceptance speech, Sarah got all lovey-dovey. This was a moment of happiness I wanted to savor. But then, the press reps converged and pulled me out to do a photo session and interviews. Of course, during the press conference, all the questions were directed to Timothy Egan, who had won the nonfiction prize for his research on the Dust Bowl. The press had heard of the Great Depression. The press had not read my book. Yet.

As Leon hugged me close he cooed: "Next run, fifty thousand. And there will be more, my friend, there will be much more. Gold seal on the cover, the works. Oh, did I mention we'll be republishing your entire backlist with new cover art in the spring?"

We exchanged conspirator's grins, as if this had been the plan all along. That we both saw this coming. Hard times are necessary to build a dynasty. Fuck Leon's other authors. I was the one.

Friendly faces crowded toward me. Someone was snapping my photo. Sarah was holding my hand. But my middle-aged bladder got the best of me and I excused myself. I slipped past the reporters double-teaming Thomas Friedman for quotes on the Iraq War. As I entered the men's room, my cell phone rang. It was Theo. Somehow he had already heard.

April 24, 1978

I live the life everyone else wants to live. I am supercharged with the excitement of my work and my writing. And I am living life to its fullest here in New York. I am out every night, I have a wonderful lover and good friends, in fact everyone I meet in the streets, at parties, in the subway, every bum, every shop owner, every cop, hooker, hot dog guy, flower lady they are all my friends.

I am like a tenth-century Persian poet, sipping the nectar from the many flowers. Wine, women, song. Delicious.

Discipline is the key. I am not hanging with Zim anymore. He is too distracting. He leaves messages on my answering machine, taunting me. He says I have no guts. He whispers accusations that I am a "schoolboy." Fuck him.

Katie encourages me. She helps me focus. She is my muse.

And I have been spending time with that *Esquire* editor, Leon. I entertain him with stories about John and the various street people I've hung with. He loves to laugh this guy. Laugh and sniff enormous volumes of cocaine. He's teaching me about vintage wines and fine brandies. He respects me as a writer.

November 20, 2006

Why can't I have a moment to enjoy my victory? Insane week. I've had to return to Boston. Dad was reencased in his hospital room suffering from some sort of problem with his bowels. The surgery did not go well and he was on a morphine drip. How did it come to this so fast? And why did it have to happen now?

His eyes were barely open, but I assumed he knew I was there. He couldn't speak, his flesh the color of old raw chicken. The oxygen sucked and blew, a relentless mechanical pulse, tugging him step by step toward the inevitable. Many machines stood guard including a device that beeped at regular intervals, meaning what? "Alive, dead, alive, dead." The nurse shuttled in every hour or so, detached his excretory bag from the catheter and carried it off to be flushed away—flush, flush—humanity is residue. So many excretions and effluvia of the dying had been dispatched in that little room, hundreds, maybe thousands of times.

Sis came and went. She's gotten good at this. Hardened. Not like when Mom passed. She'd brought a box of Dunkin' Donuts and they had ended up unopened beside a foul wad of paper towels on a tray by the bed. The paper towels were there to wipe humidity from Dad's oxygen mask. I tried to remember the name of the funeral director I had met at Sadie's.

I was sitting there because . . . why? For him? He was barely conscious. I was there so I could tell everyone I met, "I was with my dad in the hospital—four hours!," then all would praise me, maybe love me? So someday the others would show up at *my* bed when it was *my* turn to die. Headline: National Book Award Winner finds time to visit sick father in hospital.

There was a text message on my cell phone. CALL ME—THEO.

November 22, 2006

Somehow the old man has survived the week. I should be happy but constant visits have interrupted my writing. Not that I'm writing anything worthwhile. Lame Thanksgiving with Sis at the local Outback Steakhouse. Been avoiding Theo. 'Gitte has called as well. I should return that call but haven't been able to find the time.

Desire has been the motivating force of my life. I guess there are other things that can serve that purpose: Love, for one. Hate, another. The prime mover has been desire. When I was small I wanted what I couldn't have. Then I wanted what *you* had. Eventually, I wanted everything. Later, I wanted a girl, then your girl, then every girl.

I would say to myself, "you play the hand you're dealt." And I prided myself in playing my hands well.

But in the long run, everyone gets more or less the same hand. Age deals it. Infirmity and death, that's all there is in the end. No matter what you've accumulated, that's what you're left with. There's no difference between him (Dad) and me.

Here I am now. I have everything I ever wanted. But the dealer won't stop dealing. And now what do I do? If I don't want, how can I "be me"? Who am I without desire?

January 15, 1979

I guess I'm not paying much attention to this journal anymore. Been very busy. But I should try to keep it up. The book came out and it got good reviews. One of the stories got published in *The New Yorker* and another is going to be published in the *Year's Best Short Stories* along with Joyce Carol Oates and Richard Ford and T. Boyle and all these other cool guys.

Very exciting. Met Philip Roth at a party. He didn't seem very interested in me, more interested in Katie, kept staring at her with his black eyes.

Life moves on. Sid Vicious killed his girlfriend. There's a new club called the Mudd Club down on White Street.

I've been seeing Katie nonstop. She takes care of me. Our sex is deeply intimate and intense. And she's very intelligent and insightful. She's good for me. She's got me to slow down on the dope and coke and booze. Which is good. I'd been pretty messed up lately and didn't even notice it.

Did another reading at the Poetry Project and this time the place was packed. Standing room only. I guess I've arrived. Ginsberg was there. It's obvious that the crowd loves my work. I'm good at reading in front of an audience. Still not making enough money.

Some people in Amsterdam are going to fly me over to work there for a month. And someone I know is setting up a string of gigs on the West Coast as part of a "New York Reads" series. They pay all the expenses plus a stipend of seventy-five dollars a day, which is pretty fucking cool. Plus the book royalties. It adds up.

I've begun a novel. The story I wrote about John was so good I'm expanding on it. Really explore the mind-set of a modern Renaissance man, circa 1977. It will be one of those "the rise and fall of" type novels. About how he put it all together when he was young, and what happened to him. How he ends up selling weed with his beautiful old lady and corrupts young impressionable minds. (Like myself.) (Did I get corrupted by him?) Oh and by the way, Leon left *Esquire.* They're giving him his own imprint at Vintage. So I'm doing this book with him. Blake is ecstatic.

March 6, 1979

I am writing like a motherfucker. I've been totally clean for a month now. This is because of Katie. She has saved me. Plus we are getting pretty serious. It's different with her now. She's someone I can be affectionate with. Someone I can be honest with. Also I want to hear what she has to say. I want to love her. She's so smart and so delicate and so sweet. It's crazy, I have feelings for her I don't think I've ever had with a woman. We can talk.

Katie is going home to visit her folks in Minneapolis next week. I promised her no boozing and no hard drugs while she's gone.

March 8, 1979

It is an amazing gift to have someone in your life you can actually communicate with. Katie was born a thousand miles away, but one way or another we've come to see the world in such similar ways. I'm not saying we don't have disagreements, but usually when I disagree with someone, I know I'm right. With Katie, it's not like that. She's that smart.

And she's so sweet to me now. Not neurotic. She brings out the best in me. When she smiles, I feel something light up deep within me. Can I use the word "love" here? We even talk about how we both love kids. I could imagine having children with this woman.

In a way, no matter whatever's happened to me, I've always been alone. And I sense that Katie knows that feeling. It's the solitude of the genuine individual. Sometimes she becomes very quiet. And I know that that quiet flows from a tremendous capacity for empathy. That she mourns the sadness of the world, of the ultimately impossible chasms between all of us.

She is a slim, delicate beauty. She is so wonderful to hold in my arms. I guess I love her because she is honest. I know that every gesture she makes means what it is supposed to mean. Who does that? No one.

We were talking about life and she said, "Life is not the big things. It is all the little things you don't notice." As I write this she is in the next room napping on the couch. I just put a blanket on her. I feel so protective of her and that's good.

March 10, 1979

Someday I will look back at this day and I will realize that it was the best day of my life. I'm in love with Katie, I have money in my pocket, I'm writing the best stuff I've ever written, my whole future is in front of me. The sun is shining, the birds are singing outside my window and I'm sober. How great is that? She leaves tomorrow and I will miss her so much.

March 12, 1979

My new editor/publisher, Leon, copped tickets to a Broadway play because he's already signed a book deal with the author, Tom Stoppard. I'm not really big on attending theater, but Leon promised we would get backstage and I'm always up for checking things out. Plus Tom Stoppard must be a cool guy.

The play was all right. About African politics. I wasn't playing complete attention, because I was distracted by the actress playing the young wife.

Anyway, after the show Leon and I went backstage. Through all these doors and stairwells, to the green room where Stoppard was meeting his director. So we're hanging out with Tom Stoppard, a nice man, a little distracted because I guess the New York previews weren't going as well as the London shows went, and we're talking about the book he's going to write for Leon and then the actress playing the young wife, Elizabeth Joel, pops her head in, to say good night to Tom, she was going back to her apartment, had to rest her voice, etc. etc.

We all got introduced and the next thing I know I was shaking Ms. Joel's hand and then the *most amazing thing happened.* She said, "You're not *the* Richard Morris, are you?" I almost did one of those Marx Brothers routines and looked behind me to see who she was talking to.

Incredibly, this beautiful actress, Elizabeth Joel, *has read my stories.* And Elizabeth Joel *loves* my stories. She's a writer herself. I told her I thought her acting was terrific and if her stories were halfway as good as her performance, then she should write a book, BLAH-BLAH-BLAH.

We agreed to call one another to discuss "our work." All this actually happened. This is not a dream. I made a date with Elizabeth Joel. Broadway star. And the way she smiled at me, it's going to be more than that, I can feel it.

We're going to see each other tomorrow night after her performance. Called Katie in Minneapolis. Told her I was being good—no drinking, no drugging. Didn't tell her about Elizabeth Joel.

March 22, 1979

Elizabeth and I have spent the last five days together. The most intense experience of my life. I'm not sure I can describe it here. I will have to write a story about it. We're talking on the phone every night. This is the brilliant relationship I've always dreamed of. We are both fully realized artists and we have each other and so we don't just fuck each other's bodies, we fuck each other's *minds.*

The book is selling really well now. Just got a check for at least three thousand dollars! Blake is negotiating options on two stories to be made into movies. And Leon makes sure I get to at least one party a week to meet people. He's introduced me to the writing of Paul Bowles and gave me a signed edition of Norman Mailer's *Advertisements for Myself.*

Elizabeth insists I come out to L.A. at some point and spend some time with her there. She's going to buy a little place in Topanga Canyon. (She has a huge movie coming out.) She says I can write there. P.S. She loves *Gravity's Rainbow*.

It's all happening. Just not the way I expected it.

Katie returned from Minneapolis and I had to be honest with her. We said goodbye on the sidewalk outside her apartment. Tearful. Very fucked up, but inevitable. I'm going to miss her. The truth is she was never comfortable with my success and that was always going to be a problem. Also, to be honest, she was too sober for me. Different styles.

January 15, 2007

I could work harder at being a good person. I know this. There have even been times when I've pulled it off. And what happens? I disappoint. I fall short. Oh, yes, they all complain when I jab and spit, but when I don't, there's nothing to talk about, nothing to engage. My duty in my life is to exist as an unsolvable problem. Because I am an artist and that is the artist's *job*. It's not an easy job, but if the artist doesn't do it, who will? To acquiesce to the conventional morality is to be a well-balanced, "nice" person. What is that but a form of cowardice? It takes courage to press on and fight the good fight. Say what has to be said, damn the torpedoes, damn the feelings of others, damn the impression you make, etc. The ultimate goal is to tell the truth. This is what I do. Personally, privately, publicly, all of it. And so I am alone. I know this is the price I must pay for being honest about my heart and my brain and my cock.

I am honest about what I *want*. I'm not going to make a convoluted, spineless run at your affection: "I'll be nice to you if you're nice to me." What crap. Crap, crap, crap.

And so this kid Theo walks into my life. Lovely, vibrant, eager, ambitious, handsome, obnoxious, self-involved Theo. He made a decision to visit the lion in his den. Thought the lion would help him out. No, Theo. Lions don't give aid, they watch the young and helpless pups with apparent disinterest. Then they eat them.

What did Theo think I was going to do? Make introductions to editors and publishers and all my buddies? But, Theo, it's *your* fight. You break down the doors on your own, just as I did. No one did it for me. I'm not doing it for you.

I see it in your eyes. The rapacious hunger for what belongs to me, for my achievement. But, Theo, you can't just walk up to me and take it. It's mine.

You buttered me up. Flattered me. You memorized all my books. Perhaps to imitate me. And perhaps you will succeed with your imitation, perhaps you will be *lauded* for your imitation. Receive a grant or two. Maybe an award! A critic will marvel at your insightful and slick style. (Because the critics can only recognize the derrière-garde.)

But, Theo, it's not just about being a "good writer." That will get you nowhere. You must go much deeper. You must scapel your flesh, dig out your own bones, sharpen them on the stones of disappointment, strop them on anger until they're keen as quills, then dip them in your own pain-thickened blood. *Then* you can go to work. Awkwardly and publicly. With no guarantees. And that's how one makes one's way, "young scholar."

You will have to get angry, stay angry, at society, at the world, at the rich and the poor, the politicians and the academy, and *me*, for years, to find your way. This is what you need and what your work needs. And still, it may not come. Without anger, you cannot be a great artist.

January 18, 2007

Been a warm winter, turned very cold in recent days. I keep the fire roaring in the fireplace. Those boring old journals make for great kindling.

Very dry, they blaze with crackling enthusiasm. It may take the rest of the winter to burn them all.

I like these days. Serene. Getting reading done. Much writing.

A few months ago, I was so alone, so abandoned. No friends. No family I could love. Even my editor wouldn't return my calls. My girlfriend had left me. Now I have a second wind. Sarah's back, nourishing me with her vigor and soft skin. Leon and I have a new understanding. The doctor says my heart is almost back to normal. Even good old Dad is stable. He promises me he's got at least ten more years!

The house is warm. The wine is good. I sit by the window watching the chickadees out by the feeder. Here comes the squirrel to steal the sunflower seeds. The phone rings. Stops. Rings again. I know it's you, Theo. And I'm not picking up.

ABOUT THE AUTHOR

Eric Bogosian is the author of the novels *Wasted Beauty* and *Mall*; and the plays *Talk Radio* (a Pulitzer finalist), *subUrbia* and *Griller* and the Obie Award-winning solo performances *Drinking in America, Pounding Nails in the Floor with My Forehead* and *Sex, Drugs, Rock & Roll*. He is the recipient of the Berlin Film Festival Silver Bear Award, a Drama Desk Award, and two NEA fellowships. He has appeared in more than a dozen feature films and television shows. Bogosian lives in New York City.